A still heat pervaded the afternoon. In the deep shade where we stood, only the drone of insects disturbed the silence. The velvet petals of the red flowers seemed to wilt and the lake lay bright as a burning mirror. Pauline and Elaine bent tightly forward over the crossbar that joined the shafts of the little carriage, their arms drawn forward at full stretch to the cuffs at the tip of each shaft. The driver took his place, confronted by a rear prospect of the full-cheeked suggestiveness of Pauline and the tomboy cheeks of Elaine. The tail of the uniform blouse impeded his view a little and he tucked this up well clear of Elaine's young backside.

LOVE LESSONS

Scenes of Romance and Reality

From Eugene Field, Edward Sellon,
James Campbell Reddie
and Others

BLUE MOON BOOKS, INC./NEW YORK

Love Lessons
ISBN 0-8216-5016-5
CIP data available from the Library of Congress

Manufactured in the United States of America
Published by Blue Moon Books, Inc.
61 Fourth Avenue
New York, NY 10003

Cover design by Steve Brower

Contents

INTRODUCTION

WAS THAT A PISTOL SHOT? It certainly sounded like one. But who on earth would be firing a gun in the middle of London's West End at such a time as this? The answer to that question involved one of the most intriguing incidents in the whole history of underground literature.

The sharp report had flurried the pigeons from their perches above Piccadilly on a bright April morning. Below them, the carriages of the rich and fashionable were rumbling sown the grand drive from the Haymarket or Regent Street towards Mayfair and the Park. It was the heyday of monarchy and empire, the eve of the famous London "Season." Lord Derby was prime minister and the ambitious newcomer Disraeli had his hands on the nation's purse strings—and his eyes on Lord Derby's back.

One or two people looked up towards the sumptuous hotels and gentlemen's clubs at the sound of the pistol-shot. And then they looked away again. The light of the spring morning struck a gloss from the polished flanks of their high-stepping horses and illuminated the quilted interiors of the carriages. Passers-by glimpsed proud and beautiful young faces as the wheels rolled past, ribboned hats and parasols. The horses trotted westwards towards the burgeoning chestnut trees and statues of the park, the elegant vistas of Knightsbridge and Chelsea. Along the path between the trees, known as "Rotten Row," the pretty horse-breakers as they were called were showing their riding skills with a display of shapely ankles and coquettish boots.

It must have been a rook-scarer going off in one of the park trees. No one in his senses would be blazing away in the middle of such a parade of elegance. The glamour of the Piccadilly morning was full of self-confidence, clever men and pretty women—not to mention a few very clever women and handsome consorts. In this particular April it seemed good to be alive.

But Joseph Challis, who kept Webb's Hotel in Piccadilly, had been much closer to the sound of the shot. It had come from a room occupied by one of his guests, a rather strange middle-aged man called Captain Edward Sellon, late of the Indian Army. No one seemed to know much about him or how he made his living. He might have been a gentleman who lived upon his private income. But there was something about the captain that suggested he was not quite a gentleman. Not quite *comme il faut,* as Mr Challis thought of it.

By the time that the door of the room was unlocked, Edward Sellon had ceased to be a gentleman or anything else. He was found dead with his gun beside him. It was surely an open and shut case of suicide.

What might have been the opening of a crime classic was, in truth, the end of one of the strangest lives in the history of erotic literature. The police were called, the stern-faced Victorian figures who sifted the evidence and gathered the clues. One of the first items that they discovered was a poem, written by the captain shortly before his death. The cause of death was unrequited love, assisted by a bullet through the brain.

> *No more shall mine arms entwine*
> *Those beauteous charms of thine.*
> *Or the ambrosial nectar sip*
> *Of that delicious coral lip—*
> *No more.*

Scotland Yard discovered that the poetic suicide-note had been written to one of the captain's girl-friends and this seemed the greatest irony of all. The man who now lay dead in Webb's Hotel had died of sexual disappointment. Yet he, among all Englishmen of his day, was best known for contriving amorous and erotic scenes, extravagant or simple, perverse or endearing. He illustrated and inspired *The Adventures of a Schoolboy*. He wrote *Phoebe Kissagen, The New Epicurean* and *The New Lady's Tickler*. The last of these was such a smash hit that it was still in circulation during World War I. Sir Maurice Bowra, then a young subaltern in the trenches, recalled how when the German bombardment started, the colonel of his regiment would call his men round and read them passages from *The New Lady's Tickler* to steady their nerves. Condemned by the Victorian censors in peacetime, the *Tickler* was conscripted for the war effort.

But there was far more to the career of Captain Edward Sellon, this strange "officer and gentleman," than appeared at first. He had written erotic novels for a London publisher who operated in Holywell Street, near the Strand. But he was also the author of straight fiction, including *Herbert Breakspear: A Legend of the Mahratta Wars*. He had written a learned monograph, *Annotations on the Sacred Writings of the Hindus*. He was typical of his rank and class, no less in his earnest literary labours than in the frivolities of his erotic dreamworld.

The "tragedy" at Webb's Hotel was hushed up for the sake of Sellon's wife and family, though he had seen little of them recently. It appears that no report of the inquest was allowed to reach the newspapers. Of course, the police had to make tactful inquiries. Who was this author of so much kissing and smacking, riding and rogering? What was his history?

Edward Sellon's life sounds like part of a novel by Thackeray or Captain Marryat. His father had died during the boy's childhood. In the tradition of England's impoverished gentry, his mother had packed him off to India from Portsmouth at the age of sixteen with an army cadetship. Moralists were apt to tut-tut when they heard that girls as young as fifteen had experienced sex at Sellon's suggestion. But there was no such objection to a boy of sixteen being made a soldier and packed off alone to the other side of the world. Sellon managed not to die in India of cholera or a dozen other plagues that wiped out the army faster than any military enemy. But then, the mounting death-toll from climate and disease was another little difficulty that imperial morality preferred to overlook. Men like Sellon soldiered in India because they could not afford to live on army pay in England. They knew the risks.

Sellon did well in the army of the East India Company, "John Company," as it was familiarly known. After reaching the rank of captain, he came back to England ten years later. He probably felt lucky to be alive. Best of all, he discovered that while he was away his mother had worked hard on his behalf. He landed at Portsmouth again to find that she had arranged a marriage for him with a young lady of beauty and fortune. The happy couple spent a winter in Paris and then returned to England once more. Only then did Sellon discover that his wife's fortune had never existed and that he was flat broke. Young Mrs Sellon remained beautiful, but poverty did nothing to improve her temper.

Things went from bad to worse and Sellon's career of sexual adventure began. His wife pursued him, discarded mistresses confronted him. He became a coachman, driving the Cambridge Mail from the ancient University city to London. For this he assumed a false name. Being a coachman was not a gentleman's occupation and he had no wish to disgrace his family's honour. Then, just as life grew easier, the opening of a railroad put his coach out of business. There was always money to be made out of genteel education. So, he ran a girls' school, but was quite unable to keep his hands off the goodies. Mrs Sellon was not amused to catch her gallant husband fondling the charms of adolescent girls.

Meantime, he fell in with an old syphilitic reprobate called Dugdale who published erotica while trying to keep one step ahead of Scotland Yard and a private army of moral vigilantes. Captain Sellon's pen and his vivid imagination sustained him for a while. Then, by April 1866, he was at the end of his tether. There were bills he could not pay and people he dared not meet. The tangle of his life was beyond unravelling. So, in the best tradition of the officer and gentleman who has blotted his copybook and disgraced his rank, Captain Sellon booked into Webb's Hotel alone with an army pistol and a bottle of whisky. He sat in his room, wrote a final letter to a friend, drew his pistol and did "the decent thing."

The police report on Sellon told the world little about him. But his books revealed a style of erotic writing which has been with us ever since, in one form or another. The setting was a sexual fairyland where the girls were innocent, willing, and beautiful. If some of them seem Lolitas to us, they were still over the age of consent by the English law of his time. Not until ten years after his death was that age raised from twelve to thirteen, in the face of opposition from many in the British parliament who saw one of their favourite sports declared illegal. The average age at death was forty. It was thought important for a girl to "get on with it" as young as possible and raise her family in a race with the Grim Reaper.

And Edward Sellon? His books were full of laughter and sniggering, secrets and naughtiness. Sex was no fun, it seemed, if it was officially approved or stamped with an "OK" from a morality council. Furtiveness and transgression was the sauce that sharpened the excitement. But it was always summer in the stories. The men and women who inhabited the fiction lived in a degree of erotic luxury that would make West Palm Beach look like an inner city slum of the worst sort.

The opening of his erotic novel *The New Epicurean* (1863) leads us gently into that world of aristocratic taste and effortless luxury where everything is of the best and finest. Sexual enjoyment of half a dozen girls at a time requires a perfect setting.

> *That I might the better carry out my philosophical design of pleasure without riot and refined voluptuous enjoyment without alloy, and with safety, I became the purchaser of a suburban villa situated in extensive grounds, embosomed in lofty trees and surrounded with high walls. This villa I altered to suit my taste and had it so contrived that all the windows faced towards the road, except the French ones, which opened on the lawn from a charming room, to which I had ingress from the grounds at the back and which was quite cut off from the rest of the*

house. To render these grounds more private, high walls extended like wings from either side of the house and joined the outer walls. I thus secured an area of some five acres of woodland which was not overlooked from any quarter, and where everything that took place would be a secret unknown to the servants in the villa.

The secret place where, even in the open air, pleasures can be enjoyed without the risk of being seen or heard by the outside world is one of the most potent settings for erotic adventure. Sellon's dreamworld gave birth to a hundred such places, from the lamplit courtyard of the Villa Rosa with its nude and strap-adorned waitresses to the reformatories where adolescent girls like Sally Fenton or Jane Mitchener languished. The events that occur in such secluded and palatial gardens are not those of socialist realism but of sheer and luxurious fantasy. Pauline Cox and her adolescent daughter Elaine are harnessed naked over the shaft-bar of a garden carriage to tow their master for several hours along wooden drives. No one asks, as in reality, whether two such "pony-girls" could actually do this or what happens if it rains. It does not rain. The sun always shines.

If it were possible to be trundled along by Elaine and Pauline bending over the bar between the shaft in toy harness, then it must be admitted that Sellon picked the perfect route.

The grounds I had laid out in the true English style, with umbrageous walks, grottoes, fountains, and every adjunct that could add to their rustic beauty. In the open space, facing the secret apartment alluded to, was spread out a fine lawn, embossed with beds of the choicest

*flowers, and in the centre, from a bouquet of
maiden's blush roses, appeared a statue of
Venus; in white marble at the end of every
shady valley was a terminal figure of the god of
gardens in his various forms, either bearded
like the antique head of the Indian Bacchus, or
soft and feminine, as we see in the lovely
Antinous, or Hermaphroditic—the form of a
lovely girl with puerile attributes. In the fountains swam gold and silver fish, whilst rare cry-
stals and spars glittered amidst mother o' pearl
at the bottle of the basin.*

Those who deplore erotic fiction on the grounds
that its readers go out and perform the acts
described should let the innocent wallow in
Edward Sellon. The wallowers would be far too
exhausted by the toils of physical labour—"First
landscape a five-acre garden and woodland"—ever
to lay a hand on a single girl.

But Sellon would recognise his influence if, for
example, he returned to that lamplit evening when
three friends are waited upon at dinner in the
expensive and secluded courtyard of the Villa Rosa.

*The courtyard of the Villa Rosa was prepared in
good time, long before the twilight of the hot
summer day and the first flutter of beautiful
moths or the metallic rasp of the cicadas. Anton
had given instructions that the table with its
white linen was to be set at the centre of the old
paved enclosure near the disused well, under
the wrought-iron of the Spanish lamps. It was
far too big for three of us, being quite six feet
square. Yet it suited Anton's purpose. We were
to be served from the stone arcade that ran
round three sides of the yard, leaving bare only*

*the wall up which the vine and the bougainvil-
lea climbed to the upper windows. Though we
had all the comforts that civilisation could devise, we were as remote from the society of that
Atlantic resort as could be imagined. The
hushed summer tide was barely a whisper.
Round the enclosed and leafy courtyard lay the
sumptuous apartments of the villa. Beyond that
the lawns and paths stretched for quarter of a
mile on every side. Then there were the screens
of poplar trees and beyond that the high walls
which the most nimble maiden would never
climb. The only gate was locked securely and
the key remained in Anton's possession. But had
the bell in the wall outside rung on that evening, it would have rung in vain.*

In such circumstances, the three diners are
waited upon by a pair of young shopgirls, a sluttish
redhead of twenty-two or twenty-three called Sian,
and Helyn, a more softly apprehensive brunette of
nineteen. But the setting is all-important. The two
heroes and their dark-skinned woman-friend Merle
are going to enjoy themselves in any way they
choose. They will not be interrupted by the outside world and not so much as a squeak from Sian
or Helyn will be heard beyond the wide lawns and
high walls of the estate.

Erotic fiction has no monopoly on this furtive
and excited setting. The success of the Gothick
novel was largely due to its location. Remote cas-
tles in the Apennines or deep in lonely woods,
where the swooning heroines languished, made the
fortunes of the popular novelists. Even though the
heroines escaped unscathed, a thrill of horror at the
possibilities appealed to thousands of eager
middle-class readers.

The triumph of such literary fantasy is that its extravagance would bankrupt the maker of Hollywood spectaculars before the first reel was shot. And all for the price of a pack of cigarettes—or in Sellon's case, "a good cheroot." Unlike realism, no one takes fantasy apart to see if it would work as a social system from Maine to the Mexican border. Even the contraptions and devices, are spared such investigations. The servants never spoil our plans for an orgy or a banquet by reminding us that it is their evening off. The wine is never sour and the food is always tasty. And the girls are never unavailable. In imagination, at least, a little of what you fancy does you good.

Perhaps, ultimately, the harem is the luxury split-level ranch of erotic daydream. A mile or two of secluded lawns and woods, paths and flower-beds, surround it. When, in the most extravagant scene, Pauline and her adolescent daughter Elaine tow their master in his garden carriage, the setting is quite as important as the action.

A still heat pervaded the afternoon. In the deep shade where we stood, only the drone of insects disturbed the silence. The velvet petals of the red flowers seemed to wilt and the lake lay bright as a burning mirror. Pauline and Elaine bent tightly forward over the crossbar that joined the shafts of the little carriage, their arms drawn forward at full stretch to the cuffs at the tip of each shaft. The driver took his place, confronted by a rear prospect of the full-cheeked suggestiveness of Pauline and the tomboy cheeks of Elaine. The tail of the uniform blouse impeded his view a little and he tucked this up well clear of Elaine's young backside.

There is no more reality in this than in a design on a piece of porcelain. But then the art of such fantasy is always to suggest what can never be attained.

The Adventures of a Schoolboy was written by Sellon's acquaintance James Campbell Reddie, but it has the stamp of Sellon's own style and it and owed much to the illustrations that he did for it. In the chapter which follows, we witness an encounter between two young men—the narrator and his friend George—and two young women— Maria and Eliza. The young men have been at school at the Abbey, presided over by the Doctor, a set-up which sounds very like the Rugby School of Dr Thomas Arnold. What follows is in part a send-up of the system of punishment in such moral institutions, where indecent exposure was shuddered at but where it was though perfectly proper for a lad to appear naked from the waist down so long as it was for the purpose of being thrashed with a birch-rod. Sellon and Reddie have a lot of fun with this moral absurdity, though not quite as much as Lytton Strachey was to do when he lit a fuse under Arnold's reputation in *Eminent Victorians*.

As the novel shows, the importance of moral discipline cannot be properly appreciated unless you first take your pants off. Especially when you need to prove the ethical point to two young ladies like Eliza and Maria.

The Adventures
OF
a School-Boy
OR,
THE FREAKS OF YOUTHFUL PASSION.

———

The tender spring upon thy tempting lip
   Shows thee unripe, yet may'st thou well be tasted.
Make use of time; let not advantage slip.
   Beauty within itself should not be wasted.
Fairflowers that are not gathered in their prime,
   Rot and consume themselves in little time.
SHAKESPEARE.

———

LONDON:
PRINTED FOR THE BOOKSELLERS.
MDCCCLXVI

In the meantime I kept up the conversation, which soon turned upon the subject of the Abbey. I said I felt myself quite at home there and could hardly persuade myself that I had entered it for the first time only three days before; I told her that George had been so fond of talking of it, and of describing everything that had occurred to him in it, that I believed I was almost as well acquainted with it as himself, for I was quite sure there was not a room in the house he had been in, not a book he had read, not a picture he had looked at, which he had not described over and over again.

As I said this in rather a marked tone, I saw Eliza's cheeks become suffused with a deep blush, and heard Maria whisper to George, "Oh, George! George! How could you?"

"Never do you mind," was his reply. "He is quite safe: you need not be afraid of him."

I took no notice of this, and soon changed the subject, adverting to our school days, and to all we had done for one another. Among other things I told them the only time we had ever got into a regular scrape was because we had refused to tell upon each other, and preferred to submit to a flogging rather than bring each other into disgrace.

At the mention of flogging they seemed greatly interested, and Maria especially pricked up her ears and put some questions on the subject as to how often we had been subjected to it and how we liked it. Seeing that they were amused with what I told them, I continued, greatly to George's diversion, to entertain them with sundry accounts of floggings, some of which were purely imaginary and the others improvements upon scenes that had actually occurred, not with ourselves, but with some of our acquaintances.

I gradually wound up their curiosity to a high

pitch and Maria especially seemed to take a great interest in the subject. Observing this, I went on to say that it was a matter which could convey no adequate idea of by mere description, and that to understand it properly it was necessary to have gone through it, or at least to have witnessed the operation itself. "I only wish," said I, "that I had you at school some day when it was going on, that you might see the thing regularly carried through."

Maria here burst out with "Oh! it would be so funny to see it."

"Well," said I, "I am afraid there is no possibility of conveying you to school for that purpose, but here is George, who is such a perfect ladies' man, that I am quite sure if he thought it would afford you any amusement he would at once submit to undergo the operation, in order merely to give you an idea of how it is done, and for my part, I shall be quite willing to act the part of the schoolmaster, and apply the birch in a satisfactory manner."

"Speak for yourself," said George, "I am not a bit fonder of it than you are."

The girls burst out in a fit of laughter, and I gave George a look which he at once understood as a hint to keep up the joke. I continued to banter him, alleging that he was afraid of the pain and that he had not courage enough to stand the punishment.

Maria chimed in, and encouraged me to go on. After some little jesting on the subject, George appeared to come round, and at length agreed that he would submit to go through the ceremony of being flogged in their presence, exactly as the operation would be performed at school. He said the only thing he did not like about the punishment was the being kept in suspense, and he therefore stipulated that there should be no delay, and that the affair should be brought to a conclusion at once. I said there was but one objection to this, which was that as the punishment was to be bona fide and not in joke, there was a risk that he might make an outcry which would distub the house and get us into a scrape.

He affected to take this in high dudgeon, and to be greated offended at the idea that he would cry out for such a trifle, and made an excuse of it for insisting that the affair should go on, in order to prove that he did not care in the least for the pain. At length he said that if we had any apprehension on this account it might easily be obviated by our going to the old schoolroom, where any noise that might be made could not be heard in the rest of the house.

At this allusion to the schoolroom, the girls exchanged a glance of alarm, and I hastened to remove any suspicion by saying it would be better to delay until the weather improved, when the scene could take place in the open air, at a distance from the house. George, however, insisted that there should be no delay, and at length a compromise was made by which it was arranged that if the rain ceased after luncheon we should go out to the park, and if not, the ceremony should take place in the schoolroom.

As the day wore on without any symptom of improvement, George and I made all the necessary preparations. After lunch, we sat for some time with the girls without referring to the subject, which occupied all our thoughts. At length Maria made an allusion to it, upon which George started up and insisted on its being got over at once.

The so-called schoolroom—or rather library— was a large oblong apartment, which had formerly been the chapel of the Abbey. At one end was the principal entrance, and at the other a large bay window, which occupied the whole of that end of the room, with the exception of a closet on each side. The portion within the recess was elevated by two steps from the rest of the floor, and the window, though on the ground floor, was thus so high that no one on the outside could look into the room without getting up on the window sill, which, though not impossible, as George and I had already ascertained, was not an easy matter without some assistance. In the centre of the room was a long library table. A great portion of one side was taken up with a large fireplace; the remainder, and the whole of the opposite side, was occupied by bookshelves, while beside the table and opposite the fireplace, was a large old-fashioned sofa, more like a bed than a sofa of modern times.

When we reached the room I at once took upon myself the character of schoolmaster, and George assumed that of the pert school-boy. I placed the girls on the sofa, and drew a large stand for holding maps across the space between the sofa and the table, thus cutting off the communication between them and the door.

I then told George to prepare for punishment. He inquired, in a flippant tone, if he was to strip entirely naked. I pretended to be shocked, and answered with a serious air, "No, sir; you know quite well that if I were about to punish you in a severe manner I should not expose you before your companions; but take care, sir, and do not provoke me too far; for though kissing a pretty girl is a grave fault and deserves the punishment you are about to undergo, still, disrespect to your master is a much greater crime, and if you continue to show it in this manner, I shall be obliged, however unwillingly, to resort to the severest punishment in my power to inflict.''

I then made him take off his coat and waistcoat, and pretended to fasten his hands above his head to the roller from which the maps depended. I then turned his handsome bottom to the girls, and taking up a birch rod which I had provided, I affected to flog his posteriors severely. He writhed and twisted his body in the most ridiculous manner, as if he was suffering greatly from the infliction of the blows, but at the same time he turned round his head, made wry faces, put out his tongue, and made fun to the girls, who were in fits of laughter and heartily enjoying the whole scene.

I rebuked him for his improper conduct, and told him that if it was continued, I must resort to severer measures with him. The more I appeared to get angry, the more he made game of me and the more outrageous he became. At length I approached him, and took hold of one hand, as if for the purpose of restraining his antics, and making him keep still, in order that I might be the better able to apply the rod; but my object was of a totally different nature. I had taken care that he should have no braces on, and his trousers were merely fastened in front by two or three buttons. These I secretly unloosened, and having satisfied myself that his beautiful organ of manhood was in a sufficiently imposing state for the exhibition I meditated, I suddenly slipped down his trousers, raised up his shirt and inflicted two or three sharp blows on his naked posteriors, pure and white as snow, saying, ''There, sir, since you will have it in this manner, how do you like it so?''

I had no sooner finished than he turned around, and as I took good care to hold his shirt well up, he exhibited to the astonished eyes of the two girls an object which they have often contemplated before, but certainly never in such a beautiful or satisfactory state. There it stood bolt upright, issuing from the tender curls which had begun to adorn it, with the curious little balls, as yet unshaded with hair, but of a slightly darker colour than the rest of his person, which made them show off in contrast with the pure white of his thighs, the pillar rearing itself proudly up towards his navel, surmounted with its lovely coral head.

The whole proceeding only occupied a few seconds, and took the girls entirely by surprise. Uttering a shriek, they started up, and endeavoured to reach the door. This movement, however, had been foreseen, and as in order to arrive at it they had to go round the table, George was enabled to reach it before them. He hastily locked it, took out the key, and then planted himself before it, with his shirt tucked up round his waist, and his trousers down to his knees, exhibiting his flaming priapus as a formidable bar to their exit, while he exclaimed, "No, no! You shan't escape in this manner. You have all had your share in the amusement, and it is now my turn to have mine, and not one of you shall leave the room till you have all undergone the same punishment as I have been subjected to. Come, Frank, this is all your doing, so I must begin with you."

"By all means," replied I, "it shall never be said that I proposed to any one else what I was afraid to undergo myself."

Prepared as I was for the scene, not a moment was lost. In a trice, my jacket and waistcoat were off, my trousers were down at my heels, and my shirt tucked up round my waist like George's, presenting, I flattered myself, as favourable a proof of my manly prowess as he had done. Taking up the rod, he applied a few stripes to my naked posteriors, while we watched the proceedings of the girls.

Finding their escape by the principal door barred by the flaming falchion which George brandished in their faces, they made an attempt to escape by the side door. This also had been guarded against. Ascertaining that it was locked, and now catching a glimpse of the new formidable weapon, which I disclosed to their sight, and which George took care should be presented in full view, they retreated to the sofa, covered their faces with their hands, and kneeling down, ensconced themselves in each corner, burying their heads in the cushions.

In this position, though they secured the main approach to the principal scene of pleasure which they probably supposed would be the first object of attack, they forgot that the back entrance was left quite open to assault. Nor were we now at all disposed to give them quarter. While George threw himself upon Maria, I made an attack upon Eliza.

Before they were aware what we were about their petticoats were turned up and their lovely bottoms exposed to our delighted gaze. Although we did not profane them with the rod, a few slaps with our hands upon the polished ivory surfaces made them glow with a beauteous rosy tint. Ashamed of this exposure, they struggled to replace their petticoats. Nor was I at all unwilling to change the mode of attack. Throwing one arm round Eliza's waist to keep her down, and pressing my lips against her cheek, I inserted my hand beneath her petticoats as she attempted to pull them down, and gliding it up between her legs, I brought it by one rapid and decisive sweep fairly between her thighs to the very entrance, and even insinuated one finger within the lips, of the centre of attraction, before she was in the least aware of the change in my tactics.

She struggled at first, and endeavoured to rise up and get away from me. But I had secured my advantage too well to be easily defeated, and after a few unavailing attempts she gave up the contest, and seemed to resign herself to her fate.

I was not slow to avail myself of the advantage I had thus gained and, after kissing away a few tears, I contrived to insert the hand, with which I did not now find it necessary to hold her down, within the front of her gown, and proceeded to handle and toy with a most lovely pair of little, smooth, firm, bubbies, which seemed to grow harder under my burning touches.

All this time I continued to move my finger up and down in the most lascivious manner within the narrow entrance of the charming grotto into which I had managed to insert it, and the double action soon began to produce an evident effect upon her. The tears ceased to flow, and my ardent kisses, if not returned, were at least received with tokens of approbation and pleasure. Presently I felt the lips of her delicious recess contract and close upon my lascivious finger, and after a little apparent hesitation the buttocks began to move gently backwards and forwards in unison with the stimulating motions of the provoking intruder. Encouraged by this and feeling convinced that her voluptuous sensations were now carrying her onward in the path of pleasure in spite of herself, I took hold of her hand and placed it upon my burning weapon. At first she attempted to withdraw it, but I held it firmly upon the throbbing and palpitating object; and after a little struggle I prevailed upon her not only to grasp it, but also to humour the wanton movements which I made with it backwards and forwards with the grasp of her soft fingers. This delightful amusement occupied us for some little time, and I was in no hurry to bring it to a close, for I found Eliza was every moment getting more and more excited, and her actions becoming freer and less embarrassed. But I felt that if I continued it longer we must both inevitably bring on the final crisis. Having already succeeded so well in my undertaking, I was anxious that she should enjoy the supreme happiness in the most complete manner possible, and I had little doubt that her excited passions would now induce her to give every facility to my proceedings. Changing her position a little to favor my object, I abandoned the advantage I enjoyed in the rear for the purpose of obtaining a more convenient lodgement in front. Inserting one knee under her thigh, I turned her over on her back, and throwing myself upon her to prevent her from rising, though to tell the truth, she did not appear to dislike the change of posture, I again tickled her up with my finger for a minute or two. Then withdrawing it from the delicious cavity and pressing her closely to my bosom and stifling her remonstrances with kisses and caresses, I endeavored to replace the fortunate finger with the more appropriate organ, which was now fierce with desire, and burning to attain its proper position and deposit its luscious treasures within the delicious receptacle. The head was already at the entrance, and I was just flattering myself that another push or two would attain my object and complete our mutual happiness, when a confounded bell rang out loudly.

I at once foreboded that it sounded the knell of all my hopes, for that opportunity at least, nor was I far wrong. However, I took no notice of it, but continued my efforts to effect the much desired penetration. But starting up with a strength and energy she had not previously exhibited, Eliza exclaimed, "Oh, Sir Francis, you must let me go! It is the visitor's bell, and we shall be wanted immediately."

I was extremely loth to lose the opportunity, and at first was disposed to try to retain the advantage I had already gained until I secured the victory. But the evidence distress she displayed affected me. I could not help feeling from the sudden change in her manner that it was urgent necessity, and not want of inclination, that forced her to put · a stop to our proceedings. When she exclaimed, "Oh, do have mercy on us! Think what would be the consequence if we were to be found in this state!" I could not resist the appeal, and allowing her to rise, I said that however greatly disappointed I might be at such an untoward termination to our amusements, I could not think of putting any contemplated enjoyment on my own part in competition with what might prove injurious to her, and that I should make no opposition to their leaving us at once, trusting that I should meet with the reward for my forebearance on some future more favourable occasion.

She thanked me warmly, and would doubtless have promised anything in order to get away, but I was not disposed to place much value upon any promises made in such a situation, and therefore did not attempt to extort any. She hastily began to arrange her dress, which had been not a little disarranged in the amorous struggle, and we then turned our glances towards George and Maria.

Whether it was that he had been more enterprising than I had been, or had met with less opposition, I know not, but when our attention was drawn to them we found Maria extended on her back on the sofa, with her legs spread wide out, and her petticoats above her waist, and George, with his trousers down about his heels and his plump white posteriors exposed to view quite bare, extended on the top of her, his legs between hers, clasping her tightly round the waist, and planting fiery kisses upon her lips, which were returned with interest. His buttocks were moving up and down with fierce heaves, and he endeavoured to effect his object and obtain admission to the virgin fortress.

At first I thought he had been more successful than I had been, but on a closer inspection, I found he was still beating about the bush, and that his weapon was still wandering in wild and hurried movements around the entrance without having yet hit upon the right spot, or managed to get within the secluded avenue of pleasure. Eliza spoke to them without producing any effect, and I was obliged to lay my hand on George's shoulder, and make him listen while I explained to him the state of matters. His answer was "Oh goodness, I can't stop now, I must get it in."

At this moment another bell rang, which Eliza told me was a signal they were wanted. There was now no help for it. I was forced to remind George that we should not only ruin the girls, but also lose all chance of having any future enjoyment with them if we allowed ourselves to be surprised on this occasion. It was with difficulty I could persuade him to get up and permit Maria to rise. He wished to keep the girls until they promised to come back to us; but as the thing must be done, I thought the sooner the better, and I therefore opened the side door and enabled them to escape to their own room where they hastened to repair the disorder in their hair and dress, which might have led to suspicion. Fortunately they were able to accomplish this and to make their appearance in the drawing room without their absence having attracted attention.

George had managed to extort a promise from Maria that they would return when the visitors departed; but not putting much faith in this, we dressed ourselves and proceeded to join them, hoping that we might be able to induce them to give us another opportunity when they were left alone. In this, however, we were disappointed. Being obliged to attend some ladies to their carriage, we found on our return that the birds had flown, nor did they make their appearance again till dinner time.

We were greatly annoyed at this unfortunate issue of our first attempt, just when it was on the very point of complete success; more especially, as every effort we could make to persuade them to give us another opportunity to accomplish our object was unavailing. It is true that all restraint among us was now removed. They laughed and joked with us, and did not take amiss the minor liberties we sometimes contrived to take with their persons. Nay, they even seemed to enjoy the fun, when occasionally, on a safe opportunity, we would produce our inflamed weapons and exhibit them in the imposing condition which their presence never failed to produce, in order to try to tempt them and to excite them to comply with our desires. Occasionally they would even allow us to place their hands upon them and make them toy and play with them; but still they took good care never to accompany us alone to any place where our efforts might be successfully renewed to accomplish the great object of our wishes.

One very hot day we took our books to enjoy

the fresh air under the shade of a tree on the lawn in the front of the Abbey. We were quite near enough the house to be visible from the window, and the place was so exposed that it was out of the question to think of attempting the full gratification of our desires.

Nevertheless, we were so far off that our proceedings could not be distinctly observed, and there were a few low shrubs around which entirely concealed the lower parts of our persons, but still not so high as to prevent us from easily discovering if anyone approached us.

There was thus a fair opportunity afforded us for indulging in minor species of amusement for which we might feel inclined. Our desires, kept constantly on the stretch as they had been, were too potent to permit us to let such an opportunity escape us. George's trousers were soon unbuttoned, and his beautiful article, starting out in all its glory, was placed in Maria's hand.

After a little pretended hesitation and bashfulness, she began to get excited and interested in the lovely object, twisting her fingers among the scanty curls which adorned its root and toying with the little balls puckered up beneath, all which were freely exposed to her inspection.

For my part, I had laid my head on Eliza's lap and, slipping my hand under her petticoats, had insinuated a finger within her delicious aperture, playing with it, and tickling it, in the most wanton manner I could devise. The effects of both these operations were soon quite apparent on the lovely girls. Their eyes sparkled, and their faces became flushed, and I had very little doubt that could it have been safely done, they would have consented to gratify our fondest desires. I knew that some visitors were expected to spend the afternoon with us, who would occupy the girls and prevent any chance of further amusement for that day at least; and it occurred to me that though it would be too rash to attempt the perfect consummation of our happiness, we might at least indulge ourselves by carrying our gratification as far as we could safely venture to do so, and at all events thoroughly enjoy all the minor pleasures which were within our power. I therefore made a sign to George, which he at once understood. Following my example and getting his finger within Maria's centre of pleasure, he operated upon it in such an agreeable manner that she became excited beyond measure. Stretching herself beside him, she convulsively grasped the ivory pillar which she held in her hand, hugging and squeezing it and indulging in every variety of tender pressure. George instantly took advantage of her excitement, and while he continued to move his finger rapidly in and out of her lovely grotto, he agitated his own body so as to make his throbbing member slip backwards and forwards in the fond grasp which she maintained upon it. His involuntary exclamations of rapture and delight appeared to touch and affect Maria, and seeing how much pleasure she was giving him, as well as receiving herself, she could not refrain from trying to do everything in her power to increase his enjoyment. A word or two from him, every now and then, regulated the rapidity of their movements, and I soon saw that they were on the high road to attain that degree of bliss to which alone we could aspire under present circumstances.

Finding them so well employed, I hastened to follow their example. Unloosening my trousers, I set at liberty my champion, which was burning with impatience to join in the sport. Taking Eliza's hand, I placed it upon the throbbing object. She started with surprise and pleasure, on feeling its hot inflamed state, but did not attempt to remove her hand from where I placed it. She was sitting on the ground, with her back leaning against a tree. I gently raised up her petticoats and, slipping my hand beneath them, separated her thighs, and pressed my lips upon her springy mount and kissed it fondly. Searching out with my finger the most sensitive part, I played with it and tickled it until it swelled out and became inflamed to the utmost degree.

I soon ascertained the successful effect of my operations by the delightful manner in which she rewarded me, compressing my organ of manhood in her charming grasp in the most delicious manner possible and meeting and humouring the hurried and frantic thrusts with which I made it move to and fro between her fingers.

Finding that she was quite willing to continue the operations, which afforded us both so much enjoyment, I raised myself up on my knees, and while I gazed in her lovely countenance, sparkling with all the fires of luxurious delight, I exhibited to her the full proportions of my foaming champion as it bounded up and down under the fierce excitement of the delicious pressure she exercised upon it. I had intended to have made her witness the final outburst of the tide of pleasure. And, therefore, while I kept up the pleasing irritation with my finger, I purposely delayed bringing on with her the final crisis. But as I felt the flood of rapture ready to pour from me, I could restrain myself no longer, and hastily drawing up her petticoats before she could make any opposition, I bent forward and threw myself down across her. My stiff and bursting instrument penetrated between her thighs, and deposited its boiling treasure at the very mouth of the abode of bliss. As the stream of pleasure continued to flow out from me in successive jets, I felt Eliza's body give a gentle shiver under me. We lay wrapt in bliss for some minutes, during which she made no attempt to dislodge me from my situation. I guessed what had happened to her; but to make certain, I again placed my finger within her aperture and found the interior quite moist with a liquid which I knew had not issued from me.

When I put the question to her, she acknowledged with burning blushes that from the excited state she had been in, the touch of my burning weapon so near the critical spot had applied the torch to the fuel ready to burst into flame, and had brought on with her the final bliss at the very same time with me.

As I wiped away the dewy effusion from her thighs, I tenderly reproached her with having allowed it to be wasted in such an unsatisfactory manner, when it might have afforded so much greater gratification to us both. I could read in the pleased and yet longing expression of her lovely eyes that such a consummation would have been no less agreeable to her than to me; and I could fancy that were a favourable opportunity to offer itself, there would now be no great objection on her part to allow the wondrous instrument of pleasure, on which she again gazed with surprise and admiration as it throbbed and beat in her fond grasp, to take the necessary measures to procure for us both the highest gratification of which human nature is susceptible.

On casting my eyes around to where George and Maria were placed, I saw that we were still in time to enjoy a delightful spectacle to which I hastened to call the attention of my companion. George was stretched at full length on his back on the ground.

The front of his trousers was quite open, disclosing all the lower part of his belly and his thighs. His charming weapon protruded stiff and erect up from the few short curls which had begun to adorn it. Maria was kneeling astride of him, grasping in her hand the instrument of bliss, and urging her fingers up and down upon it with an impetuosity that betokened the fierce fire that was raging within her. George's operations upon her we could not discern, for his head was buried between her thighs, and was entirely concealed by her petticoats, which fell over it. But that he was employed on a similar operation was quite evident from the short hurried movements which her posteriors kept up, no doubt in response to the luxurious and provoking touches of his penetrating finger. Maria's face was bent down within a few inches of the object of her adoration, upon which she was too intent to take any notice of us.

We enjoyed for a minute or two the pleasing contemplation of her delightful occupation and of the libidinous heaves of George's buttocks, which increased in strength and rapidity as the critical moment began with him. At length it arrived, and accompanied with an exclamation of rapture, the creamy jet issued forth from him with an energy that made it fly up, and bedew the countenance of the astonished Maria. Retaining her grasp, she gazed for an instant with rapture on this unexpected phenomenon; but her time was come too, and almost before George's tide had ceased to flow, she sank down upon him, pressing his still stiff and erect weapon to her lips, and showering kisses upon it while, as we soon found, she repaid George's exertions with a tender effusion from her own private resources, which somewhat calmed her senses and restored her to reason.

When we had a little recovered ourselves, the girls appeared to be rather ashamed of the excesses which they had committed. And as George continued to tease them not a little, regarding the sacrilege they had been guilty of in thus wastefully pouring out both their own and our treasures, they soon took refuge in the house to hide their blushes and confusion.

We soon found, however, that though still too frightened to allow us to proceed to the last extremity, they would have no objection to a renewal of our late exploit. But this did not suit the purpose of George and myself, and we were determined not to allow them thus to tantalize us and slip through our fingers, now that we had obtained such a hold over them.

CHAPTER TWO: FLOSSIE

FLOSSIE MADE HER DEBUT from the underground press of Charles Carrington in about 1900. A rumour gathered that this high-spirited romp was the work of the poet Swinburne, though no proof of this was ever produced. Long burnt out by poetry and drink, he was living as a man of sixty-three in a suburban villa at Putney, watched over in case he made another grab for the bottle. He certainly knew Carrington to the extent of exchanging letters with him but the notion that Swinburne (once tipped to become Her Majesty's poet laureate) was the pen behind the romance of Flossie and Jack Archer seems unlikely.

On the other hand, among his more famous sado-masochistic tastes, he had once shown an interest in girls of tender years, even trying to marry one of them, Jane Faulkener. There was a certain difficulty about this since Jane was not yet of consent and her admirer was a long way past it. And past it he remained. He might enjoy reading *Flossie* but there was no apparent truth to the rumour that he begat her.

Whoever its author, the novel is one of the smash-hits of its kind. Flossie's candid revelations and even more candid comments hit off with great accuracy the slangy and easy-going fashion that succeeded the more earnest Victorians. She is descended from the *Kama Sutra* on one side and from P. G. Wodehouse's heroines on the other. There is no furtiveness or shame about Flossie. She knows what she wants and gets on with it—to the delight of Jack Archer. If she had a career after the novel was over, it was probably that of an elegant young lady, riding to hounds and being presented at court. She talks like the beauties and the young wives whose photographs appeared in society magazines like the *Tattler*. For all her friskiness, Flossie wouldn't be caught dead showing a thigh or a nipple in a scandalous glamour magazine.

Carrington published the book, along with *Dolly Morton, The Horn Book,* and several others in his series "Social Studies of the Century." And so it is. Not the more frowning accounts of social problems but the lid off a raffish and fast society of the banquet years. There are rooms at the Albany and dinner at Romano's, summers at "Monte" and a box at the opera. You might look for Flossie in the Royal Enclosure at Ascot races or watching the croquet tournament at the Hurlingham Club. You would look in vain for her among the girls whose darkly made-up eyes solicited their customers along the gaslit pavements round Piccadilly. Flossie, however outrageous and mischievous her conduct, is a lady. No mistake about that.

She also torpedoes the contemporary myth that women permitted men to make love to them only as a favour and purely in order to have children, finding the whole business unappetising. Flossie is game for anything and anything is a game to her.

And what about our hero, Captain Jack Archer of the 174th Regiment? It was a name already known to readers from *Jack Archer,* a novel by the war correspondent and flag-waving scribe of Empire, G. A. Henty. Henty died in 1902 and probably never read the outrageous continuation of his hero's escapades. All the same, the figure of the imperial warrior caught with his pants down in Flossie's bedroom was just of the kind to appeal to Carrington and his more subversive authors. If Flossie was *persona non grata* in America and England, it wasn't just a matter of her erotic capers.

Stories of this sort come in as many forms as

their respectable counterparts. The best one can say of Jack Archer's memoirs is that surely they are meant to be read with a smile on the face.

FLOSSIE

A VENUS OF FIFTEEN

BY

One who knew this Charming
Goddess and
Worshipped at her Shrine

PRINTED FOR
THE EROTICA BIBLION SOCIETY
OF
LONDON AND NEW YORK

BIRTHDAY FESTIVITIES

The next morning there was a note from Flossie asking me to come as soon as possible after receiving it.

I hurried to the flat and found Flossie awaiting me, and in one of her most enchanting moods. it was Eva's birthday, as I was now informed for the first time, and to do honour to the occasion, Flossie had put on a costume in which she was to sell flowers at a fancy bazaar a few days later. It consisted of a white Tam-o'-Shanter cap with a straight upstanding feather—a shirt of the thinnest and gauziest white silk falling open at the throat and having a wide sailor collar—a broad lemon-coloured sash, a very short muslin skirt, lemon-coloured silk stockings and high-heeled brown shoes. At the opening of the shirt, a bunch of flame-coloured roses nestled between the glorious breasts, to the outlines of which all possible prominence was given by the softly clinging material. As she stood waiting to hear my verdict, her red lips slightly parted, a rosy flush upon her cheeks, and love and laughter beaming from the radiant eyes, the magic of her youth and beauty seemed to weave a fresh spell around my heart, and a torrent of passionate words burst from my lips as I strained the lithe young form to my breast and rained kisses upon her hair, her eyes, her cheeks and mouth.

She took my hand in hers and quietly led me to my favourite chair, and then seating herself on my knee, nestled her face against my cheek and said.

"Oh, Jack, Jack, my darling boy, how can you possibly love me like that!" The sweet voice trembled and a tear or two dropped softly from the violet eyes whilst an arm stole round my neck and the red lips were pressed in a long intoxicating kiss upon my mouth.

We sat thus for some time when Flossie jumped from my knee, and said:

"We are forgetting all about Eva. Come in to her room and see what I have done."

We went hand in hand into the bedroom and found Eva still asleep. On the chairs were laid her dainty garments, to which Flossie silently drew my attention. All along the upper edge of the chemise and corset, round the frills of the drawers and the hem of the petticoat, Flossie has sewn a narrow chain of tiny pink and white rosebuds, as a birth-day surprise for her friend. I laughed noiselessly, and kissed her hand in token of my appreciation of the charming fancy.

"Now for Eva's birthday treat," whispered Flossie in my ear. "Go over into that corner and undress yourself as quietly as you can. I will help you."

Flossie's 'help' consisted chiefly in the use of sundry wiles to induce an erection. As these included the slow frigging in which she was such an adept, as well as the application of her rosy mouth and active tongue to every part of my prick, the desired result was rapidly obtained.

"Now, Jack, you are going to have Eva whilst I look on. *Some* day, my turn will come, and I want to see exactly how to give you the greatest possible amount of pleasure. Come and stand here by me, and we'll wake her up."

We passed round the bed and stood in front of Eva, who still slept on unconscious.

"Ahem!" from Flossie.

The sleeping figure turned lazily. The eyes unclosed and fell upon the picture of Flossie in her flower-girl's dress, standing a little behind me and, with her right hand passed in front of me, vigorously frigging my erected yard, whilst the fingers of the other glided with a softly caressing motion over and under the attendant balls.

Eva jumped up, flung off her nightdress and crying to Flossie *"Don't leave go!"* fell on her knees, seized my prick in her mouth and thrust her hand under Flossie's petticoats. The latter, obeying Eva's cry, continued to frig me deliciously from behind, whilst Eva furiously sucked the nut and upper part, and passing her disengaged hand round my bottom, caused me a new and exquisite enjoyment by inserting a dainty finger into the aperture thus brought within her reach. Flossie now drew close up to me and I could feel the swelling breasts in their thin silken covering pressed against my naked back, whilst her hand quickened its maddeningly provoking motion upon my prick and Eva's tongue pursued its enchanted course with increasing ardour and many luscious convolutions. Feeling I was about to spend, Flossie slipped her hand further down towards the root so as to give room for Eva's mouth to engulph almost the whole yard, a hint which the latter was quick to take, for her lips at once pressed close down to Flossie's fingers and with my hands behind my fair gamahucher's neck, I poured my very soul into her waiting and willing throat.

During the interval which followed, I offered my congratulations to Eva and told her how sorry I was not to have known of her birthday before, so that I might have presented a humble gift of some sort. She hastened to assure me that nothing in the world that I could have brought would be more welcome than what I had just given her!

Eva had not yet seen her decorated underclothes and these were now displayed by Flossie with countless merry jokes and quaint remarks. The pretty thought was highly appreciated and nothing would do but our dressing Eva in the flowery garments. When this was done, Flossie suggested a can-can, and the three of us danced a wild *pas-de-trois* until the breath was almost out of our bodies. As we lay panting in various unstudied attitudes of exhaustion, a ring was heard at the door and Flossie, who was the only presentable one of the party went out to answer the summons. She came back in a minute with an enormous basket of Neapolitan violets. Upon our exclaiming at this extravagance Flossie gravely delivered herself on the following statement:

"Though not in a position for the moment to furnish chapter and verse, I am able to state with conviction that in periods from which we are only separated by some twenty centuries or so, it was customary for ladies and gentlemen of the time to meet and discuss the business or pleasure of the hour without the encumbrance of clothes upon their bodies. The absence of *arrière-pensée* shewn by this commendable practice might lead the superficial to conclude that these discussions led to no practical results. Nothing could be further from the truth. The interviews were invariably held upon a Bank of Violets (so the old writers tell us), and at a certain point in the proceedings the lady would fall back upon this bank with her legs spread open at the then equivalent to an angle of forty-five. The gentleman would thereupon take in his right (or dexter) hand the instrument which our modern brevity of speech has taught us to call his prick. This, with some trifling assistance on her part, he would introduce into what the same latter-day rage for conciseness of expression leaves us powerless to describe otherwise than as her cunt. On my right we have the modern type of the lady,

· 38 ·

on my left, that of the gentleman. In the middle, the next best thing to a bank of violents. Ha! you take me at last! Now I'm going to put them all over the bed, and when I'm ready, you, Eva, will kindly oblige by depositing your snowy bottom in the middle, opening your legs and admitting Mr. Jack to the proper position between them."

While delivering this amazing oration, Flossie had gradually stripped herself entirely naked. We both watched her movements in silent admiration as she strewed the bed from end to end with the fragrant blossoms, which filled the room with their delightful perfume. When all was ready, she beckoned to Eva to lay herself on the bed, whispering to her, though not so low but that I could hear:

"Imagine you are Danaë. I'll trouble you for the size of Jupiter's prick! Just look at it!"—then much lower, but still audibly—"You're going to be fucked, Eva darling, jolly well fucked! and I'm going to *see* you—*Lovely!*"

The rose-edged chemise and drawers were once more laid aside and the heroine of the day stretched herself voluptuously on the heaped-up flowers, which sent forth fresh streams of fragrance in response to the pressure of the girl's naked body.

"Ah, a happy thought!" cried Flossie. "If you would lie *across* the bed with your legs hanging down, and Jack wouldn't mind standing up to his work, I think I could be of some assistance to you both."

The change was quickly made, a couple of pillows were slipped under Eva's head, and Flossie, kneeling across the other's face, submitted her cunt to be gamahuched by her friend's tongue which at once darted amorously to its place within the vulva. Flossie returned the salutation for a moment and then resting her chin upon the point just above Eva's clitoris, called to me to "come on." I placed myself in position, and was about to storm the breach when Flossie found the near proximity of my yard to be too much for her feelings and begged to be allowed to gamahuche me for a minute.

"After that, I'll be quite good," she added to Eva, "and will only *watch.*"

Needless to say I made no objection. The result, as was the case with most of Flossie's actions, was increased pleasure to everybody concerned and to Eva as much as anyone inasmuch as the divine sucking of Flossie's rosy lips and lustful tongue produced a sensible hardening and lengthening of my excited member.

After performing this delightful service, she was for moving away, but sounds of dissent were heard from Eva, who flung her arms round Flossie's thighs and drew her cunt down in closer contact with the caressing mouth.

From my exalted position, I could see all that was going on and this added enormously to the sensations I began to experience when Flossie, handling my yard with deft fingers, dropped a final kiss upon the nut, and then guided it to the now impatient goal. With eyes lit up with interest and delight, she watched it disappear with the soft red lips whose movements she was near enough to follow closely. Under these conditions, I found myself fucking Eva with unusual vigour and penetration, whilst she, on her part, returned my strokes with powerful thrusts of her bottom and exquisitely pleasurable contractions of her cunt upon my prick.

Flossie taking in all this with eager eyes, became madly excited, and at last sprang from her kneeling position on the bed, and taking advantage of an outward motion of my body, bent down between us, and pushing the point of her tongue under Eva's clitoris, insisted on my finishing the performance with this charming incentive added. Its effect upon both Eva and myself was electric, and as her clitoris and my prick shared equally in the contact of the tongue, we were not long in bringing the entertainment to an eminently satisfactory conclusion.

The next item in the birthday programme was the exhibition of half a dozen cleverly executed pen and ink sketches—Flossie's gift to Eva— shewing the three of us in attitudes not to be found in the illustrations of the "Young Ladies' Journal". A discussion arose as to whether Flossie had not been somewhat flattering to the longitudinal dimensions of the present writer's member. She declared that the proportions were "according to *Cocker*"—obviously, as she wittily said, the highest authority on the question.

"Anyhow, I'm going to take measurements and then you'll see I'm right! In the picture the length of Jack's prick is exactly one-third of the distance from his chin to his navel. Now measuring the real article—Hullo! I *say,* Evie, what *have* you done to him!"

In point of fact, the object under discussion was feeling the effects of his recent exercise and had dropped to a partially recumbent attitude.

Eva, who was watching the proceedings with an air of intense amusement called out:

"Take it between your breasts, Flossie; you'll soon see a difference then!"

The mere prospect of such a lodging imparted a certain amount of vigour to Monsieur Jacques, who was thereupon introduced into the delicious cleft of Flossie's adorable bosom, and in rapture at the touch of the soft flesh on either side of him, at once began to assume more satisfactory proportions.

"But he's not up to his full height yet," said Flossie. "Come and help me, Evie dear; stand behind Jack and frig him whilst I gamahuche him in front. *That's* the way to get him up to concert pitch! When I feel him long and stiff enough in my mouth, I'll get up and take his measure."

The success of Flossie's plan was immediate and complete, and when the measurements were made, the proportions were found to be exactly twenty-one and seven inches respectively, whilst in the drawing they were three inches to one inch. Flossie proceeded to execute a wild war-dance of triumph over this signal vindication of her accuracy, winding up by insisting on my carrying her pick-a-back round the flat. Her enjoyment of this ride was unbounded, as also was mine, for besides the pleasure arising from the close contact of her charming body, she contrived to administer a delicious friction to my member with the calves of her naked legs.

On our return to the bedroom, Eva was sitting on the edge of the low divan.

"Bring her to me here," she cried.

I easily divined what was wanted, and carrying my precious burden across the room, I faced round with my back to Eva. In the sloping glass to the left, I could see her face disappear between the white rounded buttocks, at the same moment that her right hand moved in front of me and grasped my yard which it frigged with incomparable tenderness and skill. This operation was eagerly watched by Flossie over my shoulder, while she clung to me with arms and legs and rubbed herself against my loins with soft undulating motions like an amorous kitten, the parting lips of her cunt kissing my back and her every action testifying to the delight with which she was receiving the attentions of Eva's tongue upon the neighbouring spot.

My feelings were now rapidly passing beyond my control, and I had to implore Eva to remove her hand, whereupon Flossie, realising the state of affairs, jumped down from her perch, and burying my prick in her sweet mouth, sucked and frigged me in such a frenzy of desire that she had very soon drawn from me the last drop I had to give her.

A short period of calm ensued after this last ebullition, but Flossie was in too mad a mood to-day to remain long quiescent.

"Eva" she suddenly cried, "I believe I am as tall as you nowadays, and I am *quite sure* my breasts are as large as yours. I'm going to measure and see!"

After Eva's height had been found to be only a short inch above Flossie's, the latter proceeded to take the most careful and scientific measurements of the breasts. First came the circumference, then the diameter *over* the nipples, then the diameter omitting the nipples, then the distance from the nipple to the upper and lower eges of the hemispheres, and so on. No dry-as dust old savant, staking his reputation upon an absolutely accurate calculation of the earth's surface, could have carried out his task with more ineffable solemnity than did this merry child who, one knew, was all the time secretly bubbling over with the fun of her quaint conceit.

The result was admitted to be what Flossie called it—"a moral victory" for herself, inasmuch as half a square inch, or as Flossie declared, "fifteen thirty-

two-ths", was all the superiority of area that Eva could boast.

"There's one other measurement I *should* like to have taken," said Eva, "because in spite of my ten years *'de plus'* and the fact that my cunt is not altogether a stranger to the joys of being fucked, I believe that Flossie would win *that* race, and I should like her to have one out of three!"

"Lovely!" cried Flossie. "But Jack must be the judge. Here's the tape, Jack: fire away. Now, Evie, come and lie beside me on the edge of the bed, open your legs, and swear to abide by the verdict!"

After a few minutes fumbling with the tape and close inspection of the parts in dispute, I retired to a table and wrote down the following, which I pinned against the window-curtain.

Letchford v. Eversley.

Mesdames,

In compliance with your instructions I have this day surveyed the private premises belonging to the above parties, and have now the honour to submit the following report, plan, and measurements.

As will be seen from the plan, Miss Letchford's cunt is exactly 3 1/16 inches from the underside of clitoris to the base of vulva. Miss Eversley's cunt, adopting the same line of measurement, gives 3 5/8 inches.

I may add that the premises appear to me to be thoroughly desirable in both cases, and to a good, upright and painstaking tenant would afford equally pleasant accommodation in spring, summer, autumn or winter.

A small but well-wooded covert is attached to each, whilst an admirable dairy is in convenient proximity.

With reference to the Eversley property, I am informed that it has not yet been occupied, but in view of its size and beauty, and the undoubted charms of the surrounding country, I confidently anticipate that a

permanent and satisfactory tenant (such as I have ven-
tured to describe above) will very shortly be found for it.
My opinion of its advantages as a place of residence may,
indeed, be gathered from the fact that I am greatly
disposed to make an offer in my own person.

> Yours faithfully,
> J. Archer,
> (Captain of the 174th Regt.)

As the two girls stood with their hands behind
their backs reading my ultimatum, Flossie laughed
uproariously, but I noticed that Eva looked grave
and thoughtful.

Had I written anything that annoyed her? I could
hardly think so, but while I was meditating on the
possibility, half resolved to put it to the test by a
simple question, Eva took Flossie and myself by
the hand, led us to the sofa and sitting down
between us, said:

"Listen to me, you two dears! You, Flossie, are
my chosen darling, and most beloved little friend.
You Jack, are Flossie's lover, and for her sake as
well as for your own, I have the greatest affection
for you. You both know all this. Well, I have not
the heart to keep you from one another any longer.
Flossie, dear, I hereby absolve you from your
promise to me. Jack, you have behaved like a
brick, as you are. Come here to-morrow at your
usual time and I think we shall be able to agree
upon *'a tenant for the Eversley property'* ".

This is not a novel of sentiment, and a description of what followed would therefore be out of
place. Enough to say that after one wild irresponsi-
ble shriek of joy and gratitude from Flossie, the
conversation took a sober and serious turn, and
soon afterwards we parted for the day.

THE TENANT IN POSSESSION

The next morning's post brought me letters from both Eva and Flossie.

"My dear Jack (wrote the former),

"To-morrow will be a red-letter day for you two! and I want you both to get the utmost of delight from it. So let no sort of scruple or compunction spoil your pleasure. Flossie is, in point of physical development, a woman. As such, she longs to be fucked by the man she loves. Fuck her therefore with all and more than all the same skill and determination you displayed in fucking me. She can think and talk of nothing else. Come early to-morrow and bring your admirable prick in its highest state of efficiency and stiffness!

"Yours,
"Eva"

Flossie wrote:

"I cannot sleep a wink for thinking of what is coming to me to-morrow. All the time I keep turning over in my mind how best to make it nice for you. I am practising Eva's 'nip.' I *feel* as if I could do it, but nipping *nothing* is not really practice, is it, Jack? My beloved, I kiss your prick, in imagination. To-morrow I will do it in the flesh, for I warn you that nothing will ever induce me to give up *that,* nor will even the seven inches which I yearn to have in my cunt ever bring me to consent to being deprived of the sensation of your dear tongue when it curls between the lips and pays polite little attentions to my clitoris! But you shall have me as your like to-morrow and all days to follow. I am to be in the future

"Yours, body and soul,
"Flossie."

When I arrived at the flat I found Flossie had put on the costume in which I had seen her the first day of our acquaintance. The lovely little face wore an expression of gravity, as though to shew me she was not forgetting the importance of the occasion. I am not above confessing that, for my part, I was profoundly moved.

We sat beside one another, hardly exchanging a word. Presently Flossie said:

"Whenever you are *ready,* Jack, I'll go to my room and undress."

The characteristic "naïveté" of this remark somewhat broke the spell that was upon us, and I kissed her with effusion.

"Shall it be . . . *quite* naked, Jack?"

"Yes, darling, if *you* don't mind."

"All right. When I am ready I'll call to you."

Five minutes later, I heard the welcome summons.

From the moment I found myself in her room, all sense of restraint vanished at a breath. She flew at me in a perfect fury of desire, pushed me by sheer force upon my back on the bed, and lying at full length upon me with her face close to mine, she said.

"Because I was a girl and not a woman, Jack, you have never fucked me. But you are going to fuck me now, and I shall be a woman. But first, I want to be a girl to you still for a few minutes only. I want to have your dear prick in my mouth again; I want you to kiss my cunt in the old delicious way; I want to lock my naked arms round your naked body; and hold you to my face, whilst I wind my tongue round your prick until you spend. Let me do all this, Jack, and then you shall fuck me till the skies fall."

Without giving me time to reply to this frenzied

· 47 ·

little oration, Flossie had whisked round and was in position for the double gamahuche she desired. Parting her legs to their widest extent on each side of my face, she sank gently down until her cunt came full upon my open mouth. At the same moment I felt my prick seized and plunged deep into her mouth with which she at once commenced the delicious sucking action I knew so well. I responded by driving my tongue to the root into the rosy depths of her perfumed cunt, which I sucked with ever increasing zest and enjoyment, drawing fresh treasures from its inner recesses at every third or fourth stroke of my tongue. Words fail me to describe the unparalleled vigour of her sustained attack upon my erected prick, which she sucked, licked, tongued and frigged with such a furious *abandon* and at the same time with such a subtle skill and knowledge of the sublime art of gamahuching, that the end came with unusual rapidity, and wave after wave of the sea of love broke in ecstasy upon the 'coral strand' of her adorable mouth. For a minute or two more, her lips retained their hold and then, leaving her position, she came and lay down beside me, nestling her naked body against mine, and softly chafing the lower portion of my prick whilst she said:

"Now, Jack darling, I am going to talk to you about the different ways of fucking, because of course you will want to fuck me, and I shall want to be fucked, in every possible position, and in every single part of my body where a respectable young woman may reasonably *ask* to be fucked."

The conversation which followed agreeably filled the intervening time before the delicate touches which Flossie kept constantly applying to my prick caused it to raise its head to a considerable altitude, exhibiting a hardness and rigidity which gave high promise for the success of the coming encounter.

"Good Gracious!" cried Flossie, "do you think I shall ever find room for all that, Jack?"

"For that, and more also, sweetheart," I replied.

"*More!* Why, *what* more are you going to put into me?"

"This is the only article I propose to introduce at present, Floss. But I mean that when Monsieur Jacques finds himself for the first time with his head buried between the delicious cushions in *there" (touching her belly)* "he will most likely beat his own record in the matter of length and stiffness."

"Do you mean, Jack, that he will be bigger with me than he was with Eva?" said Flossie with a merry twinkle.

"Certainly I mean it," was my reply. "To fuck a beautiful girl like Eva must always be immensely enjoyable, but to fuck a young Venus of fifteen, who besides being the perfection of mortal loveliness, is also one's own chosen and adorable little sweetheart—*that* belongs to a different order of pleasure altogether."

"And I suppose, Jack, that when the fifteen-year-old is simply dying to be fucked by her lover, as I am at this moment, the chances are that she may be able to make it rather nice for him, as well as absolutely heavenly for herself. Now I can wait no longer. 'First position' at once, please, Jack. Give me your prick in my hand and I will direct his wandering footsteps."

"He's at the door, Flossie; shall he enter?"

"Yes. Push him in slowly and fuck gently at first, so that I may find out by degrees how much he's going to hurt me. A little further, Jack. Why, he's more than half way in already! Now you keep still and I'll thrust a little with my bottom."

"Why, Floss, you darling, you're nipping me deliciously!"

"Can you feel me, Jack? How lovely! Fuck me a little more, Jack, and get in deeper, that's it! now faster and harder. What glorious pleasure it is!"

"And no pain, darling?"

"Not a scrap. One more good push and he'll be in up to the hilt, won't he? Eva told me to put my legs over your back. Is that right?"

"Quite right, and if you're sure I'm not hurting you, Floss, I'll really begin now and fuck you in earnest."

"That's what I'm here for, Sir", she replied with a touch of her never absent fun even in this supreme moment.

"Here goes, then!" I answered. Having once made up her mind that she had nothing to dread, Flossie abandoned herself with enthusiasm to the pleasures of the moment. Locking her arms round my neck and her legs round my buttocks, she cried to me to fuck her with all my might.

"Drive your prick into me again and again, Jack. Let me feel your belly against mine. Did you feel my cunt nip you then? Ah! how you are fucking me now!—fucking me, fu . . . u . . . ucking me!"

Her lovely eyes turned to heaven, her breath came in quick short gasps, her fingers wandered feverishly about my body. At last, with a cry, she plunged her tongue into my mouth and, with convulsive undulations of the lithe body, let loose the floods of her being to join the deluge which, with sensations of exquisite delight, I poured into her burning cunt.

The wild joy of this our first act of coition was followed by a slight reaction and, with a deep sigh of contentment, Flossie fell asleep in my arms, leaving my prick still buried in its natural resting-place.

Before long, my own eyelids closed and, for an hour or more, we lay thus gaining from blessed sleep fresh strength to enter upon new transports of pleasure.

Flossie was the first to awake, stirred no doubt by the unaccustomed sensations of a swelling prick within her. I awoke to find her dear eyes resting upon my face, her naked arms round my neck and her cunt enfolding my yard with a soft and clinging embrace.

Her bottom heaved gently, and accepting the invitation thus tacitly given, I turned my little sweetheart on her back and, lying luxuriously between her widely parted legs, once more drove my prick deep into her cunt and fucked her with slow lingering strokes, directed upwards so as to bring all possible contact to bear upon the clitoris.

This particular motion afforded her evident delight and the answering thrusts of her bottom were delivered with ever increasing vigour and precision, each of us relishing to the full the efforts of the other to augment the pleasure of the encounter. With sighs and gasps and little cries of rapture, Flossie strained me to her naked breasts, and twisting her legs tightly round my own, cried out that she was spending and implored me to let her feel my emission mix with hers. By dint of clutching her bottom with my hands, driving the whole length of my tongue into her mouth I was just able to manage the simultaneous discharge she coveted, and once more I lay upon her in a speechless ecstasy of consummated passion.

Anyone of my readers who has had the supreme good fortune to fuck the girl of his heart will bear me out in saying that the lassitude following upon such a meeting is greater and more lasting than the mere weariness resulting from an ordinary act of copulation 'where love is not.'

Being well aware of this fact, I resolved that my beloved little Flossie's powers should not be taxed any further for the moment, and told her so.

"But Jack", she cried, almost in tears, "we've only done it *one* way, and Eva says there are at least *six!* And oh, I do *love* it so!"

"And so do I, little darling. But alas, I love *you*, and I'm not going to begin by giving you and that delicious little caressing cunt of yours more work than is good for you both."

"Oh, dear! I suppose you're right, Jack."

"Of course I'm right, darling. To-morrow I shall come and fuck you again, and the next day, and the next, and many days after that. It will be odd if we don't find ourselves in Eva's six different positions before we've done!"

At this moment Eva herself entered the room.

"Well, Flossie. . . ?" she said.

"Ask Jack!" replied Flossie.

"Well Jack, then. . . ?" said Eva.

"Ask Flossie!" I retorted, and fled from the room.

The adventures I have, with many conscious imperfections, related in the foregoing pages, were full of interest to me, and were, I am disposed to think, not without their moments of attraction for my fellow-actors in the scenes depicted.

It by no means necessarily follows that they will produce a corresponding effect upon the reading public who, in my descriptions of Flossie and her ways, may find only an ineffectual attempt to set forth the charms of what appears to me an absolutely unique temperament. If haply it should prove to be otherwise, I should be glad to have the opportunity of continuing a veritable labour of love by recounting certain further experiences of Eva, Flossie and Yours faithfully, "Jack".

CHAPTER THREE: SWEET DREAMS

THE STORY OF *Sweet Dreams* might happen to anyone—anyone, that is, who was rolling in money and could afford to spend most of his time observing the curiosities of human behaviour. As a narrator, the technique of the central character is something like the camera's eye, peeping and spying, recording the pictures of love in action. Unlike Jack Archer, he talks to the reader as if sharing his experiences with a friend. And, despite his involvement with the teenage girls whose guardian he becomes, there is a fastidious detachment about him. No doubt his worldliness as well as his discrimination comes from life in Paris, where he has made his home.

No one could accuse him of being a sex-crazed philanderer trembling to get his hands on a victim. His first encounter, for example, is with leather-jacketed pillion girl Angie, whom he photographs on the platform of a train station without ever speaking to her. He is fascinated and even obsessed by this teenage redhead, though he never sees her again. For several months he goes to great lengths to learn the details of her private life and adventures. But his curiosity about Angie is quite as psychological or even sociological as it is sexual. Her story is pinned out for display, like an exotic butterfly under glass.

This life of detachment and speculation ends abruptly when he leaves Paris and spends a summer in England. Performing a reluctant favour for a friend, he agrees to supervise a household in a seaside villa. It consists of the two teenage girls, their young governess, and a randy nineteen-year-old stable-maid. Of the sisters, Sharon at seventeen is a "languid sensualist," and Victoria at fifteen is a hard and cynical little minx. Neither of them would appeal to him as a girl to be wooed or seduced.

The novel is all about oddities of sexual feeling in a man confined under a roof with several women. Even Digon the circus clown must reconcile his passion for red-haired Angie with the fierce sexual jealousy of the creole girl Brigitte who shares their caravan but not their enjoyments. Later on, in England, our hero must come to terms with the reality of life at close quarters with four very different women. He cannot quite trust his own judgment. In the end he discovers that it is the younger Victoria rather than the older sister Sharon who excites him increasingly, despite his wish to the contrary. He does not even like her very much. And when he has occasion to punish seventeen-year-old Sharon by whipping her bare bottom, the aftermath is vividly described.

The visual account matters little, by contrast with the psychological curiosity. What intrigues him is the strange and ambiguous domestic relationship between an adult and a girl he has chastised. The next week is passed in an angry silence, strengthened by the fury of Sharon's younger sister on her behalf. But the adult disciplinarian has had an intimate view of Sharon during the punishment and her uncertain glances at him across the silent dinner table show that she knows it. He has heard Sharon scream as she would probably never do before or after that evening. When their eyes meet, it seems plain that she is thinking of this too. Sharon hated every minute of it and yet, paradoxically, she and her chastiser shared an intense intimacy during the process. They are bound closely together for the rest of their lives by such memories. The oddity was noticed elsewhere. In the stylish 1944 film *The Curse of the Cat People,* when the head of the family goes upstairs to whip his daughter's bottom for misbehaviour, one female character calms the apprehension of the other by assuring that "a first spanking is a special occasion." It is this kind of quirk that *Sweet Dreams* exploits in such incidents.

The realism of the novel is in its psychology rather than its plot. There is not much chance of most of us finding ourselves suddenly in possession of a pair of teenage sisters and a young governess. But the way in which so much that happens in the story is fortuitous or accidental does ring true. Life lurches unpredictably from one crisis to the next. But on the seashore of a sunlit English summer, it lurches quite agreeably.

The following selection combines three incidents from the time covered by the story, a first encounter; the mentor as disciplinarian; and the first unexpected realisation of mutual passion.

SWEET DREAMS

* * * * *

A SUMMER ROMANCE
By "A Parisienne"

SOUS LE SIGNE D' EROS

Like her younger sister Sharon has a firmness of chin and profile, a calm and self-possessed beauty in the rounded oval of her face. Though Sharon's is the paler complexion and Victoria the sun-kissed child of nature, they have a perfection to make you sigh. Their brown eyes give you an enigmatic and quizzical look, something almost eastern about them like the sly harem odalisque. Yet Sharon's gaze is calm and indifferent, while Victoria's is fierce and intense, her lashes dark as if the little teaser had used Joanne's mascara brush upon them!

Sharon's lightly-waved and silky brown hair is worn loose like a veil to frame her face, its fringe parted on her forehead and its length lying in a luxuriant and rounded sweep down her back. Vicky's rather hard and shrewd young face is softened by the little curve of brown hair on one side of her forehead. The length of her hair is straight, trimmed back to lie over her collar an inch or two and sometimes to fall more softly forward on her lapels. It is certainly young Vicky who appears the tomboy of the pair, while Sharon is already the paler and more languid sensualist.

In personality, they share the same self-possessed and indifferent attitude to the adult world, like daughters who have been brought up in affluence but not cured of wilfulness. Sharon is quiet and self-obsessed, self-loving and secretly indulgent of her own vices. You would recognise her as a brooding, self-absorbed girl with her quiet brown eyes and the heavy silken slant of the brown hair across her forehead. I think Sharon probably makes love to herself a good deal or at least spends languid hours of self-caressing in bed or in the bath. Vicky is a harder little minx, vivacious at times but equally given to spurning affection in a mood of adolescent independence. She will shrug off a kiss or a hug and turn her face silently away.

I watched them dismount and took a private survey of their figures. As you would expect, the blouse and jeans showed Victoria at fifteen to have the taut, unfledged thighs and hips of a girl hardly at the threshold of womanhood. What an advantage two more years have given to the older girl! Sharon is almost a young woman who has not quite shed the last sheen of her adolescent puppy-flesh. As they dismounted, I made my study of her seventeen-year-old figure in the smooth tautness of her jeans. Sharon's legs are quite long and resilient but not with the slender grace of a nymph, for though she is averagely tall there is a hint of weight in her thighs. I raised my eyes and studied the firm rounded oval of her pale face and the enigmatical indifference of her brown eyes for so long that she pointedly turned away from me.

This was no great hardship, for her rear view has something to recommend it. The sleek and silken spread of brown hair down her back, long enough to cover her shoulder-blades, has a strongly sensuous appeal. As for her figure, Sharon likes to wear jeans that are smooth and tight-fitting, perhaps enjoying the friction of the seam between her legs as she walks. The light blue jeans-cloth was drawn into little sheaves of wrinkles behind her knees by its tightness. Several more creases gathered across the back of each thigh's weight at the top, from the rear opening of Sharon's legs.

I look forward to the chance of punishing her and thus of making moody seventeen-year-old Sharon bend over, for the sight would be extremely provoking. At present she has certainly not lost that puppy softness which gathers round a girl's hips and seat at adolescence. There is a full soft swell to the cheeks of Sharon's bottom, though they are nicely rounded. However, the man who wishes to enjoy Sharon at her best should lose no time. Even in her young womanhood those thighs and buttocks may fatten sooner than one would wish. However, I was so pleased that she and the colonel's younger girl had honoured my arrival by wearing such tight riding-pants. They stood together, the tight unfledged rounds of Vicky's trim little buttocks in their tense youthfulness and the fatter softer delights of Sharon's bottom-cheeks, which shimmered a little with the impact of jumping down from her horse.

* * *

They returned and presently I was alone with Sharon. She stood before me in her singlet and jeans, the veil of brown hair freshly combed and settled on her shoulders, the careless fringe of it on her forehead and the sweep of it framing the firm pale oval of her face. She stood there with arms folded, her straight look suggesting that though she would not resist me, she would do nothing to assist in her own punishment. A girl of eighteen like Sharon is capable of at least that much self-possession.

I turned to the cupboard, taking out the slim black switch and the rather frayed cord of the horsewhip. She stared at them, still not able to guess the degree of torment they might inflict upon her. At the centre of the room was a heavy oblong library table of dark wood.

"Go over and stand facing the table, Sharon," I said quietly.

She turned and walked slowly across, still with her arms folded as if to show her indifference. I promised myself that she would show little indifference or self-possession in half an hour more.

"Lie forward over the table, Sharon. Bend forward over it."

She did as she was told, still without a word, lying forward along it.

"Give me your hands."

She reached them out in front of her, above her head as she lay there. I slipped a strap round her wrists and drew it tight. Then I ran a length of stout cord round the strap, drew her arms out at full stretch and tied the cord firmly to the legs at the far end of the table. Sharon turned her face aside and shook her dark brown hair into place, her cheek resting on the table.

I pulled the singlet hem free of the waist of her jeans. Now that I had Sharon bending over, the rear view of her jeans was of two quite fatly-swelling young bottom-cheeks with the outline of her panties clearly ridged. I undid her at the waist and eased the denim down, making her step out of the jeans when they had fallen to her ankles. She now bent in the usual pair of briefs in white elasticated cotton, a clean pair put on just before dinner.

"Now your knickers, Sharon," I said, "You must be properly undressed for this."

Sharon's bottom gained its seductive fullness from the slight pale sheen of adolescent puppy fat, for it suited her figure and her character. I ran my hand upon it and gave a light cheek-smack, causing Sharon's soft pale arse-flesh to jump and quiver.

"Never had the whip before, Sharon?"

She bit her lip and said nothing.

"Answer when you're spoke to!"

There was a pause and then the answer came

almost as a gasp.

"No!"

I gave the same bottom-cheek another light smack.

"You shall have a taste of the stable-switch first, Sharon, and then the whipcord to finish you off."

Though her face was hidden, her body now betrayed Sharon's panic. Her knees were pressed together and she was trying to compress her rear cleavage. I stood over her, put one arm round her waist and closely inspected her young backside and the rear opening of her thighs.

"Relax your body, Sharon. I must have a good look at you first."

And so I did, admiring the rear aspect of her sex. She tried to tighten again presently, when I pressed hard apart and considered the little vortex of Sharon's posterior tightness. I straightened up, gave her another light slap on her bottom and went across to the desk where the slim black switch was lying. I picked up the switch and a leather belt. The latter went tightly round Sharon's bare waist, for I intended her to remain very firmly lying over the table.

I cut the air with the switch and the sound of it made her jump with fright. The soft pallor of Sharon's buttocks tightened instinctively.

I spent a little while taking my aim, touching the cold leather of the switch one way and another across Sharon's bare and flinching rear cheeks. My purpose had begun to harden and I very much wanted to make this a long session. I raised the long slim switch and brought it down hard with a flick of the wrist, catching Sharon's squirming young backside expertly aslant its cheeks. The room rang with the smack of leather on the soft flesh of Sharon's bottom. Sharon gasped and then her gasp rose to a cry as if the anguish increased for a moment after the impact. The silky length of her brown hair slithered clear as she tried to twist her face round to me. The whip cracked keenly, making her young bottom-cheeks quiver again and then again.

Sharon bent one knee up quickly and desperately as if that might ease the lingering smart of the whip, something I was later to see Vicky do. I caught her again with a cut that touched the searing red of the first stripe and Sharon yelled wildly. Her silky hair was spilling in confusion and the brown eyes were filled with dismay. Sharon had never dreamt that anyone would hurt her like this in reprisal for her conduct. Her legs were squirming and jigging. The whip smacked low across her bottom-cheeks. Sharon uttered a wild and wordless soprano shrillness.

The pale swell of Sharon's bottom-cheeks still jumped and quivered a little under the force of each impact. She performed arse-contortions that a professional belly-dancer might have envied. The slim black switch whipped and whipped again across her young backside until Sharon made the walls ring after every cut. She kicked out with her bare legs this way and that, receiving six measured cuts across the backs of them to discourage such conduct. Her knees seemed to give at this point. Had she been merely bending over to touch her toes, Sharon would have collapsed on the floor. How wise I had been to position her over the table so that she had to take what was given her, whether her legs would support her or not.

I do not know if she was sorry for all her previous misconduct but she looked extremely sorry for herself. From its deep blushes and crimson streaking, Sharon's seventeen-year-old bottom now looked as if she had made to sit all day in a *vase de nuit* filled with a boiling brew of sharpest thorn-twigs.

I stood back and gave her six for luck, such that in her desperation she pushed herself up from her knees and balanced by her shins on the chair's edge. Then, with some reluctance, I laid down the implement. I freed her and she burst out in a heaving lament. I undid her and let her stand up. Like a little girl who has had a smacked bottom, she wanted only to be out of her chastiser's presence and safe in her own room.

"Have you had enough, Sharon?" I asked.

She would not answer me, her head bowed, her face scalding with tears, and her brown hair hanging forward.

"No answer, Sharon? Want some more, then? I can ask the grooms to put you over the table again and hold you. Would you like that, Sharon?"

She shook her head vigorously but would neither look up at me nor speak.

"Have you learnt your lesson, Sharon?"

Still nothing. Before I could repeat the question or warn her of the penalty for dumb insolence, Sharon snatched up her briefs and jeans. Without pausing to put them on, she uttered a wild sob, ran from the room, and made the house echo to her running footsteps on the stairs.

Despite such discourtesy, I did not resume after the culprit was released. Sharon spent an hour in the bathroom and in the toilet before throwing herself on the bed, sobbing and sleeping at last.

* * *

I cannot believe there is a stranger relationship than that between a man and a girl he has whipped for some domestic offence. At any rate, I have found it to be so. The culprit and her chastiser have been antagonists and ought to be the greatest of enemies. But they have also been on terms of strange intimacy that can allow the girl nothing to hide nothing from him. I had viewed Sharon's most secret anatomy more closely, perhaps, than ever her bridegroom would on her honeymoon night. I had seen the soft quiver of Sharon's pale bottom-cheeks as her thighs squirmed in an almost sexual manner under the torturing impact of the whip. I had heard Sharon scream as, perhaps, no one would in the rest of her life. We were linked forever by sharing such highly-wrought moments and an intimate experience of her body.

During the days that followed I was aware of the manner in which she watched me when she thought I was not looking—and then turned quickly away as I glanced at her! It was plain that she thought of nothing during these encounters but the display she had offered and the manner in which she had behaved privately during her punishment. Once or twice, before she looked suddenly away in her parade of teenage temper, I caught a half-formed appeal in her brown eyes, as if she was begging me not to reveal to the others the things I had heard and seen while I was dealing with her.

After a day or two her resentment faltered. When our eyes met, she seemed to search my own gaze as if anxious to know what I thought of her. I believe she wished for an end to her silence but did not quite know how to accomplish it. The state of "not speaking" during family quarrels is not easy to terminate. I believe, however, that she also needed reassurance and affection. When Sharon was forced to take her knickers down and bend over for a man, on that first occasion, she had been confronted abruptly by the challenge of grown womanhood and all its emotions. Self-loving and childishly self-indulgent as she was, she could not, for the life of her, find a way to meet that challenge. Yet being whipped had made Sharon conscious of a new dimension and intensity of her feminine emotions. I could tell that she knew the time for adolescent sulks and moods was long past.

*　*　*

After a day or two, I noticed that they were reading several pages from *Pearls of the Orient*. Judge for yourself from the page they had been reading.

Mandy was a tousled fair-skinned brunette who had been brought up as a common working-girl. She was now a housewife, a young woman of the people, a mature young Amazon with long legs, strong thighs and hips. One might admire her firm features, brown eyes and the tresses clustering on her forehead and round her collar. It was decided to require such a strapping young wench as "cabin-boy" to Mr Bowler. Skin-tight boots came up to her knees. A short singlet ended at her waist. Day and night in his cabin, her sturdy hips, thighs and backside were always bare. It was her duty to tempt him constantly. As he reclined on his back, Mandy must clamber, tall and statuesque, on top of him, threading herself, thighs squirming and buttocks clenching. Next night Mr Bowler lay on his back again, manhood erect, while the smiling groom showed Mandy a pony-whip. She must pay a price for her pleasure as he spurred her on.

*Unhesitatingly, the eager young Amazon
mounted. This robustly-shaped brunette lay forward, comforted by Mr Bowler between her
thighs and displaying her bare buttock-swell to
the groom. The groom began his wickedly-
accurate target-practice. The blushes upon
Mandy's backside would have made the whip-
maker smile and the turnkey lick his lips with
envy. Only when first light lit the waves, did the
groom lay down his tickler, leaving Mandy to
sprawl glowing and exhausted over the divan.*

You would think that after I had tanned Sharon
the sisters must be repelled by a description of
such events. So they were if the recipient was a girl
in her teens. They showed contempt for an
account of the reformatory birch used on the
pretty young cheeks of Sally Fenton's bottom. But
they grinned with delight if it was Susan Webb,
Mandy or Trish. Had Joanne been the book's
heroine, they would have been agog with excitement.

Their adolescent clannishness and teenage
resentment dictated their tastes even in such things
as this.

* * *

When the meal was over, they both pleaded that
the afternoon's ride had exhausted them. They
positively must go to bed at once. I made no
objection. When they had been gone a few
minutes, however, I went silently up the stairs and
into the dressing-room. The recital of how the
overseer avenged himself on Sian and Helyn had
recommenced.

You may imagine how it went on, the same

voice reading all the time. There was also a continuation, or rather the conclusion, of Mandy's story. It was a sombre scene in which a harem vizier gave the sturdy young wench her quittance. Suffice it to say that she was fastened bottom-upwards over a trestle in a room where a lover's marking-ring glowed in the sparkling brazier coals, where the whips and the long-nozzled bellows were suggestively placed, and where the leather collar was capable of sinister and fatal adjustment.

At the end of this adventure, there was a pause.

"Now," said the same voice teasingly while the others protested at the interruption, "I must take the books back and lock them in the cupboard before Mr Busybody or anyone else misses them. Give me the key, Sharon."

It was, of course, the lewd young maid, Tania Jennings, who had pilfered the key to the cupboard and laid hands upon the forbidden fruit. I went back down to the study ten minutes later. The cupboard key was where I had hidden it—and where Tania had discovered it!—on top of the book-case. *Belle Sauvage* and *Pearls of the Orient* stood on the locked shelf, just where I had left them.

You may think that I summoned Tania herself to judgment at once. I did not. One does not punish a stable-maid when a young lady of the house is the prime instigator. I was going to confront Sharon for the second time within a month.

*   *   *

The world would stand aghast at the example of teenage sisters dwelling on such lurid accounts as the demise of a sturdy young trollop like Mandy. In the case of my two *protégées,* I was no less perturbed. It is no bad thing that they should read of such matters in some shape or form, as a caution against the evils of the world. It was the sniggers and gloating with which they consumed the story that worried me more than anything else. But since I am confessing the truth, I am obliged to add that the prospect of having Sharon to myself in the study—and at my disposal—was uppermost in my mind just then. Compared with that encounter, I do not suppose I cared whether she was reading randy tales or the works of Shakespeare.

I was sitting in the leather armchair by the tall minster fireplace when she came in. She did not knock for admittance. Young girls do not do that nowadays, regarding the entire house as Liberty Hall, coming and going as they please. She had not gone to bed, of course, for it was still not ten o'clock, and she was dressed in her jeans and blouse as usual. Even at Beechy Lodge, the days were gone when such teenage girls would put on a simple but becoming dress in the evenings.

"Come here, Sharon," I said, looking up and indicating the hearth-rug in front of me. She walked across and, I think, she was genuinely in doubt as to what she might have done wrong. She stood in front of me, the silky brown tresses combed aside on her forehead from their central parting, a rather pudding-faced dullness on the oval pallor of her face.

"What is it?" she asked, trying to sound indifferent but her voice betraying the lightest tremor.

I looked up at her from my chair.

"Your maid has developed a habit of stealing the key to the cupboard by the bookshelves. You are old enough, Sharon, to know that small acts of dishonesty among girls of her class will lead to more serious ones."

"It was Tania," she said indifferently, "Not me."

"She removed from that cupboard various books belonging to Sir Harry," I said insistently, "You took them from her. What is much worse, you then encouraged Victoria . . ."

To my astonishment, her sullen bravado gave way to a look of despair. Sharon bowed her head and put her hands over her ears, as if she could not bear to listen. It was so utterly out of character that I could not explain her action at all. She looked up once at the table beyond me, then bowed her head again and gave a slight self-pitying sob.

To my greater astonishment, she sank to her knees on the hearth rug, buried her face in my lap and emitted another dry sob. Was it to be like this every time I found fault with her? It was quite unlike her previous conduct—the contemptuous adolescent. I was lost for words. In that moment, I looked about me, thinking that this was scarcely the most convenient posture in which to hold a discussion on moral duty! As I turned my head, towards the table that she had been gazing at while I spoke to her, I saw that the slim leather switch was lying across it.

Now this was pure coincidence. Until that afternoon I had forgotten that it was propped against the pale stone of the minster fireplace, where it had remained since I had thrashed Sharon so soundly a few weeks before. That afternoon, I had picked it up with an intention of telling Tania to return it to the stables. But the breaking of my cuff-link chain and all that followed had quite put the business out of my mind. But the switch still lay on the table where I had put it several hours before.

Sharon, of course, standing before me and hearing my reprimand, naturally supposed that she was about to receive another taste of it. That was not my intention but the threat filled her with horror. After the previous tanning, Sharon's bottom had been bruised and swollen for several days. But it was not this discomfort that she remembered. Her mind recalled the naked agony of the whip across her bare backside and thighs, the screaming and frenzy, the torture she had undergone.

I did not—and do not—regret that, for she thoroughly deserved it. But this was another matter. However, I sat with Sharon's silky brown veil of hair overspreading my thighs and her face still buried from view. I believe I should have found the right words in a few seconds more. I had already formed a vision in my own mind of raising Sharon gently to her feet, reassuring her, reprimanding her a little for her conduct, and then establishing a calm affection between us. I did not think it possible that there could be any other outcome that evening.

Looking back on the incident, I now see that Sharon was more frantic than I could have imagined. Having tasted the agony of leather across her bare backside, it now held a terror for her that she would do anything in the world to avoid. I approve of that, naturally, for what is the use of such punishment otherwise? But the consequence was that before I could respond she placed a hand on my thigh with another sob and drew open a significant button.

Well now, I am too much the man of the world to jump up like a scalded cat each time a girl of seventeen or eighteen helps herself in this way. Sharon led on the warm sleeping serpent that was now to be her household pet and whose bulk stirred a little into stiffness at the gentle and cool touch of her fingers. She raised her head a little and the rounded silken veil of brown hair slid from her shoulder-blades and fell about her face as she looked down at what she had done.

I craned my head down for a better view, so that I could watch what Sharon was doing. By this time, I had not the least intention of interfering with her submissive display of affection. That being the case, it was sensible to enjoy it to the full. She turned her head on one side, holding the fine specimen in her hand and I stroked the hair back from her face so that I could watch more clearly still.

She touched her lips to the proud head with a little peck of a kiss, not quite able to bring herself to the vital point. Then she settled her head on my lap, kneeling up with her hips raised from her heels. Sharon studied the proudly raised creature thoughtfully and without dismay. I do not think she had ever familiarised herself with such before but instinct was her teacher and she acted as sensibly as any grown woman. Indeed, it was upon this evening that she seemed to accept the status of adult womanhood without reserve.

Again she kissed the head and, holding the demanding fugitive up, kissed it along its length. But still she was not quite ready to abandon herself. Then she paused, drawing her face back, her brown eyes looking steadily at the monster. As if committing herself before she could have any further doubts, Sharon opened and rounded her lips and took the first plunge. I felt the wet satin warmth of her soft tongue comfort my yearnings. Despite the books she had read so furtively, Sharon needed no instruction or education as to what to do next. It was natural in her as it has been in women since time began.

Sharon drew up and down the length with the eager but awkward skill of an inquisitive girl with a stick of rock. I was certain it was the first time and

I do not think Sharon would have done it then, had it not been for her dread of the torture with which the whip threatened her. That torture of the whip across her bare bottom and the backs of her legs had driven her almost out of her mind by its intensity. She would do anything to escape it this time. She paused and drew back so that the head of the prisoner was still confined. Then she moved her tongue and used its tip to tickle the head. All her childish sullenness and adolescent resentment was put aside. She did what she imagined I would expect Joanne to do.

One has little conscience when a situation of this kind develops so far. As her veil of brown hair cascaded about my lap, I led Sharon to the conclusion in one way or another. I might oblige her to swallow her pride at last. It was important for Sharon that she should make her amends in some way.

I stilled her from time to time, laying my hands on her head in its sleek swathing of hair. I wanted Sharon to endure for as long as possible and, if it could be prolonged, for the better part of the night. By no means was she to spend half an hour in the study and then return to bed forgiven.

I cannot say how long it was before I made Sharon pause again and drew myself back.

"Stand up," I murmured, "Stand up, Sharon."

She did as she was told, glancing at me uncertainly once or twice but slipping off her briefs without further ado. She could not forget that the last time she was like this in the study it was to receive a good hiding! But still she pulled off her jeans and her cotton briefs. I tucked up the hem of her blouse above her waist and made a gesture which, I suppose, was ambiguous.

To my surprise, Sharon walked across and bent over the table in much the same posture as when I had tanned her. The reason was simple enough, I suppose. She had seen that I had been excited to have her in that position on the previous occasion and she thought that I would like it now. I walked across and stood over her. But though I stood where I had done before, on this occasion my hand was empty. I circled her waist with my left arm and bowed my face to her rear as she remained bending over the table. I kissed the backs of her soft pale thighs and Sharon gave a little quiver. I coaxed back her feminine warmth and fondled it gently. By doing this firmly and certainly I quietened her tremors. All the same she gave a little involuntary shudder when I kissed and trilled my tongue against the warm humidity of the sensitive flesh.

"I think it will be better if we both kneel down and lie on the carpet, Sharon," I said gently, coaxing her to sink to the floor and strip off her blouse. I wanted to do a good many things but at this stage it was necessary to be prudent. It would never do for Sharon to have a curiously swollen belly and produce an infant nine months after my time of being in authority over the household at Beechy Lodge! She lay down presently, according to my suggestion, drawing her legs up and parting them widely so that her feet hovered in the air like pretty white birds. It was not that Sharon had any experience with those boys who were her admirers. Feminine intuition told her that this was the way to hold herself when she was about to be loved and comforted.

With some caution, I knelt down and took my place in her very gently. It would have been more difficult had she been chaste in the strictest sense. But though Sharon had not yielded the pleasures of that place, her inclinations towards self love had made her easier in that way than she might have been otherwise. So I toiled over her and, at the same time, kissed her bare breasts and teased their nipples with my teeth. Sharon was gasping and, though it was I who was the active partner, the sweat gathered in the hollows of her body on that warm night, as if she was labouring to achieve her climax.

She gave herself slightly to the rhythm of love, pressing and relaxing alternately so that she felt it more deeply and with greater vigour. I hoped that I might bring her off, for it is important that such a girl should associate her first proper experience with ecstasy of that degree. I could see from the way she fluttered her eyes and drew breath through parted lips that Sharon was floating high with the delicious and dreamy feeling of being ridden by a man. But it was necessary to prolong this so that she might have time to overcome her teenage misgivings and join in the fun properly. By that means she would be more likely to triumph properly.

But I knew that it would be most imprudent for me to let go within her. There was a point at which I withdrew and heard such a forlorn and bereft little cry from Sharon. She had been parted from the thing she adored most in the world! The beloved object without which she could not live! In her present state she was beyond reason or restraint of any kind.

Well, I had no intention of playing the barbarian with her by denying her the relief she sought and which I owed her as a duty of love. I turned her over gently on her side and lay behind her. The slightly waved gloss of her brown hair lay in a rounded cut to cover her shoulder-blades and was so abundant that it covered most of the width of

· 74 ·

her back. I slipped my stiffness between her thighs from the rear, not entering her but ensuring that the rod stroked along her sex as I moved to and fro. She shuddered and moaned at this for she found that the sensitive lips and the exquisite button of feminine release thrilled to such caresses. At the same time I slipped my arms round her so that my hands fondled her breasts and her belly.

Sharon was in a dream of bliss as all this was done to her and I had not the least doubt that she would find her fulfilment in a moment more. I was more concerned about my own approaching crisis, for the pressure of it was building fast and would scarcely be denied. I drew back to avoid the mischances which sometimes follow from releasing it between a girl's legs. I laid myself down in the warm valley between the soft pallor of two pearly rear hills.

"I shall certainly put you to a little inconvenience in a moment, Sharon," I said breathlessly. "Will you mind?"

She could not bring herself to speak but shook her head most emphatically. My right hand descended and slipped between her legs from the front as we lay clamped in this posture. I soothed and tickled and stroked, feeling her shiver and gasp with the excitement of it. A mad idea it was that had seized me and yet I could not honestly say I regretted it just then. As my passion boiled over, I directed it first to the firmly shut postern. While the vagrant knocked for admittance at the bottom gate, the custodian of the forbidden rear portal hesitated a moment and then turned traitor to herself. She made a supreme effort to throw open the defence, yielding with a will and holding the happy traveller tight enough to squeeze the last drop of life from him . . .

I believe we came almost at the same time. Sharon was gasping and crying and shuddering, keening in ecstasy, spiced by alarm at the feeling of the lodger who occupied such a large space in so small an entry. My own instinct was to press in as far as I could. As I did so, she seized my hand which had played and teased her, kissing and tickling it with her tongue.

We lay for a moment with my manhood still ensnared and Sharon kissing the beloved hand. I realised that my power was not even waning, thanks to Sharon's bottom and the excitement in my brain. She lay very still. Indeed, she was watching us in one of the mirrors, in which I was also able to see that firm oval beauty of her face with its parted fringe and veil of brown hair.

Sharon could feel this too and was well aware of my continued vigour. After a moment, I sensed the unmistakable movement of her haunches. It was not the act of expulsion. Sharon was permitting and even enabling me to continue.

"In this way, Sharon?" I asked, amusement and surprise in my voice.

She nodded quickly, as if to still her own doubts.

"But I shall have to go up when you've finished," she said, half turning her head and brushing back the hair from her face.

I smiled and held her steady with a hand on each flank of her bare hips. Then the movements began. Sharon folded her arms and buried her face in them. This time she could only be passive, receiving but unable to yield any more. She leant forward a little, the soft pallor of her bottom-cheeks swelling out. During this, she held herself a bit tense and uneasily, which added to the drama of the situation. At last I warned her gently to expect her reward, which amounted to quite as much as the first had done. This time she evicted me gently when it was over, turned into my arms and thanked me for what I had done.

I raised her affectionately and led her across the the hearth-rug. I sat down in the same chair and pressed her to her knees before me, allowing her to admire the cause of her "ruin" more closely. She held the wanderer in her hand and turned it this way and that, until it began to respond again. To my astonishment and delight, she lifted her hips from her heels, bowed her face and once more cocooned the homeless fellow in the sensual delights of her young mouth.

I had never had any intention of using discipline upon her, it would have been absurd. But while she gave tongue, I reached for the switch and used it to tickle her bare bottom and give her a menacing little thrill. The result was that she worked much harder than on the first occasion, joining in the game and pretending to be fearful that she might not have escaped retribution after all. When the moment came, I whispered to her, reminding her that she must not shrink from her duty. I was almost as profuse as before while Sharon consumed me and was consumed in her turn.

It was past midnight. She got to her feet looking a little confused. She snatched up her briefs, just as she had done after her punishment.

"I must go upstairs," she said breathlessly, not even waiting to put them on, for I guessed they would only have to be taken off again in a moment more. And so she rushed from the room, holding her other hand over her bare bottom in a charming gesture of reticence.

I got up from my chair. But I did not go at once to bathe and change into my smoking jacket.

Instead I opened the study door, turned the light out, and waited. A minute or two went by. Then the main door opened softly and was locked again. A figure crossed the hall towards the stairs. To my surprise it was Victoria, who had kept her vigil on the terrace for us.

After this, it seemed to me that Victoria was almost as softly confiding and quietly affectionate towards me as Sharon. While I was Sharon's enemy, the chastiser of the elder girl, Vicky sparkled with hatred. But now I had become the lover and adorer of Sharon, so that Victoria was obliged to change her view as well.

I was glad that matters had been resolved. There are those, I daresay, who will stand aghast and deplore my hours as Sharon's lover. But let me say this. Sharon was the better for it in many ways. She required an escape from the prison of her teenage emotions. Before that evening, Beechy Lodge was a place of sulks and jealousies, resentment and furtive laughter. From now on it became a far more agreeable house in which to live.

Vicky, as well as Sharon, became a little more serious and level-headed. They talked about the affairs of the day as if they might be mature young women. They were no such thing and yet they played at maturity and womanhood, which was a vast improvement.

I sat alone with my cigar and hock an evening or two later, when the others had gone to bed. I thought of the irony of my situation. The world would see me as a libertine, a seducer led by his tool. Sex was all I thought about. Shall I tell you the truth? Had Sharon been repulsive to me and had I had no interest in her sexually, I would still have rated those hours of seduction as an evening well spent. They gave me the very thing that discipline and repression often fail to produce. At last I had an affectionate and obedient household in which a man could enjoy peace and quiet.

It seemed a small price to pay.

CHAPTER FOUR: A SUMMER AMOUR

ONLY A BOY, OR A SUMMER AMOUR was published in Paris by Charles Carrington in 1908. It forms the second half of a volume, the first part being taken up by a facetious lecture of sexual instruction. Lacking a snappy title, Carrington called that preliminary lecture, *Love and Safety,* or *Love and Lasciviousness with Safety and Secrecy—A Lecture delivered with Practical Illustrations by the Empress of Austria (The Modern Sappho) Assisted by her Favourite Lizette and Others.*

With a title like that, there wasn't much more for the lecture itself to say. The French government, having had enough of Carrington's antics already, was not best pleased by a public lampoon on the Empress of Austria. She, poor lady, had died in 1898 having been stabbed by an Anarchist at Geneva. But then it turned out that the lecture was actually a translation of a French sex-education spoof that had been going round since the 1860s.

So the sensible reader skipped over *Love and Safety* and came instead to *Only a Boy, or A Summer Amour.* It was a short novelette, well written and sensitively pitched in its tone. This was no fly-by-night pornography but the work of a real writer, Eugene Field, who had died in 1895 at the age of forty-five. He was a celebrated columnist for the *Chicago Morning News,* well known for his humorous writing and his verses, many of them for children. *A Little Book of Western Verse* (1889) was among his best known.

During his lifetime, Field published nothing that would rate as a work of underground fiction. It is a fair indication of the repressive censorship in America as well as England at the time that *Only a Boy, or A Summer Amour* had to find its home in the Rue du Faubourg Montmartre along with the rest of Carrington's stock.

Eugene Field's story is the reminiscence of a man at the end of his life, though he was only in his forties when he wrote it. He looks back at a youthful idyll of erotic awakening. The novel is unusual among the literature of its kind in being set in California, though it is a California far removed from the one we know today. Its balmy innocence seems remote as some tropical island.

The story's theme belongs to that age of innocence. How is the boy, as hero of the story, to learn the ways of womankind? That problem no longer concerns us. A few lessons in sex education and let him get on with it among his own contemporaries. The romantics had another vision, which owed more to France than California. In his teens he would meet an older and sexually experienced woman. She would not be that much older, perhaps twenty-five or thirty. Taking as much pleasure in it as he, she would gently teach him the ways of love. The relationship would not be permanent, of course. But he would always remember her with love and gratitude.

Perhaps it never worked anywhere except in a novel, but the idea of it appealed strongly in a less cynical age than our own. The reality in Europe was that a good many young men went off to the brothels of Paris or Berlin, London or Madrid, and took a crash-course in sex from women who might be quite a bit older. But that was the world of Maupassant and Zola rather than of the California idyll. So here, complete and unexpurgated, is Eugene Field's story. True or not, it remains the embodiment of a wistful and romantic idea.

ONLY A BOY OR A SUMMER AMOUR

OR

LOVE AND LASCIVIOUSNESS
WITH SAFETY AND SECRECY

THE EROTICA BIBLION SOCIETY
OF
LONDON—NEW YORK

ONLY A BOY OR A SUMMER AMOUR

The thorns which often prick us most
Are found 'mong sweetest flowers.

An incident in my boyish life to-night passes before me in all the tinting of a panoramic view; and as my thoughts run back over the checkered pathway of forty years, which has sprinkled my hair with gray, filled my life with thorns and orange blossoms, to a month that has left its imprint on my whole life, I wish that I possessed the power to reproduce the picture in all its colors, and do justice to the work which, at your request, I undertake to-night. I regret that the favor you ask is one which compels me to write of myself. To a modest man, lacking that phrenological enlargement that as a rule in men and women predominates in such a lamentable degree, the position is embarrassing; and in the perusal of this, I trust your eye will rest on the unpleasant character I am, as little as possible.

I was born 'neath a warm sun and pleasant skies; where the air was frighted with the blended odor of the magnolia and jessamine that heightened the senses; where everything had its bud and blossom almost at his birth, where the dreamy languour of the voluptuary seemed inherent in all; where even in those which here in the North would be termed children, the sexual spark only waited for contact to flame up in its power; where girls were mothers at thirteen and grandmas at thirty. But up to my eleventh year, I had known only books and sketching—a sweet-tempered, linen-dressed boy, who lived out of the sunshine and ignored the innocent deviltries of youth; who looked upon girls as horrid; whose life was rounded by a pony, books, pictures, and the flowers in the conservatory. But changes for good or evil take place in every life. It came to mine; and on that sweet, sighing summer day in my twelfth year, when Cupid threw apart the silken curtains, revealing beauties of which I had not even dreamed, my hand lost its cunning; to books I said farewell, and ambition was dead. That was a day of fate. How bitterly have I cursed it since; how cursed her who snatched me from my little heaven with its delightful anticipations and chaperoned me through the hot-house of passion, where every beautiful flower was filled with a subtle poison which racked the nerves, sapped the life and deadened the brain. My introduction to the pleasures and mysteries that have ever been associated with the couch of Love—the keen relish for which has blasted the family hearthstone and overthrown empires—was not entrusted to a novice; no timid, simpering girl, taking her first steps toward the realization of the anticipation of forbidden pleasures, but to a woman—a woman of thirty, who being an apt pupil under the skilful manipulations and teachings of a husband for a term of years, had herself become a preceptor in all those delicate points that surround an amour with such delights and rosy tints.

How plainly do I see her to-night! How much keener my appreciation of the wonderful piece of anatomy that time only still deeper imprints upon my memory; the standard by which from that time all female perfections and loveliness has been gauged. Ah! she is before me again, and this time unveiled. Look at her! Is she not beautiful? Note the poise of her head, from which her glinted golden hair falls in such a wealth. See those amber eyes; those wonderfully chiselled lips, so red, pulpy and moist; her fair cheeks tinted by their reflection. Her shoulders—how perfectly and exquisitely moulded—rounded with the same finish of her beautiful, swelling globes, so daintily pinked and tipped. What belly, back and hips ever had the graceful curves of thine? And you! Rounded arms, white swelling thighs and full dimpled knees (in your warm, fond pressures of years ago I feel you again tonight) was the mould broken with your completion? Gone? Yes! Only in memory now.

> We all of things
> For the first time taste
> Whether sorrow, pain or bliss.

The house on the Sound those with whom I lived had taken for the summer months was very small, only large enough for three and the servant, but it was delightfully situated in a perfect Eden: where all was soft air, perfumes, flowers and singing birds, and as I recall it now, just the spot for lovers and the complete enjoyment of stolen sweets. One day a carriage rolled up the gravel walk to the door. A beautiful woman was handed out, and everything tended to show that we had an unexpected guest. As I stood there with my black, long curling hair neath a broad palmetto hat, dressed in white pantaloons and a green jacket with brass buttons, my face reddened with the sun's rays on the water, she stopped down and kissed me tenderly many times; and as I remember now they produced a very different sensation from any kisses I had ever known before—I liked them; but I did not know why it was that I hung around her all day and thought her so nice. After she had visisted all the forenoon in the house, during which time I had learned that she was the wife of a gentleman who was a friend of my father, but who had gone to California for his health—I am willing to gamble ten *now* that he had consumption—she took my hand, and we went for a stroll around the place, along the beach and up into the lovely woods, with their tangled grasses and wild flowers. What to me then was all that snowy linen; those beautiful ruffled skirts, as she pulled them up to step over some stick or bramble—she did not seem to care how high—revealed the daintiest of feet and legs of such matchless beauty that even a cigar store Indian would lose his head at the sight of them. Ah! how many thousands have longed to live over again the first part of a life with a knowledge they had acquired in the last. Could this happen to me, what a different color the picture of which I am writing would have.

In a dense shade, where the sun could not penetrate, we sat down on a log; and after she had taken off my hat and run her dainty white hands through my hair, she placed my head in her lap, and, pulling me close to her panting bosom, she placed her pretty lips on mine and held them there, with her eyes shut, until sometimes I stifled and almost lost my breath; then she would take her lips away while her eyes sparkled and her cheeks reddened clear to her hair. There was something about it all that I liked, for I would ask her to do it again; and she, exclaiming "Bless my little man," would press me to her again and kiss me until my lips and face were all wet from her lips. Each attack and each pressure seemed to create for me some new and delightful sensation I had not known before, and then, where my little pantaloons buttoned in front, I had a pain and a great hard lump that hurt me, and in my innocence I told her about it. "Let me see," she said kindly; and one of her hands, that had so many pretty rings on her fingers, stole down and unbuttoned my pants; and then, what I had never seen more than two inches long, and soft as a baby's flesh, was standing out full five inches and terribly swollen. I was awfully frightened at the sight and the pain, but she took it in her hand, telling me "it was no matter," and I seemed to get better right away. Then she kissed it four or five times and bit it gently, after which, she put it back and buttoned my pantaloons again. I wanted her to hold it some more, but she said "No," we must go back; and before we reached the house, she made me promise on my life that I would never say what she had done or would choose to do. I would have done anything for her, for I tell you she had made a willing slave of me in the few hours that had followed since her arrival.

During the time between tea and the hour for retiring, and while she was in conversation with the older ones, I hung about her knees playing with her beautiful hands and looking into her wonderful eyes; but I soon felt that I was not as much to her as I had been out in the woods, and signifying my intention to retire, I was informed at the foot of the stairs that I was to sleep across her bed at the foot.

I took off my clothes, then had my regular evening sponge off, put on my little short nightshirt, and then turning back the coverlet very carefully, as per last instructions, placed me a pillow and crept in. I lay for some time, thinking of my afternoon's experience, and the strange and delightful sensations that had been awakened by my newlyfound acquaintance, but I could not solve the problem; and, while wishing that the night would be very short, so that when day came she would take me walking again, I fell asleep.

I do not know how long I slept, but I seemed to be dreaming that some one was tickling one of my ribs; and I awoke only to find that I had a bedfellow, and that it was a pretty pair of feet that had been playing with me. I was wide awake in an instant, and had them in my hands. How soft they were. Gradually my hand stole higher up than her feet—up her limbs so round and smooth, but I did not know why I did it, unless they were so soft and felt so warm. The moon was shining brightly through the window, and the room was light as day. I turned over and there was her pretty face and those great eyes looking at me.

"Come up and I will take you in my arms," she whispered, and I was less than a second getting there.

Oh! How she hugged and kissed me, and how nice her plump bare arms felt to my face and neck.

Then she carelessly unfastened her chemise and I saw what I had never seen before in that way— two beautiful bosoms at once. How pretty they looked, so white and so round, in the soft moonlight. She rubbed them, panting and heaving, over my face and lips, and then whispered to me to "bite them," and as my lips fastened over the little hard tips, her breath almost burned my face, and I felt a new joy that I had not learned in the woods, and realized that I was swelling again as I had in the afternoon of the day before. Then I felt one of her warm hands steal down and take it, while with the other she took my hand, rubbed it up and down on the big part of her soft legs, and then to the softest, prettiest thing I had ever felt in my young life, where she left it.

Oh, what a plaything I had found, so soft, curly and juicy; and as my hand found a delicate opening, she jumped as though I had hurt her. Then I felt her open her legs wide apart, after which she whispered to me to get in there and lie on top of her, which I did; and, as she pulled my little shirt up, I felt my bare belly fitting close to hers, and that her chemise was clear up to her arms. Then she kissed me and hugged me again—I thought that she would break me in two; and whispering to me to do just as she told me, she reached down and took the little fellow that was killing me with pain and placed it where I had my finger when I thought I had hurt her. "Now you make it go in," she whispered, and she raised her body clear from the bed with my weight on her, and when she settled back it *was* in; and she gave a great sigh, as I had heard people do who were in trouble. Then she squeezed me and bit me, and seemed to be trying to rock me in a new kind of cradle; and taking me by the hips, she would push me off and pull me back, never letting that little fellow get out of the nest where she had placed him; and while I felt a tingling sensation in my fingers and toes and up and down my back, she would roll her head on the pillow from side to side, saying, "Oh, oh, oh!" I whispered to her that I thought I would have to get up to "pepe," but she said "No," and, putting a towel under her hips, she suddenly locked her legs over my back; then, bending her back high from the bed, she panted and held me so for a second, trying to reach my lips, but I was too short—then I lost my senses and everything got green, and I felt that I was bleeding in and all over that pretty little plaything on which I had been lying for ten minutes. Her arms and legs unloosened and I rolled off from her shaking like a leaf; but she kissed me and whispered that I would feel better in a few minutes, and I did. Then she got up carefully and taking the towel, she went to the washstand and did something, I did not know what (then), and coming back to the bed she took me in her arms, telling me that I *must never tell;* and asking me if it wasn't awful nice, she kissed me a few times, made me kiss her, and with my head on her pretty bosom, we fell asleep.

"Wasn't it awful nice?" Well, I should say it was; the little heaven I had created had all been knocked into a cocked hat by the one she had created for me. I smile when I think of my innocence—smile when I reflect what a public benefactor I was at that tender age.

The next morning, after a kiss and a look at the pretty bosom and white bare arms, I received my instructions as to how I should act; and putting on my clothes, I went down stairs, *kicking gently* for having to sleep across the bed.

She was a lady of culture and refinement, saw things to be done and did them with a will; could prepare the choicest of pastries, and by her winning way was soon a welcome guest at our cottage on the beach; but who dreamed of the bond—those most intimate of relations—that had so suddenly been established between us.

Breakfast over, at which she was asked the usual questions as to how she had rested, and if I had made her any trouble, etc., all of which received the proper replies, I took her out in my boat in the cool of the morning for a ride; and more than once I caught sight of her pretty legs peeping out from her snowy drapery, that had suddenly grown to have such significance for me. She sang to me on the water, while I rowed and watched what little of her limbs were in sight; but I had a strange desire, for one of my age, to see more, and I said: "Mrs. B—, you have such pretty legs, would you let me see them higher up?" She said: "Why, certainly my little man, I will do anything for you," and reaching down, she gathered her dress skirts and ruffles and held them clear up over her face. Gods! What a picture—the tight-fitting stockings; the blue garters above her knees, and the white, bare thighs. Then the skirts went down again, but the picture was left in my mind.

In the afternoon, we strolled out into the woods and sat in the same place as the day before, when she sang to me and told me stories. She was silent for a while, then turning to me she said: "My little man, for you are a man, what we did last night is what those do who get married. My husband is sick and for nearly a year has been gone for his health, and for months I have been almost dying for the pleasure your little body gave me last night," and drawing me to her she kissed me rapidly. I felt very proud of myself after what she said, and immediately asked her if I might do it again when she came to bed; and with a smile she kissed me and said she "would see about it."

She knew the power her beautiful legs had brought upon me, and on the way back she revealed them at every opportunity; and when I asked her if I might put my hand on the little beauty-spot, she said: "Yes, but be quick," and I was; but I did, and she liked it as well as I; and the reaching down, and putting my hand up under her rattling skirts to the mossy charm, created the same intense thrill that characterized the same attempt in my later years.

Before we reached the cottage, she charged me to be sure and eat a hearty supper, and to always eat plenty of meat and eggs and to drink milk.

Ah! How well do I know now why she was so careful in looking after my diet. Meat, eggs and milk! Oh, yes. I think I have followed those instructions every day from that time—from then til now—thirty long years with their lights and shades.

After tea was over, I for the first time in my life, experienced a high degree of restlessness and impatience. What was it I wanted? I got out my drawings; they had grown dull and stupid. I turned to my books, but they were unsatisfying, and bidding all good-night, I went to bed, but not to sleep. 'Twas she and only she. In the bed, with its tender memories of the night before, I grew even worse, tossing and longing, the moments stretching into hours, while I waited for her coming.

How my heart beat when at last I heard her footsteps on the stairs. As she came in, I feigned sleep, and bending over me, she kissed me with her hot lips and I was happy. Then she went to the mirror and began taking down her beautiful hair, which loosened, fell below her hips. After she had unhooked her dress and taken it off, she unfastened her skirts and stepped out of them, and taking off her corset, she stood before me in her short ruffled chemise, while she toileted and coiled up her lovely hair.

How beautiful and fascinating she was as she stepped about here and there, and as she stood to pick up this and that from the floor. I peeped under her little skirt and saw the white bare thighs that I had seen in the boat—that had held me so tightly the night before. Then she sat down and unlaced her shoes, and drawing the stockings from her beautiful legs, stood up again.

"I like you," I said to her in a low tone, and she stepped to the bed, whispering, "You little rascal, have you been awake all this time and watching me?" I inclined my head, and putting my arms around her neck whispered that I had been waiting so long for her to come, and that I thought she was so nice and pretty.

"Bless your heart," she replied, "do you think so?"

I answered "Yes," and asked if she wouldn't please take *all* off, and, looking at me a second, she shrugged her lovely shoulders and the chemise slipped down to her feet; then I saw her all at once from her full neck to her toes—saw what I had longed to see—that little beauty with golden hair which had almost killed me with joy the night before. "Now are you satisfied?" she asked, and she bent over me, while her bosoms rested on my face; and as I put my hands on them as though to keep them, she put on her chemise—then took it off again—and putting out the light, came to bed.

I was less than a minute getting by her side and she was less in getting me in her arms. I knew now what she wanted; what I wanted; the ice had been broken. I was an apt pupil, and the secret fire of my youth had burst forth in all its fury. I bit her arms, her belly, her legs; bit and sucked her rosy nipples; kissed her from head to foot; tickled her little beauty with golden curls; got on to and off from her; put my head between her hot, fat thighs; which pressed it until I thought it would split, sported from knees to lips in a wild delirium of newfound ecstasy, her breath burning my cheeks as I rested for a moment with my head on her beating bubbies.

Then, holding me tightly, she put a sudden stop to my gambols, and sliding her hand down to her little friend, who had attained his majority—and was no slouch for twelve years, I assure you—she put me on my back, and bending over me she nibbled him gently with her red, damp lips; and then, falling on her back, she lifted me, as though with iron force, above her, and opening her quivering thighs, let me down gently, saying, "All ready," and taking in her hand the pet who was eager for his duty, she gently parted the golden hairs, and having fitted him, locked her arms around my body, and, raising her buttocks from the bed, I pressed gently down and she fell back with a smile and glowing cheeks.

The motion she had produced in her way the night before, I now felt that I could perform without assistance, and as I did so she tried to kiss me, and whispered, "That's right," her voice fluttering so that I thought she was choking. I had found the secret of her pleasure, and hers was mine; and as I alternately tickled her, briskly, then gently, I remembered a supressed, fluttering moan, which I now know was the acme of bliss. But I grew tired and fell where I lay; yet linked together the bliss went on in a delicious throbbing, that can never be told. Soon she gasped, "More! more!" and I, loving her so strongly that I would do anything for her, began again the gentle movement.

She whispered to me, but I was getting deaf and blind with rapture; and then I whispered to her that it was coming; she straightened her snowy legs, drew them together, threw her belly up against mine, loosened her arms, quivered from head to foot, gasped "Now then!" and as a thick mist gathered in my eyes, I felt the hot stream go from me to her and all was over.

"Oh, you sweet boy," she said, as she pulled me to her lips, kissing me and biting my neck, "you don't know how happy you have made me to-night—how you have satisfied my restless, burning fever," and getting up, she went to the washstand, where she remained a second or two; then, putting on her chemise, she came back to bed and taking me in her arms, I fell asleep while she was smoothing my hair.

On the following morning, I awoke as bright as a dollar and happy as a lark, and, after raising and peeping under the thin cover, through which the sun was shining, lighting her beautiful, velvety skin with a rosy tint, I ran my hand all over her beauties here and there, petted the little flaxen-haired darling, crawled up to her bubbies and nibbled then awhile, and then, with her morning kiss upon my lips, I went downstairs and out to see my pony, that for two days had seen less of me than he had at any time, since the day he was given to me as a reward for my diligent course at school.

How many times, since the days which I am recalling, have I thought of that little cottage and wondered if fate had ordained that my room should be above the close-curtained parlor that was seldom used, and never after the sun was down.

Ah! Wise heads, I would that your confidence in the innocence of your boy had been less strong; then the seeds of an engrossing passion which have ripened and borne fruit these long years would never have been sown.

How long it seemed to me before she came down to breakfast. I could think of nothing but her and the many beauties she had unveiled to my young eyes and vivid sense; my only thought to feel her kisses and dally with the pretty charms concealed beneath her whitest of skirts and pretty embroideries. But she came and I was happy.

That day, she complained of headache and we neither went boating nor walking, but remained at the house all day; and when she came to bed, she took me in her arms, but did not kiss me much, and told me that I must go to sleep and not think of that, as she was feeling badly. Her words cast a gloom over my young life, but I did as I was told and bore my grief in silence. On the following day she was well again and in her usually happy mood.

We bless that which antidotes pain.
And sunshine is sweetest after rain.

After dinner, the sun being behind the clouds and not too warm, we went down to the boat for a ride. She talked to me while I rowed and kept my eyes on her, and observing that once in a while my eyes glanced towards her little feet, she seemed to know by intuition what was in my thoughts, and up went all that hid what I longed to see. The sight sent the blood to my white face, and, as she put down her skirts, she looked at me and, smiling, said; "My little sweetheart, if you will row to some nice, quiet little spot, where no one goes, and we can be alone, you can lie between the legs you think so pretty and like so much." I was a little tired of the oars, but at her words I grew suddenly strong, and being near a long strip of land that ran out into the Sound, I pulled up to the point and we got out, and had walked but a few steps when we came to a nice little grass plot, on which we sat down, after she had spread out a light shawl that I had observed on her arm as we went down to the boat.

With the exception of the twittering birds and the water washing up against the shore all was as still as death. The great pines and cedars that moon so in the summer air were even still, while the absence of the sea breeze among the jessamine and honeysuckle made their odor almost stifling there under the dense foliage.

"Oh! little one, ain't this nice?" she said to me as she took off her hat and tossed it to one side;

"what a nice time we will have alone in the lovely shade"; and putting her arm around me she fell back on the shawl, taking me with her. We were both on our backs, looking up among the green leaves. Soon she drew me closer to her and asked me what I wanted, and as I placed one of my hands on the bosom of her dress, she began to unhook it at the neck one by one, until all were undone, and I saw them peeping out over her chemise so white and round. Then she unclasped her corset. By this time, I was on my knees, and unbuttoning her chemise, I turned the corners back and took the pretty things, all undressed, in my hands. Then I bent over them and kissed them, bit them gently, then sucked them, and it seemed to me then that I would have given my life to have one of them all in my mouth.

I was feeling good all over as, she pulled me down to her and kissed me in such a new way; she seemed to cover my whole mouth with her lips and sucked it all in between them. I felt her hot tongue in my mouth and almost down my throat, while her breath came hot and her bubbies rose and fell. I turned and saw her skirts above her knees, and as with one hand I reached down to pull them up higher so as to feast my eyes, I felt her hand working into my pants and tickling the little eggs that I thought would burst with pain. I had just got my hand on the little bird's-nest, that was such an infatuation to me, when she said: "Jump up quick and take off your pants."

As I arose to do her bidding, and unbuttoned my pants from my jacket, what a delightful view I had of her many charms; and those bare thighs! how intensely inviting do I remember them. My pants off, I walked to her and stood over her, the little soldier standing hard and proud. She put out one of her hands and took hold of it, and then raised herself until her lips could touch it. Oh! how she squeezed and bit it, all the time muttering some little words of affection. Then, springing from her, I put my head down between her white legs and kissed little goldy until she rolled and moaned and said she could stand it no longer, "Do it now! do it now!" she said, and as she threw her thighs apart, I crawled between them and rested my weight on her belly. Then I felt her warm fingers arranging things; and when she had placed her pet as she wanted him, I felt him among the parted curls that seemed all wet, gliding so smoothly until it was all in, and our bodies close together. "Oh! what delight!" She seemed to be doing the same thing with her mossy lips that she had with the others when she kissed me a few moments before, and I felt that she would draw me to her very heart, body and all, as she lay there murmuring: "Oh, you sweet boy!" "No, you do it to me nice," she said, as I drew him back gently and then plunged him back quickly. I felt her body drawing and writhing under me with some new motion of her buttocks that I had not felt before, which was highly electrifying to us both; but how wet and smooth she was there. Soon she began to draw her legs up and then straighten them out again, her hands squeezing her bubbies, while, with her eyes shut, she rolled her head from side to side, a gentle moan escaping her half-open lips.

"Now! Now! Quick! Quick!" she said, as she opened her eyes and started suddenly. I felt that I was dying with delight, but I immediately began knocking more vigorously at her little gateway, and as she locked her legs over my back, holding them so tight that I could not move, I felt a tingling, twitching sensation of delight, and in a second her velvet-lined lips were sipping the hot stream of my youthful passion. Her arms fell lifeless at her sides; her fat legs dropped from my back, and the smile on her beautiful face spoke more than words.

While I was putting on my pants, she went away, but was soon back again, and, kissing and hugging me a few times, we went down to the boat and home.

Ah! how that woman in three days had crept into my life; I was hers, body and soul; she was my sunshine, my life; no thought that was not of her, no act but that tending to gain her smiles. I could look in her face and eyes for hours and never weary of it. Little did I know then what the heart was; what it could suffer; what it could stand; and yet how short was the time until mine was put to the test.

The days came and went, but there was no abating in my desire to see her charms; to know the delightful intoxications that I found in her arms. She did not always humor me in my desires, however, knowing that for her pleasure I must have time to recruit to be equal to her passion, but she was always kind and gentle, and outside of the *act,* never denying me a wish in the looking at or feeling what I chose. How often, while standing, has she allowed me to stoop down and get under her skirts, and with my arms around her hips, let me bury my face high up between her swelling thighs until I almost suffocated.

Yes, the mould was broken after those hips and legs so well shaped.

> *Unexpected pleasure*
> *Doth highest pleasure round.*

Two weeks had almost elasped since the day she

came, and still our relations were unsuspected.

One day she wished to go to the city and return in the evening. On her promise to take good care of me, I was allowed to accompany her.

On arriving we went to a hotel and were placed in a lovely room. We ran about the stores until noon and then to the room, and after putting off our things, went to dinner. She ordered for me just what she said I must eat, and while there were things that I wanted, I did not let her know it, but obeyed her in everything. After we had finished our dinner we went to our room, and after closing the lower shutters, she began taking off her clothes, while my eyes were wide with wonder. One thing and then another were taken off, until finally she stood with nothing on but her stockings and chemise. She seemed to hesitate a second, and then taking those off, she threw herself on the bed with her hands over her head.

How sweet she was, and as I stood looking at her, she said: "Come, my little man, ain't you going to take yours off and come and lie with me?"

I was going to be in heaven again, and I had mine off in half the time she had taken, and was as naked as she when I stepped up and stood beside her.

Taking her playmate in her hand, so soft and white, she tickled him awhile and saw him grow, and after nibbling me a little on my belly, she threw her arms around me and tossed me over on the bed, and, straightening me out full length, she drew me close to her hot skin and covered me with kisses. As soon as she loosened her embrace, I had my mouth on one of the nipples of her snowy breast (and as I remember now, that act struck every electrical wire in my body—it does yet); one hand over the little "poulter" nestling in the soft of her thighs; and as my finger found its way in slowly, she rather liked the two sensations; her cheeks growing redder each moment, she grasped the fellow who, at his full size, was throbbing at her side, then, jumping up quickly, she took the pillows and throwing them together on the bed, told me how to lie on them. When she had me bent over them to her idea, that which she was longing to feel wedged in her mossy lips was standing up hard and proud. Then getting over me in the right position, I felt her place it between the hot lips, and after a gentle motion on her part, it was all in where she seemed so delighted to have it. "There, now! ain't that nice?" she asked, with a look of mingled joy and pride, and then she began to slide up and down on it (in a peculiar way that I have not known since), her bosoms jumping with every move that seemed to send fire through my veins to my brain. I could feel that she was making me awful wet where we were linked, but the sensation was hot and delightful; and as she kept at work, I saw her grasp her bosoms as though she would crush them; her motion became more rapid, her lips swelled, she shut her eyes and threw back her head, flung out her arms and drew them back again, and as she trembled all over, my delight reached its height; and as my love messenger took wings and flew, she fell forward on me with all her weight, almost crushing my bones. She lay panting and gasping for a moment, and as she jumped to the floor I saw that he who had given her so much comfort, also my belly, bore delicate crimson stains. She saw it, and blushing deeply said it was no matter, and sponging me off, I put on my shirt and lay with my face to the wall as she had asked me to do. Soon she came with her chemise on, and taking me in her arms, we went to sleep, my face resting on her white bosom. After awaking we arose and dressed, and at eight were at the cottage.

Ah! naught so bright
But sometime will lustre lose.

That night brought a change in her. When she came to bed, she as usual let me get in her snowy arms, but the kisses I had learned to love were missing. She allowed me freedom with her bosom, but with any attempt to put my hand under her chemise she took it away, saying: "No; no more."

Ah! in those boyish days, I did not know that nature had ordered an armistice in favor of the little citadel which had so often been stoned, stormed and entered. The last rapture that I ever knew lying between her voluptuous swelling thighs was on that day she took me with her to the city, and that night my young, boyish heart felt its first aches and trouble.

Two days after, she kissed me sweetly at the gate, saying that she would never forget me (it has been mutual); and when the carriage that took her away was out of sight, the sky seemed darkened, the grass was dead, the flowers had lost their perfume and beauty.

My heart seemed like a lump of ice. My life followed on after that carriage—followed her for days and weeks out on the long miles that lay between us. I grew nervous, pale and restless. I could eat nothing, and that bed was so big and lonesome that I could not sleep—only lie and toss, while my fevered brain sketched and re-sketched the beautiful life figures which she had unveiled to my eager eyes. Books, flowers, drawing, pony—all things of the past. The juice of the orange I had sucked was still in my mouth; the spark she had discovered and fanned was burning me alive. The strain at last was too much; memory was lost in unconsciousness; and on the same bed, so hallowed by the lingerings of the past, I was battling with death.

After long weeks, I was victorious, and when strong enough, returned to school. But ah! in those few days, she injected into my veins the sweet poison which has remained for years.

I sacrificed health and ambition, but in exchange took my first lessons in an art that has puzzled the world, which in later years has been held in high appreciation; which now I sometimes think repays me for all.

Trusting that in the perusal of this you will be rewarded with all the pleasurable emotions that you anticipated—that I have written nothing to burst the front buttons from the pantaloons of my gentlemen friends, or bring the dear girls to the use of a long-necked cologne bottle to quench the flame in their electrical generators, my task is finished.

CHAPTER FIVE: LIFE IN PARIS

NO ONE LIKES TO BE REPRESSED, censored or gagged. But censorship has one by-product which not only shows the futility of censorship itself but provides people with a lot of fun. The difficulty about telling the human race to shut up and do as it's told is that, in the end, people won't shut up. And the more vigorously certain topics are banned, the faster the furtive whispers, the giggling, and the sniggering spread. What is forbidden becomes enjoyable and amusing. Thanks to the efforts of the censors, *Fanny Hill* or the Marquis de Sade may be read by people who wouldn't know the eighteenth century if it fell on their heads. Promoted by the same asininity, *Lady Chatterley* is gulped down and, goodness, how did Lawrence of Arabia ever find the time?

Underground fiction has always been rich in books that exploit the consequences of taboo. Pretty girls are shielded from the terrible truth of you-know-what. But pretty girls, like their mothers before them, are going to find out that truth or die in the attempt. As a matter of fact, all the peeping and prying, the poking and prodding, the sniggering and blushing, turns out to be much more fun than solemn classroom lectures on sexual biology.

So our teenage heroines are initiated into the facts of life. But how do they spread the good news? Well, in erotic fiction they write letters to one another. The giggles almost burst off the page. There is a delicious soufflé whisked up from feminine innocence and knowingness, laughter and wonder, combined with an eagerness to get in there and try it for oneself.

Thirty years before the present book, in *Un Été à la Campagne,* Adèle and Albertine had exchanged a few dozen hilarious letters on the subject. Sent to stay with her aunt while her uncle was away with his regiment, Adèle spied on this beautiful creature in her boudoir and saw her with legs apart applying some strange instrument between them, an upright device with a rounded knob. What could it be? Adèle had been far too properly brought up ever to have heard of such a thing as her aunt's dildo.

On the other hand, she guessed that it was a substitute for her aunt's absent husband. And so the quick-witted girl decided to call it "Uncle." In no time at all "Uncle" is much in demand, not least in Albertine's Parisienne school for young ladies. In his velvet-lined box, "Uncle" travels by post to the French capital, satisfies a few dormitories full of girls, and then travels back again. At last, of course, Adèle and her aunt are consoled by the real thing and "Uncle" goes into honourable retirement in his velvet lining.

There is a good deal of a similar kind in *School Life in Paris*. Without censorship, would it have been possible? In an age when sex is on the school curriculum and everybody knows everything, there is less room for fun of this kind. But *School Life in Paris* preserves it, even in the case of the little girl and "dolly" who is sick. Unfortunately it is just such passages over which the censors muse, frowning and grumbling. To such earnest and industrious officials, it seems impossible that it could be a joke. Perhaps that it just as well. If there is one thing officialdom dislikes more than erotica, it is a joke.

Meanwhile, in that chattering and intimate world of teenage girlhood, the hothouse gossip of the finishing school, Blanche takes up her pen and writes a very private letter to her "Dearest Ethel" back home.

School Life in Paris

A Series of Letters from Blanche, aged seventeen, who has just been sent to a Paris finishing School, to her Cousin Ethel, in England, with whom she had formerly been at School.

LETTER II

My dearest Ethel,

I promised in my last letter to give you an account of the life we live here, so to begin with, I had better explain that we elder girls do no real "lessons"; the object of our education being simply to fit us, as far as possible, for taking a position in society as fashionable young ladies. This being the case, our only studies are the French language, music, dancing and gymnastics, and—in Madame's eyes the most important point of all—the care and development of our personal charms.

We are called at 8:30 in the morning by maids who bring us cups of steaming coffee or chocolate with delicate sandwiches and bread-and-butter which we consume luxuriously in bed. After this we get up and go in pairs to the bathroom, where there is an immense bath, surrounded with mirrors on every side, and large enough to allow for two of us being in it at the same time comfortably. At first I felt very shy of finding myself naked in a bath with another girl in the same condition, especially as the mirrors gave the effect of a perfect crowd of nude figures; but since my initiation as a "Lesbian" I enjoy it immensely, and, as we intertwine our naked limbs and bodies in the hot water, it is delightful to watch the reflection of our lascivious postures in the glasses on the walls. The eldest girl—Bertha—whom I mentioned in my last letter, is generally my companion in the bathroom; and, when the luxurious feeling of the scalding water, aided by the contact of our moist bodies, has made us begin to feel "hot" and wicked, she tells me the most delightfully improper stories, one of which I will reproduce here, for your benefit:

One very hot summer afternoon a young man of

about five-and-twenty went up to his bedroom, took his coat and trousers off, and flung himself down on his bed, where, being very tired, he very soon fell sound asleep. Presently his little five-year-old niece found her way into the room, and, coming close to her uncle, caught sight of his "prick," with its head hanging down between his legs. Not knowing what it was, she touched it and began to play with it, and was immensely astonished to find it immediately begin to grow big and stiff as she fondled it with her little hands. Very soon, by some inherent instinct of vice, she found that by playing with the hairy "balls" with one hand, and briskly rubbing the point of the "ramrod" with the other, it stood up so tall and thick that she could hardly meet her baby fingers round it.

Meanwhile the man was dreaming that he was "on top" of a lovely girl, enjoying the most exquisite "poke" that he had ever had in his life. Child as she was, perceiving that the more she rubbed and tickled his instrument, the more her uncle's sleeping body writhed about in a perfect ecstasy of pleasure, she worked it so with her little hands that in due time the hot flow of manly "sperm" spurted from the end with extra randy force, and the mighty "prick" sank down exhausted with the violence of its sensuality.

Frightened at this, the little girl ran out of the room, shutting the door behind her, and thereby making a noise which woke up her uncle, who came to the conclusion that he had just had the most delicious "wet dream" that he had ever experienced.

The little girl, however, ran downstairs to her mother, when the following conversation took place:

"Mummy?"

"Yes, dear."

"Uncle Harry has got a dolly."

"Has he, dear?"

"Yes, such a dear little dolly: he keeps it between his legs."

"Nonsense, dear, what do you mean?"

"Well, I found it lying asleep, but when I began to play with it, it jumped up and began to play with me."

"Did it, dear?"

"Yes, but Mummy, when I had played with it a good time, I don't know how it was, but *(confidentially)* Dolly was sick."

Since we heard that story, we always call a man's instrument "Dolly," which is ever so much nicer than its real names—tool, or cock, or prick, don't you think so?

After the bath we put on a few clothes and our dressing gowns, as we do not make our *toilette* for the day till after the twelve o'clock *déjeuner.* When we are ready, we go downstairs to Madame's sitting room, where we find her also *en peignoir,* and we then have our French lesson, which consists of reading aloud some French novel, and as we are allowed to choose what book we like, you can imagine that we pick out something pretty spicy—not of course the extra-smutty "suppressed" books that the girls read to one another in their bedrooms, but still books which would be considered awfully wicked in England—all about married women who spend half the day in bed with their lovers, and men who spend all their time with mistresses or *cocottes,* as the French call them, whose refinments of luxurious vice and voluptuousness are described in a marvellously outspoken manner. To give you some idea of the sort of thing, I will tell you at the end of this letter about the book we are reading this week, but first I will finish the account of our day.

When we have finished the reading, and have discussed the words we don't know (we always pretend not to know the naughtiest words, so as to embarrass Madame by making her explain them!), we have *déjeuner,* which is a sort of lunch and breakfast in one, and after that the most serious business of the day—the making of our toilette—begins, and generally occupies us from about one till nearly three. When we are duly arrayed, we go out with either Madame or one of the governesses, and we are so well known for our smart getup that we often find some of the smartest and most fashionable of the Parisian "mashers" standing about on the lookout for us and throwing us the most audacious glances of lustful admiration from their wicked eyes as we go by. When we have admired the shops and been sufficiently admired by the men, we go back to afternoon tea, and from then till dinner at 7:30 we practise our music, or have drilling and gymnastics in awfully fetching knickerbocker-costumes.

It is only we elder girls who have the privilege of late dinner with Madame, and we have to wear low dresses for it every night, so as to accustom our constitutions to the displaying of naked busts and shoulders in the evening.

After dinner we generally dance for a little while, and about a quarter-to-ten we begin going to bed. I say "begin" because our toilette for the night takes almost as long to make as that for the day.

When this is completed, and we have made our sacrifices to the "pomps and vanities of this wicked world," we are expected to say our prayers, as Madame considers that it is "good style to be religious." As, however, kneeling is considered bad for our knees, we say our prayers in bed, where they get rather mixed up with the naughty stories we have heard during the day. And this reminds me that I promised to tell you something about the book we are at present reading aloud to Madame.

It is by Victor Joze, and is called *Le Demi-monde des Jeunes Filles*. I need not tell you that *demi-monde* is the name given to the *cocottes* or "tarts" as a class, and the name of the book therefore implies that young girls of good society are rapidly beginning to resemble the "tarts" in their knowledge and practise of vice.

The last chapter which we read this morning contains an account of a *rendez-vous* between Cesar Blond, a writer of erotic and lustful poems, about forty years of age, and Bianca—a very hot Society girl, half Italian and half French, who has just turned eighteen. He met her first at a smart dinnery party, where he sat next to her at dinner and soon found out, by slyly touching her foot with his to begin with, and afterwards by bolder squeezings of her leg between his own, etc., that she was fully alive to the pleasures of sensuality, in spite of her presumed innocence and piety. Later, in conversation, he found that she had read all the smuttiest of his own poems, as well as a number of other books of a similar character. He was immensely struck with the beauty both of her face and figure, the latter being displayed by an evening *corsage* cut so generously low that, as she leaned forward over her plate, he could clearly see the points of her breasts thrusting themselves out erect and stiff in answer to the contact of his leg against hers, while, from the sensuous smile she gave him as she caught him looking at them, he realized that her motion forward had been made with the deliberate intention of showing him the voluptuous fullness of her splendid bust.

Before the end of the evening she gave him a *rendez-vous* for the following afternoon, and the chapter I speak of describes what happened when they met.

She arrived at the meeting-place exquisitely dressed, though, knowing what was likely to happen, she had displayed even more care and taste over the selection of her underclothing than upon her outdoor *toilette*.

He came in his brougham, into which he at once handed her, telling his coachman to drive slowly and by a roundabout route to his own house.

Drawing down the blinds of the carriage, he placed one arm round her waist, and having raised her veil, began to kiss her passionately upon the lips. She pretended to resist, but showed by the ardent way in which she returned his kisses that she was really longing for him to go further.

Murmuring words of the most lawless and lustful passion in her ear, and still clasping her waist with one hand, he began with the other to feel his way slowly but deliberately up her leg, under her skirt, delicately fondling the open-work silk stocking, until he reached the satin garter above the knee.

The gentle action of his practised fingers only caused her to thrill with pleasure—a thrill which was accentuated a moment later, when she noticed the triumphant smile upon his face as the naked flesh of her thighs, with which his fingers came in contact above the stocking, told him that, evidently out of compliment to him, she had omitted to put on any drawers. In another moment he had reached her nest of Venus where, without actually entering it, his experience enabled him, by judicious touchings and ticklings in its neighbourhood, to excite her to the highest pitch of sensual expectation. As a proof of this, he felt her daintily gloved hand involuntarily placing itself between his own legs, where his "dolly," in a violent state of erection, was making itself clearly visible beneath his trousers.

A younger and less experienced man would probably have unbuttoned his trousers and engaged the poking of her then and there, but he was far too experienced to risk losing any of the enjoyment, owing to the cramped position of the carriage, while at the same time he knew how much a sensual pleasure of this kind is prolonged and increased by anticipation.

Somewhat therefore to her disappointment they reached his house without her ardent desires having been in any satisfactory way assuaged.

Conducting her to his sitting room, they found an exquisite repast of champagne and the most delicate sandwiches; and while they were partaking freely of these, he called her attention to the paintings on the walls, which were beautifully executed by first-rate artists, but which were all of the most improper mythological subjects.

One represented Leda yielding to the amorous embraces of the Swan, while another showed Jupiter in the form of a Bull inserting his immense prick into the blushing nest of Europa. Many of them were scenes from Rabelais, in which groups of naked girls in the most lascivious postures were mingled with naked men, whose "dollies," in the highest state of erection, testified to the effect which these feminine charms were exercising upon them.

Having thus waked up the heat of his fair partner's body and also her imagination to such a pitch that she could scarcely contain herself, he opened the door leading into his sumptuous bedroom, and having rapidly divested her of all her clothing except her absolutely transparent chemise of pink chiffon, her long kid gloves, her long open-work silk stockings and high-heeled shoes—for to an experienced sensualist, a girl in this costume excites his lust far more than if she were absolutely naked, the stockings and shoes being in particular an added charm as the legs intertwine in the amorous struggle!—he laid her on the bed, her large dark eyes gleaming at the prospect of the pleasure she was about to experience.

In another moment he had undressed himself, and, with his "dolly," which was of an unusually large size, standing so erect and stiff that it evidently required no further stimulating, he approached the bed, Bianca opening her legs in amorous invitation as he did so.

Kneeling before them, he endeavoured to thrust his "dolly" into her palpitating "cunnie," but the latter was so small and the former so large that his first attempts were quite unsuccessful. Moreover, when she tried to guide it to its destination, the touch of her kid-gloved fingers upon his excited prick only caused it to grow stiffer and thicker than ever.

Finding his efforts fruitless, he withdrew from her embraces for a moment, and proceeded to anoint his ramrod's point with a liberal allowance of vaseline. Then, twining his legs round hers, and clasping his hands beneath her back while she did the same to him, they both pushed with all their force until, to their mutual delight, his organ of sex slid gently forward into hers, and, in spite of its great size, pressed onward further and further in, until its passage was stopped by the pressure of his swelling balls against the mount of her cunt. So tight was the fit that at first he could scarcely move it up and down at all, but the intense pleasure caused by this friction soon made her organ expand, and then the amorous contest began with a series of contortions and struggles which would have offered a most alluring picture to a spectator, had any been present. That practised sensualist Napoleon III is reported to have said that, in making love, he much preferred the knowing sidestroke of the professional to the ineffectual wriggle of the amateur. But though Bianca was an amateur, she had the instinct of sensuality, and owing partly to the tightness of her "pussie" and partly to her adroit movements, Cesar Blond was of the opinion that he had never before enjoyed a more delicious "poke." His skill, on the other hand, enabled him to prolong the pleasure in such a way as to repay her fully for her efforts on his behalf. Long before he was ready to "come," he felt the muscles of her organ contracting for the spasm of ecstatic delight, and his quickened workings brought her not only to the swoon of pleasure, but beyond it, and, to the delight of them both, it was not until she "came" for the fourth time that his own gush of sperm, shooting out with immense force through having been withheld so long, joined with her own flow to water her very entrails, thereby at last deliciously assuaging the fire of her burning lust.

You can easily imagine, my dear Ethel, what an effect the reading aloud of such a chapter as this had upon us, and, in spite of Madame's presence, it was all we could do to prevent our hands from stealing down to tickle one another's "pussies," as the description of the "poke" grew hotter and hotter. Madame herself laid down her embroidery and listened as intently as any of us, and, though when the chapter was ended she said she did not think it was at all a proper book for us to read, it was easy to see from her gleaming eyes how much she had enjoyed the voluptuous scene. Moreover, when the girl who was reading it said that the book had been recommended by her aunt, the Countess de B***, she at once said that, in that case, she was perfectly satisfied with it, as the Countess de B*** is one of the leaders of fashion in gay Paris.

It will be my turn to read tomorrow, and I mean to try reading that chapter over again, just to see what Madame will say. Of course it sounds a good deal coarser in English than it does in French, which seems to have an endless supply of naughty words that are quite pretty and poetical, whereas ours are nearly all ugly and dirty!

From the extract I have given you of this French novel *you* will think it a most awful book, but the books which the girls have locked up in the bedrooms are even worse, because they deal not merely with women being "poked" by men, but also with men poking boys, which is called Sodomy or buggery, and women making love together, which, as you have gathered, is called Lesbianism or Sapphism.

These books also have illustrations showing not only men but boys with their "pricks" in erection, and small girls ten years old in the most wanton and lascivious positions, revelling in the delights of "poking" and tickling quite as much as older women. One of the books I have seen contains most realistic pictures of a great many ways of "making love," but Bertha, who has a young man-cousin who often "pokes" her in the holidays, says that the best way of all is to make the man stand up by the bed, while the girl is on her back, in such a way as to bring her "cunt" just to the edge of the bed. She opens her legs and clasps them behind his back while he thrusts in his "dolly," the fact that he is standing firmly on the floor enabling him to "poke" with far greater force than when he is lying on top of her in the ordinary way.

I have rambled on so long that I have no time left to tell you of the second meeting of our Lesbian Society, which was so delicious and exciting that I must reserve it for another letter.

I will send you a copy of *Le Demi-monde* when I have time to get one, as I am sure it will be a perfect revelation of naughtiness to you, and yet it is said to be a very fair picture of the fast Society girls here in Paris!

Ever your loving,
Blanche.

LETTER III

My dearest Ethel,

I told you in my last letter that I would describe the second meeting of our "Lesbian Club," but now I come to think of it, it was very little more than a repetition of the first, with the exception of the fact that being no longer the innocent "Saint" that I was on the first occasion, I was better qualified to play my part as a giver, as well as a receiver, of pleasure. The third meeting, however, was of a very different kind, and well merits a description, which I will now endeavour to give you.

The Sunday started well, for being a very fine day, we had taken exceptional care with our Church costumes, which, as you may well believe, caused somewhat of a sensation during the service, to Madame's great delight.

When we went to our rooms to dress for dinner, we found that Madame's feeling of satisfaction had shown itself in placing a lovely corsage-bouquet of flowers in each of our rooms; and when we reached the dining room, duly arrayed in our strongly scented bouquets, we found that a still further surprise was waiting for us, for Madame had ordered up a plentiful supply of champagne—a luxury hitherto almost unheard-of in the establishment!

Thanks to the fact that Madame plied us, as well as herself, liberally with this fascinating beverage, we were all very lively by the time dinner was ended; and I was therefore a good deal surprised when, immediately after dinner, Madame proposed that we should all, herself included, go at once to bed. On Sunday nights, I must tell you, we are let off everything in the way of "night *toilette*," which

· 118 ·

was the reason why the "Lesbians" chose that night for their meetings.

When I got to my room I quickly undressed, but to my surprise the other girls did not arrive for nearly half an hour. Throwing off their hastily put-on dressing gowns, they explained that the reason for their delay was that they were waiting to give Madame time to get to bed, so that she might not come and disturb us. They were all crowding round in a naked group, admiring my figure, etc., when to my horror, in walked Madame, wearing a lovely pink and white opera cloak instead of a dressing gown, and bearing in her hand a birch-rod.

To my surprise the other girls, on seeing her, did not seem in the least astonished or dismayed, but took her arrival quite as a matter of course.

"What is the meaning of this, girls?" she asked in a severe voice. "Not only do I find you in Blanche's room, but you are all huddled together naked, which is most indecent."

Immediately the girls ran to the bed and bent over it, with their backs to Madame, motioning to me to do the same.

She then applied the birch to the plump "cheeks" and thighs of each of us in turn, but it was done so gently that, without hurting in the least, it made the blood run towards our "pussies," making us feel awfully hot and naughty. When we were all writhing, not with pain but with randiness and lust, she put down her birch, saying "There, that will do for the present."

Saying this, she threw off her opera cloak and disclosed a costume which amazed me more than anything in the world. It consisted of silk openworked tights of a deep violet hue, the open-work being so wickedly arranged as to leave her "pussie," with its fringe of flame-coloured hair, completely exposed to view. Above the tights she wore a tiny evening-corset of white satin, above which her large rounded breasts stood out firm and high like twin hills of snow. A pair of high-heeled white satin shoes and white satin garters just above the knee completed the costume, except for her hands and arms, which I now for the first time perceived were delicately gloved in white kid, sewn with broad violet stitching at the back to match the tights.

Nothing could have displayed her magnificent figure to better advantage, and I found it hard indeed to realize that this glorious looking "Angel of Vice," with the gleam of lust fired by champagne in her eye, was really the staid school mistress, whom I had looked upon as a model of propriety and virtue!

From a pocket inside the opera cloak, one of the girls produced a large morocco case, which, with a smiling permission from Madame, she proceeded to open. The contents consisted of three rods of ivory of various sizes, rounded at one end, while to the other end were attached two india-rubber balls, like small tennis balls.

I was at a loss to imagine what these could possibly be, when my friend Bertha exclaimed, "Oh Madame, you have brought the 'dildoes!' How charming of you!"

At this you may be sure I pricked up my ears, for Bertha had several times explained to me the nature of a "dildo," which is nothing more nor less than an artificial model of a man's "dolly."

The smallest was only about three inches long, not much thicker than my forefinger, and had a much sharper point than the others. This I gathered was nicknamed "The Baby," for it was evidently not the first time the girls had seen and handled these treasures.

The next one, known as "The School-boy," was about half as large again, being covered all along its length with obscene carvings in low relief, the object of which was to cause a greater amount of tickling than a smooth surface would have done.

The third was "The Captain," which was quite twice as long and more than twice as thick as "The Baby," being covered like the last with carvings, while the balls were of a considerably larger size.

Bertha, after a short consultation with Madame, darted off to the latter's bedroom, whence she returned bearing a lighted Etna, which evidently contained some steaming liquid.

Under her arm she carried another leather case, this time looking like a large pistol case, at the sight of which Madame pretended to be much displeased; but she nevertheless opened it and displayed its contents to all of us, the evident astonishment of the girls clearly showing that this, at any rate, was something they had never seen before.

It was a dildo made exactly like "The Captain," but of such gigantic proportions that it positively took our breath away. It was at least ten inches long, and quite as thick as my wrist, the balls being about the size of cricket balls.

"Surely, Madame," said one of the girls, "no one in the world has a cunt large enough to admit that?"

It gave me rather a shock of surprise to hear her use such a naughty word as "cunt" in speaking to Madame, but I soon found out that the latter could be the smuttiest of us all, when she felt inclined, as it was evident she did on the present occasion; in fact she only smiled at the question and said:

"It comes from South America, where the women are accustomed to being poked by negroes who, as I daresay you know, have far bigger 'pricks' than European men."

"But surely no European girl could use it?"

"That all depends on the way in which it is done," she answered. "Of course, if a girl in cold blood were to thrust this into her 'cunnie,' she would simply fail to get it in, in the first place, and in the second she would about kill herself if she succeeded. But if the 'cunt' had previously been excited, first of all by Lesbian kisses, and then by an ordinary dildo, you would find, I think, that, with the help of some vaseline and a good deal of pressure, 'The Giant,' as I have named it, would not only go in, but would cause the most exquisite pleasure to the 'pussie,' in which it would undoubtedly be a most amazingly tight fit!"

While she was saying this, Bertha had taken out "The School-boy," and had filled the balls with the hot liquid, which, I gathered, was a mixture of milk and ising-glass.

I had forgotten to tell you that each of the dildoes had straps attached to them for the purpose of fastening them round a female's body, so as to make her resemble a man. "The Baby" was fastened to one girl, while Bertha made herself into a pretty boy by means of "The School-boy."

"Now Blanche," said Madame, approaching me, "as we do not allow Virgins in this society, we are going to take your maidenhead."

I was laid on the bed, my "tiddies" were kissed as before by two of the girls, while Madame herself, putting her head between my legs, began, with a far more expert tongue than Bertha's, to tickle my "pussie." Her tongue several times touched my membrane of virginity, which was to be pierced by

"The Baby."

When Madame had excited me sufficiently, "The Baby" girl, climbing on me as a man would have done, slid the instrument into my "cunt," causing me an exquisite sense of pleasure, which made me clasp her towards me with all my force, and in a moment I felt a thrill, half of pleasure and half of pain, and I knew that my virginity had gone.

As soon as Madame perceived this she signaled to "The Baby" girl to come out of me so as to make room for Bertha, who with the larger dildo, which penetrated into regions which were now entered for the first time, gave me the liveliest pleasure, and caused me to "come" with a feeling of exquisite enjoyment, different from the enjoyment I had felt when the girls had "kissed me down," and which I now experienced for the first time. When she saw that the supreme moment had arrived, Berta gripped the "balls" between her legs, and squeezing them again and again, squirted up the hot liquid through the tube in the centre of the dildo, so as to produce exactly the same effect inside my "cunt" as if a man's "sperm" were being poured into me.

Madame was delighted to see how much I enjoyed the experience, and assured me that, for her part, she much preferred a dildo to a man, because one can make the dildo "spend" when one chooses, whereas the man has to "come" when he can.

The girls were now all begging Madame to let them try if they could get "The Giant" into her in the way she had explained, and, though she at first resisted, she soon took my place on the bed, where she lay with her legs apart, still in her fancy costume, panting with the anticipation of the voluptuous experience she was about to undergo.

Two of the girls started at once to suck her "tid-dies," while I began with tongue and finger to tickle her delicious "cunt," and very soon had the satisfaction of seeing that we were causing her to thrill with delighted sensuality.

Bertha and another girl were meanwhile filling the immense balls of "The Giant" with liquid, and getting "The Captain" ready to be used first.

When I had started Madame successfully upon her voyage of pleasure, I motioned to "The Captain" girl, who at once got on top of her, and, inserting the dildo, proceeded to work it up and down as knowingly and as quickly as if she had been a man.

I, meanwhile, was aiding Bertha to gird on "The Giant," with the result that, when it was adjusted, she looked like a delicate boy endowed by nature with the most monstrous prick that ever was seen. I smothered the point in vaseline, and we then stood and waited by the bed. Very soon it was evi-dent from Madame's lascivious movements that "The Captain" was rapidly conducting her to the supreme pleasure of "coming" and a few moments later we saw that "The Captain," as he slid in and out of her "pussie," was covered with a thick frothy moisture, showing that the flow of "sperm" had begun. This was evidently the moment for "The Giant," and as "The Captain" slipped out, I instantly inserted my fingers, so that the sensation of pleasure might not slacken for a moment.

With wonderful speed and adoitness Bertha took the place vacated by the other girl, and while I held the lips of the "cunt" as wide apart as ever I could with my two hands, Bertha pushed and shoved with all her force, until to our great satisfac-tion, it began to move slowly inwards. Then fol-lowed the most extraordinary scene that can possibly be conceived. Madame, having already reached the highest pitch of enjoyment to which she had ever attained, could scarcely believe that there was still greater delight yet to come: but as Bertha pushed "The Giant" steadily onwards, at the same time working it gently in and out in the proper manner, the distension and irritation of the "cunt" was so extreme and the delightful feeling of tickling so immensely in excess of anything she had ever felt before, that her body rocked and swayed about in a perfect agony of enjoyment, and her voluptuous movements caused us onlookers to feel as randy as possible. As "The Giant" went steadily further in, Bertha quickened the movement, and finally, pushing it right home, she sqeezed the balls repeatedly, sending into her very soul a flow both far hotter and far more plentiful than any man's "prick" could possibly have produced. As Bertha withdrew the dildo from the palpitating "pussie," Madame swooned away in a dead faint, utterly exhausted by the immensely prolonged and artificially exaggerated scene of enjoyment, of which she had been the delighted heroine.

On seeing this, one of the girls ran downstairs and soon returned with some champagne, which speedily revived her, and she immediately began to give us an account of the exquisite sensations she had been experiencing. She assured us that from the moment "The Giant" began to make its way in, the pleasure was absolutely heavenly, causing her to "come" twice before the final injection of the fluid, but that at times the feeling became so strong as to be scarcely bearable.

This recital, in addition to the voluptuous scene we had witnessed, aroused our sensuality to a high pitch of expectation; and Madame herself, having recharged "The Captain" with liquid and having fastened it on, was very soon on top of Bertha, vigorously "poking" her, while I did the same to one of the other girls with "The School-boy"; and, as the other three girls were doing the "Trio of the Graces" with mutually tickling fingers, the goddess of sensuality was soon reigning supreme over our naked bodies.

When I was at last left alone in bed, I could not get to sleep for a long time, owing to the heated and excited state of my brain and blood, and as I lay awake, I could not help feeling amazed at the part our dignified school mistress had taken in the proceedings. Later on, however, I found that she had long been an ardent devotee of "Lesbianism," and had only become a school mistress in order to have plenty of opportunities of satisfying this entrancing lust.

There, my dear Ethel, you have a full and true account of our third meeting, and if it does not make your hair stand on end, fringe and all, I shall be surprised! I wonder, by the way, if my former letters have made you sufficiently curious to induce you to try the experiment of tickling your own "pussie"? If so, I have no doubt you have discovered the little "button," the incitation and tickling of which causes such exquisite pleasure. At the same time I can tell you from experience that it is not half so nice to do it to oneself as to get someone else to do it, and I am told that to have it done by a nice boy is the most voluptuous thing of all.

Good-bye, dearest, for the present, and I hope you will not be shocked by this awfully naughty letter from

Your ever loving,
Blanche.

CHAPTER SIX: VENUS IN INDIA

FAR REMOVED FROM THE FINISHING SCHOOLS of Paris or the idylls of California was the life of imperial grandeur. Edward Sellon knew it in reality and a few other heroes knew it in fantasy, though much of the fantasy was quite close to the truth. Jean de Villiot's *Woman and her Master* (1904) chronicles the British defeat at Khartoum and the fate of Grace Marjoribanks in harem slavery. Other adventures, like Charles DeVane's *Nights of the Rajah,* dated 1906, or Charles Devereaux's *Venus in India, or Love Adventures in Hindustan,* published in Brussels in 1889, describe the heated passions and amorous intrigues of the British Raj in its greatest imperial possession.

From the Palladian splendours of Viceregal House, Calcutta, to the cool hills of Simla with English tea-rooms and cricket pavilions faithfully rebuilt in the middle of Asia, successive Viceroys of the Queen Empress administered a kingdom of their own. But however much the young subalterns might console themselves with cool beer known as "India Pale," or with hock and seltzer, there was one home comfort in very short supply. English girls. For those who were available there was hot competition. Wives of junior officers and daughters of senior officers had all too many followers. The most rigorous self-control was needed to prevent a sexual free-for-all. It was not a matter of being celibate for a year or two. Some young officers posted to India at twenty-five might not see home again until they were almost forty. They had an even chance of being dead by then. Edward Sellon, who was out and back again by twenty-six, was fortunate in that respect.

The solution for many was to take an Indian

girl—or several Indian girls—as mistress. It was inexpensive and the talent was plentiful. Or else there were the Eurasian girls of mixed English and Indian descent. The notion that young Englishmen crossed their legs and thought of home and duty got a nasty knock as early as 1846 when Sir Richard Burton reported that "every officer" in his unit had a local bed-companion.

Our hero Charles Devereaux is obliged to leave his young wife behind him in England as he sails for Bombay. Cousin Fred in *My Secret Life* suggests why when he explains to the narrator his reluctance to take a wife or mistress there. "All the regiment would be sniffing at her tail," he says bluntly. Arriving safely at Bombay, however, Captain Devereaux travels on with a railway warrant to Allahabad and then by yak towards the outpost of Cherat. No one expects him, no one particularly wants him. Brigade-majors and others have enough problems of their own already. He gets stuck in a village short of Peshawar because no one can provide horses to get him further. He finds a billet in a screened-off part of a public bungalow. The sense of chaotic military administration under impossible conditions seeps through the erotic storyline of the book. So far, during the long sea voyage and overland journey, Captain Devereaux has kept his spirits up by reading a few French novels, notably, *Mademoiselle de Maupin*.

The war in Afghanistan has just ended and the British regiments are straggling back from the North-West Frontier. No one seems to know what the hell is going on or who is supposed to be where. There are native brothels, "knocking shops" as Devereaux calls them, with enlisted men standing in line, holding their erections in their hands and yelling at the Indian girls inside to get a move on.

In other words, there is a good deal in Devereaux's account that rings true. We find him at last, standing there in this desolate village of north India with no transport and precious little accommodation, wondering what to do next.

———

Reader dear, do you know what it is to feel that somebody is looking at you, though you may not be able to see him, nor are aware for a fact that somebody is looking at you? I am extremely susceptible to this influence. Whilst sitting thus idly looking at the most distant thing my eyes could find to rest upon, I began to feel that someone was near, and looking intently at me. At first I resisted the temptation to look round to see who it was. What with the hot wind, and what with the circumstances of the sudden halt I was compelled to make, I felt so irritable, that I resented, as an insult, the looking at me which I felt certain was going on; but at last this strange sensation added to my unrest and I half-turned my head to see whether it was reality or feverish fancy.

My surprise was unbounded when I saw the same lovely face, which I had caught a glimpse of that morning, looking at me from behind the slightly opened chick, of the room next to mine, I was so startled that instead of taking a good look at the lady I instantly gazed on the hills again, as if turning my head to look in her direction had been a breach of good manners on my part; but I felt she was still keeping her eyes fixed on me, and it amazed me that any one of the position which I imagined she held, for I was firmly convinced that I was right as to my surmise that my unknown beauty was a lady, and a Colonel's daughter, she should be guilty of such bad manners as to stare at a perfect stranger in this manner. I turned my head once more, and this time I looked at this lovely but strange girl a little more fixedly. Her eyes, large, lustrous, most beautiful, seemed to pierce mine, as though trying to read my thoughts. For a moment I fancied she must be a little off her head, when, apparently satisfied, with her reconnaissance, the fair creature let the chick fall once more against the side of the door and so was lost to my sight. From that moment my curiosity was greatly aroused. Who was she? Was she alone? Or was she with the unknown Colonel in that room? Why was she staring at me so hard? By Jove! There she is at it again! I could stand it no longer. I jumped up and went into my own room and called the Khansamah.

"Khansamah: who is in the room next to mine?" and I pointed to the door which communicated with the room the lady was in, and which was closed.

A Mem Sahib! Now I had been in India before, this was my second tour of service in the country, and I knew that a Mem Sahib meant a married lady. I was surprised, for had anyone asked me, I should have said that this lovely girl had never known a man, had never been had, and never would be had, unless she met the man of men who pleased her. It was extraordinary how this idea had taken root in my mind.

"Is the Sahib with her?"

"No, Sahib!"

"Where is he?"

"I don't know, Sahib."

"When did the Mem Sahib come here, Khan?"

"A week or ten days ago, Sahib!"

"Is she going away soon?"

"I don't know, Sahib!"

It was plain I could get no information from this man, only one more question and I was done.

"Is the Mem Sahib quite alone, Khan?"

"Yes, Sahib: she has no one with her, not even an Ayah."

Well! this is wonderful! How well did my young friend, who had only gone away this morning, know her? You, gentle reader, with experience, have no doubt your suspicions that all was not right, but for the life of me I could not shake off the firm notion that this woman was not only a lady, but one exceptionally pure and highly connected.

I went back to my seat on the verandah, waiting to be looked at again, and I did not wait long. A slight rustle caught my ear, I looked around and there was my lovely girl showing more of herself. She still looked with the same eager gaze without the sign of a smile on her face. She appeared to be in her petticoats only, and her legs and feet, such lovely, tiny, beautiful feet, and such exquisitely turned ankles, were bare; she had not even a pair of slippers on. A light shawl covered her shoulders and bosom, but did not hide either her full well-shaped, white arms, her taper waist or her splendid and broad hips. These naked feet and legs inspired me with a sudden flow of desire, as much as her lovely face and its wonderful calm, yet her severe expression, had driven all such thoughts from my mind. Jacques Casanova, who certainly is a perfect authority on all that concerns women, declares that curiosity is the foundation on which desire is built, that, but for that, a man would be perfectly contented with one woman, since in the main all women are alike; yet from mere curiosity a man is impelled to approach a woman, and to wish for her possession. Something akin to this certainly influenced me. A devouring curiosity took possession of me. This exquisite girl's face inspired me to know how she could possibly be all alone here at

Nowshera, in a public bungalow, and her lovely naked feet and legs, made me wonder whether her knees and thighs corresponded with them in perfect beauty, and my imagination painted to my mind a voluptuous motte and delicious slit, shaded by dark locks corresponding to the color of the lovely eyebrows, which arched over those expressive orbs. I rose from my chair and moved towards her. She instantly withdrew and as instantly again opened the chick. For the first time I saw a smile wreathe her face. What a wonderfully different expression that smile gave it! Two lovely dimples appeared in her rounded cheeks, her rosy lips parted and displayed two rows of small perfectly even teeth, and those eyes which had looked so stern and almost forbidding, now looked all tenderness and softness.

"You must find it very hot out there in the verandah!" she said, in a low, musical voice, but with a rather vulgar, common accent which at first grated on my ear, "and I know you are all alone! Won't you come into my room and sit down and chat? You will if you are a good fellow!"

"Thank you!" said I smiling and bowing, as I threw away my cheroot and entered whilst she held the chick so as to make room for me to pass. I caught the chick in my hand, but she still kept her arm raised, and extended; her shawl fell a little off her bosom which was almost entirely bare, and I saw not only two most exquisitely round, full and polished globes of ivory, but even the rosy coral marble which adorned the peak of one of them. I could see that she caught the direction of my glance, but she was in no hurry to lower her arm, and I judged, and rightly, that this liberal display of her charms was by no means unintentional.

"I have got two chairs in here," said she,

laughing such a sweet sounding laugh, "but we can sit together on my bed, if you don't mind!"

"I shall be delighted," said I, "if sitting without a back to support you won't tire you!"

"Oh!" said she, in the most innocent manner, "you just put your arm round my waist, and then I won't feel tired."

Had it not been for the extraordinary innocent tone with which she said this, I think I should at once have lain her back and got on top of her, but a new idea struck me; could she be quite sane? And would not such an action be the very height of blackguardism?

However, I sat down, as she bade me do, and I slipped my left arm around her slender waist and gave her a little hug towards me.

"Ah!" she said, "that's right! Hold me tight! I love being held tight!"

I found that she had no stays on at all. There was nothing between my hand and her smooth skin but a petticoat body, and a chemise of very light muslin. She felt so awfully nice! There's something so thrilling in feeling the warm, palpitating body of a lovely woman in one's arms, that it was only natural, that not only did my blood run more quickly, but I began to feel what the French call the "pricking of the flesh". There she was, this really beautiful creature, half-naked and palpitating, her cheeks glowing with health, though paler than one is accustomed to see in our more temporate Europe, her lovely shining shoulders and bosom almost perfectly naked, and so exquisite! The nearer I got my eyes to the skin the better did I see how fine was its texture. The bloom of youth was on it. There were no ugly hollows to show where the flesh had receded and the bones projected. Her beautiful breasts were round, plump and firm looking. I longed to take possession of those lovely, lovely bubbies! To press them in my hand, to devour them and their rosy tips with my mouth! Her petticoats fell between her slightly parted thighs and showed their roundness and beautiful form perfectly as though to provoke my desire the more, desire she must have known was burning me, for she could feel the palpitating of my agitated heart, even if a glance of her eyes in another and lower direction did not betray to her the effect her touch and her beauty had on me, she held out one and then the other of her fairy feet, so white and perfect, as though to display them to my eager eyes. The soft and delicious perfume which only emanates from woman in her youth, stole in fragrant clouds over my face, and her abundant wavy hair felt like silk against my cheek. Was she mad? That was the tormenting thought which would spring up between my hand and the glowing charms it longed to seize! For some few moments we sat in silence. Then I felt her hand creep up under my white jacket and toy with the buttons to which my braces were fastened behind. She undid one side of my brace and as she did so said:

"I saw you this morning! You were in a dark gharry and I just caught a glimpse of you."

Her hand began to work at the other button. What the deuce was she up to?

"Oh yes!" I said, looking into her small eyes and returning the sharp glances which shot from them, "and I saw you too! I had been fast asleep, and just as I opened my eyes my sight fell upon you! and I . . ."

She had unbuttoned my braces behind, and now stole her hand round and laid it, back up, on the top of my thigh.

"And you what?" said she, gently sliding her extended fingers down over the inside of my thigh: she was within a nail's breadth of the side of my rod which was now standing furiously!

"Oh!" I exclaimed, "I thought I had never seen such a lovely face and figure in the world!"

The fingertips actually touched Johnnie! She slightly pressed them against him, and looking at me again with the sweetest smile, said:

"Did you really! Well! I'm glad you did, for do you know what I thought, when I saw you lying inside the gharry?"

"No, dear!"

"Well! I thought that I would not mind if I had been travelling with such a fine looking, handsome young man!"

Then after a short pause she continued, "So you think me well made?" And she glanced down proudly on her swelling breast.

"Indeed then I do!" I exclaimed, quite unable to restrain myself any longer. "I don't know when I ever saw such a lovely bosom as this, and such tempting, luscious bubbies!" and I slipped my hand into her bosom and seized a glowing globe and as I pressed it gently and squeezed the hard little nipples between my fingers, I kissed the lovely upturned mouth which was presented to me.

"Ah!" she cried, "who gave you leave to do that? Well! Exchange is no robbery and I will have something nice of yours to feel for myself too!"

Her nimble fingers had my trousers unbuttoned, my braces undone in front too, and with a whisk of her hand she had my shirt out, and with it my burning, maddened stallion, of which she took immediate and instant possession.

"Ah!" she cried, "Ah! oh! what a beauty! How handsome! bell topped! and so big! Isn't he just about stiff! He's like a bar of iron! and what fine big eggs you've got! My beautiful man! Oh! How I would like to empty them for you! Oh! you'll have me now! Won't you? do! do! oh! I feel that I could come so nicely if you only would!''

Would I have her? Why! Gods in Heaven! how could mortal man brimful of health, strength, youth and energy like myself, resist such an appeal to his ears and senses, and not comply, even if the fair petitioner were not half nor a quarter as beautiful as this lascivious and exquisite creature, whose hands were manipulating the most tenderly sensitive parts which man possesses! For all reply I gently pulled her on her back, she still kept a firm but voluptuous hold on her possessions, and I turned up her petticoat and chemise, and gliding my burning hand over the smooth surface of her ivory thigh, up to, I think, the most voluptuous bush I had ever seen or felt in my life! Never had my hand reposed on so voluptuous and full a motte! Never had my fingers probed charm so full of life and so soft outside, so smooth and velvety inside as it did now, that this most perfect place, and the domain around and above it, were in my possession! I was eager to get between her lovely thighs, and to snatch my almost painfully strained organ from her hands, and bury it up to its hilt, and further, in this melting charm, but she stopped me. With her face and bosom flushed, her eyes dancing in her head, and a voice choked with the greatest excitement she cried:

"Let us put on our skins first!"

I was standing before her, my sword at an angle of at least seventy degrees, my sack and groin aching, for the most vigorous action had set in, and my reservoirs had already been filled to the utmost they could hold. I felt I must either have this beautiful wild girl or burst!

"What do you mean?" I gasped.

"I'll show you! See!"

And in a moment she had, as it were, jumped out of her clothes, and stood, all naked and glowing, and radiant with beauty, real by all that is voluptuous and erotic before me.

In a moment or perhaps a little longer, for I had boots and socks as well as coat, shirt and trousers to take off, but at all events, in a brace of shakes, I was as naked as she! I can shut my eyes now and there before me I see this exquisitely formed creature, surely, quite the equal of the beautiful Mademoiselle de Maupin, standing in all her radiant nudity before me. That form so purely perfect so inimitably graceful, those matchless limbs! That bosom with its hills of living snow topped with rosy fire and that more than voluptuous motte, a perfect "hill of Venus", clothed with the richest dark bushes of curly hair, sloping rapidly down, like a triangle standing on its point, until its two sides, folding in, form the deep soft-looking and inside line, which proclaimed the very perfection of a Goddess. The only thing which slightly marred this perfect galaxy of beauty was the occurrence of some slight wrinkles, which like fine lines crossed the otherwise perfect plain of her fair belly, that exquisite belly with its dimpling navel!

Gods! I rushed at this lovely creature, and in another moment I was on top of her, between her wide-opened thighs and resting on her beautiful bosom. How elastic did her beautiful bubbies feel against my chest! and how soft, how inexpressibly delicious, did her cavern feel, as inch by inch I buried Johnnie in it, until my motte jammed against hers, and my eggs hanging, or rather squeezed, against her lovely white bottom, I could get in no

further. And what a woman to have! Every movement of mine brought forth an exclamation of
delight from her! To hear her you would have imagined it was the very first time her senses had been
powerfully excited from their very foundation! Her
hands were never still, they promenaded over me,
from the back of my head to the intimate limits of
my body to which they could reach. She was simply perfect in the art of giving and receiving pleasure. Every transport of mine was returned with
interest, every mad thrust met with a corresponding buck which had the effect of taking my engine
into its extreme root! And she seemed to do nothing but "come" or "spend"! I had heard of a
woman "coming" thirteen or fourteen times during
one session, but this woman seemed to do nothing
else from beginning to end. But, it was not until I
had arrived at the exciting, furious, ardent, almost
violent short digs, that I knew to what an intense
degree my Venus enjoyed pleasure! I thought she
was in a fit! She almost screamed! She gurgled in
her throat! She half-crushed me in her arms, and
putting her feet on my behind, she pressed me to
her motte, at the end, with a power I should never
have thought she possessed. Oh! the relief! the
exquisite delight of the spend on my part! I inun-
dated her, and she felt the spouting torrents of my
love darting in hot, quick jets, and striking against
the deepest part of her almost maddened cleft! She
seized my mouth with hers, and shot her tongue
into it as far as she could, touching my palate, and
pouring her hot, delicious breath down my throat
whilst her whole body from head to heel literally
quivered with the tremendous excitement she was
in! Never in my life had I such a fling! Oh! why are
there no better words to express what is really
heaven upon earth?

The tempest past, we lay in one another's arms; tenderly gazing into one another's eyes. We were too breathless to speak at first. I could feel her belly heaving against mine, and her throbbing cunnie clasped my tool as though it had been another hand, whilst her motte leaped and bounded! I looked into that angelic-looking face, and drank in the intense beauty of it, nor could I believe it could be an abandoned woman, but rather Venus herself, whom I held thus clasped in my arms, and whose tender and voluptuous thighs encircled mine! I could have wished that she held her peace and let me dream that I was the much desired Adonis, and she my persistent, longing Venus, and that I had at length won her amorous wishes, and found the heaven in her arms of which, before I entered her matchless cleft, I had no notion. But my airy fancies were dispelled by her saying:

"You are a good poke and no mistake! Oh! You know how to do it! No fellow ever rams like that without he has been taught!"

"Yes!" I said, pressing her in my arms and kissing the ruby lips which had just spoken so coarsely but truly, and pointedly, "I have been well trained! I had good lessons in my boyhood, and I have always tried to practice them as often as possible!"

"Ah!" she said. "I though so! You do the heel-and-toe better than any man I've ever had, and I've had, I dare say, many more men than you've had women!"

Frank and how!

"What do you mean by heel-and-toe, my pet!"

"Oh! Don't you know? You do it at any rate! And splendid! Heel-and-toe is to begin each stroke at the very beginning and end it at the very end. Just give me one long stroke now!" I did so. I withdrew until I was all but out of her panting orifice, and then gently but firmly drove it home, as far and as deep as I could, and then I rested again on her belly.

"There," she cried, "that's it! You almost pull it out, but not quite, and never stop short in your thrusts, but send it home, with a sharp rap of your cods against my bottom! and that's what's good!"

And she appeared to smack her lips involuntarily.

At length I withdrew, and my fairest nymph at once commenced a most minute examination of that part of me and its appendages which had pleased her so much. Everything was, according to her, absolutely perfect, and if I were to believe her there had not passed under her observation so noble and handsome an organ, and such beautiful, well balanced stones as I had and she was the mistress of! My stones especially pleased her! She said they were so big! She was sure they must be full of spend, and she intended, she told me, to empty them before she would consent to my leaving Nowshera!

This first sacrifice simply whetted our appetites, and still more inflamed with the minute examination of one another's charms, we fell to again, and writhed in the delicious agonies of another amorous combat! It was about two o'clock before I left her, and we had not been at any one time more than ten minutes "out of action." The more I had of this exquisite creature, the more I longed to have her. I was fresh, young, strong, vigorous, and it was nearly two months (a long time for me) since I had last indulged in the delights of Cyprian pleasures. No wonder my Venus was pleased with me, and called my performances a perfect feast.

They say that love destroys appetite for food. Perhaps it does when it is love unrequited, but I give you my word, dear reader, that I was ravenous for my tiffin after my morning's work. I was really glad to get something to eat, for what with the heat of the combats I had been through, and the parching effect of the terrible hot wind blowing, I was dried up, as far as my mouth was concerned, though far from being so as regards the proceeds of my sack. I never felt so fit for woman as I did that day, and I never probably have had so much joy with so little loss of physical force. Doubtless my steady married life with its regular hours, regular meals, and regular, never-excessive sacrifices on the altar of Venus had much to do with the steady power I felt so strong in me, but over and above that, was the fact of my new lady love being extraordinarily beautiful, and voluptuously lascivious, and the erotic excitement raised in me, was, of course, great in proportion to the cause which gave birth to it. In spite of my hunger for food, I would certainly have remained with her on that most genial of beds, and have revelled on in her joyous arms, and filled her with quintessence of my manly vigor, but she told me she always slept in the afternoon, was hungry herself, and, doubting my power, she wished me to reserve some good portions of my force to be expended between her lovely thighs that night and for the solace of her liveliest of crannies.

Whilst the Khansamah was laying the table I saw a note addressed to me, leaning against the wall, on the mantelpiece (for in Northern India the winters are sharp enough to render a fire not only pleasant but sometimes quite necessary), and taking it and opening it, wondering who the writer could be, as I was perfectly unknown in this part of the world, I found it to be from my young officer friend who had quitted Nowshera this morning, it ran thus:

"Dear Devereaux:—In the room next to yours is one of the loveliest of women and best of pokes! Verbum Sap!*

Yours,
J.C.

P.S.—Don't offer her any rupees or you will offend her mortally, but if you are inclined to have her, and I think you will on seeing her, just tell her so and you won't have to ask twice."

* Probably J. C. means to quote Terence, 'Dictum sapienti sat est' (A word to the wise is sufficient.)

Ah! Dear young chap, now I understand why you were so reticent this morning and did not like to tell me that I had a lady for my next door neighbor! Well! Poor girl! I am afraid that you must be put down as one of the "irregulars", although it is a shame to think ill of one who has given me the first few hours of real delight since I left home!

These thoughts naturally brought my beloved little wife into my recollection and I was somewhat staggered to feel I should so completely have forgotten her and my marital vows! But I was altogether too full of desire. Desire only just whetted and crying for more! More! I was in fact half mad with what some call lust and others love and, wife or no wife, nothing short of death would, or should, prevent my poking that heavenly girl again, and again, until I really could not raise a stand. I longed for evening. I burnt for night. I ate my tiffin like a ravenous tiger, hungry for food, but thirsting for the sweet savour of the blood of a victim he knew to be within reach. Tiffin put away, I lit a cheroot, and began wandering round and round my room, balancing impatiently at the door which closed the communication between it and that of my supposedly now sleeping Venus, and like Wellington wished and prayed for night or—not Blucher—her awakening! Suddenly it struck me as very funny that—supposing some catastrophe were to separate this girl and me, neither would be able to say who the other was! We had not exchanged names. My young friend the officer who signed his initials "J.C." had not told me. I did not even know his name, though he knew mine, probably from seeing it painted on my baggage. Of a surety this lovely Venus must have a history, and I resolved to try and get her to give me her version of it, from which no doubt I could make out what was true and what was invention, for that she would tell me the exact truth I hardly expected. Oh! when would she awake?

Should I go and peep and see? By Jupiter, I would . . .

Throwing away the fresh cheroot I had lighted I crept, in my stocking feet, to her chick, and pulled it slightly open, and there on the bed fast asleep, I saw my lovely enslaver. She had simply put on a petticoat and was lying on her back, with her hands clasped under her shapely head, her arms, bent in a charming position opened out, showing the little growth of hair under the arm pit next to me; hair the same in tint, but not so rich in color, as that magnificent bush I had moistened so liberally, aided by her own offerings this morning; her bosom bare and naked, with its two priceless breasts, so beautifully placed, so round, polished and firm, and her entire body down to her slender waist, quite nude! One knee, that next to me, was bent, the small graceful foot planted on the bed clothes, each gem of a toe straight and just separated from its neighbor, a foot that would have charmed the most fastidious sculptor that ever

lived, whilst the other leg, bare almost from the
groin downwards, was extended at full length, the
lovely foot, which terminated it, resting against the
edge of the bed, so that her thighs, those lovely
voluptuous and maddening thighs, were parted!
Gods! could I remain outside while so much beauty
was freely displayed, on which I could feast my
burning eyes whilst its lovely owner slept? I went
gently and noiselessly in, and passing round to the
other side of the bed, so that my shadow might not
fall on that exquisite form, and hide the light,
already softened by the chick, from it, and gazed in
silence on the beautiful girl who had made me
enjoy the bliss of Mahomet's heaven in her voluptuous embraces that forenoon. How lovely was her
sleep! Who, looking on that face so pure in all its
lines, so innocent in all its expressions, could imagine that in that soul there burnt the fire of an
unquenchable Cytherian furnace. Who, looking on
those matchless breasts could imagine that lovers
innumerable had pressed them with lascivious
hand or lip and been supported by them when
they trembled in the agonies and the delight of
having her?

The fair broad plain of her belly was still hidden
by the upper portion of her petticoats, but the fine
lines, which I had noticed when she "put on her
skin", had told me the tale, that perhaps more than
once it had been the breeding place of little beings,
who, cast in such a beauteous mold, must needs be
as beautiful as their lovely mother! I, who, looking
at those virginal breasts which seemed as if they
had never been disturbed by pent-up milk, and
whose rose-bud-like nipples seemed never to have
been sucked, by the cherry lips of babies; who,
gazing in the girlish face, could connect such
charms with the pains, the caress, and duties of

maternity? No! surely, like the fair Houris of Mahomet's paradise, she must have been created for the fulfillment of the pleasure only, not for the consequences of the kiss of love! But the wrinkles told a different tale, and I should like to examine them more closely. It would be near the groin, and all that I had to do was to lift, gently, so as not to disturb her sleep, the part of her petticoat which still hid her there, and lay the garment back upon her waist.

With a hand trembling with excitement, I did so! lo! my nymph almost as naked as she was born! God of Gods! What a blaze of exciting beauty! I had uncovered the sweet belly to look at the wrinkles, but my eye was captured before it lifted its gaze so high! As the bird is caught in the snare surrounding the luscious bait exposed for it, so were my eyes entangled in the meshes of that glorious hair, which from the forest-like bush growing on that voluptuous motte, and shading the slit, the like of which for freshness, beauty, and all that excites desire, could not have existed in that to anybody but that of the great Mother of love, Venus herself. It seemed to me impossible that this beauteous portal to the realms of bliss, could have been invaded by so many worshippers as her speech of the morning had led me to believe. It looked far from having been hard used. What grand full lips it had. How sweetly it was placed. How pretty did the fine dark hairs which crossed it look against the whiteness of the skin, whose infoldings formed that deep and perfect line. What a perfect forest overshadowed it, and how divine were the slopes of that glorious hill, the perfect little mountain, which led up the sweet descent to the deep vale between her thighs, and ended in that glowing grotto in which love delighted to hide his blushing head, and shed the hot tears of his exulting joy.

But what is that? What is that little ruby tip I see beginning to protrude, near the upper meeting of those exquisite lips? She moves. See! I think she must be dreaming! She slightly closes her bent leg towards that one outstretched! It is her most sensitive clitoris, as I live! See! It grows more and more! And by the Gods! it actually moves in little jerks, just like an excited stem standing stiff, and mad at the thoughts of hot desire!

I gazed at the tranquil face of the sleeping beauty, her lips moved and her mouth opened slightly showing the pearly teeth! Her bosom seemed to expand, her breasts to swell, they rose and fell more rapidly than they had been doing before this evident dream of love fulfilled or about to be, invaded the soft heart of this perfect priestess of Venus! Ah! Her bubbies do move! Their rosebuds swell out, they stand, each like an eager sentinel perched on the snowy tip of his own mountain, watching for the loving foe who is to invade this dreaming girl to the soft and sharp and hot encounter.

Again those thighs close on one another. Heaven! again they open to show the domain of love, excited, moving, leaping, actually leaping! That glittering ruby clit is evidently striving to feel the manly staff of which my charmer dreams. Why not turn the dream into a sweet and luscious reality?

I do not hesitate. I swiftly strip and in a moment I am as naked as I had been that morning, but I would like to see whether, as when I raped my cousin Emily, my second love, I could actually get into this sleeping girl, before she woke to find me in her glowing orifice.

So I gently got over her thigh next to me, and

with knees between hers I supported myself upon my hands, one on each side of her and stretching out my legs backward, kept my eyes fixed on the sweet and burning cranny I intended to invade. I lowered my body until I brought the head and point of my agitated and jerking tool exactly opposite its lower half, and then I maneuvered it in!

Gods! The voluptuousness of that moment! I could see myself penetrating that seat of love and luxury! I could feel the cap fall back from the tingling head of my member and fold behind its broad purple shoulder! For a moment I glanced at her face to see if she had perceived the gallant theft I was making on her secret jewel! No! She was asleep, but in the excitement of an erotic dream! Little by little I pressed further and further in, only withdrawing, to give her more pleasure. I am nearly all in—her thick and lofty bush hides the last inch or so of my spear from my eyes, our hairs comingle, my eggs touch her, and she wakes with a start!

In a moment her eyes met mine with that keen, almost wild glance, which had so impressed me when I saw her out of the gharry, but in a moment they changed and beamed with pleasure and affectionate caresses.

"Ah! Is it you?" she cried. "I was dreaming of you! You darling man to wake me so sweetly!"

Some burning kisses, some close, close hugs, some little exclamations of delight, and then breast to breast, belly to belly, mouth to mouth, we play for the ninth or tenth time. I really don't know which, that same excited tune which had sounded all that morning so melodiously to our ravished senses. Heel-and-toe! as she called it: delicious movements mingling in every part, hot, quick, thrilling short digs, and then the torrents of two volcanoes of love burst forth simultaneously and mingled their lava floods in the hot recesses buried below the sylvan slopes of the Hill of Venus.

The gong on which the non-commissioned officer of the guard sounds the hour of the day in India, rang five o'clock. We had been in intense action nearly a whole hour, and my charming beauty was for the fifteenth time examining what she called my "wonderful" member and stones, wonderful, because the first showed no symptoms of fatigue, and the second no signs of exhaustion or depletion.

"I don't believe this can be a proper tool at all!" said she feeling it, pressing it, and kissing its impudent looking head, first on one side and then on the other.

"Why?" I asked laughing.

"Because it's always stiff as a poker—always standing!"

"That is because it admires your delicious cranny so much, my darling, that it is always in a hurry to get back into it after it has been taken out!"

"Well! I never saw one like it before! All other men that I have had always grew soft and limp, after the second go at any rate, and generally took a good deal of coaxing to get to stand again, unless one gives them lots of time! But yours! I never, never, met one like it! It will give me a lot of trouble, I can see, to take all the starch out of it!"

"Oh! but I assure you my most lovely girl, that with ordinary women I am just as you describe the men you have known. I can assure you it must be your extraordinary beauty which has such a powerful effect upon me! Come!" I continued opening my arms and thighs. "Come and lie on top of me and let me kiss you to death!"

Enraptured by the lavish, but not unmerited, praise of her beauty, she threw herself, with a cry of delight, on top of me, and my manhood found a sweet resting place between our respective bellies. She took and gave me the sweetest kiss, murmuring little words of love and passion like a cat purring, until I was just going to propose that she should put her thighs outside mine, and let me have her a la St. George, when a sudden idea seemed to strike her. She raised herself on her hand and asked me:

"I say! Have you reported your arrival to the Station Staff Officer?"

What an idea! Fancy talking of such commonplace things just as I was about to propose the most delicious thing a woman can have from man, the very poetry of life and love! I could not but think of Mrs. Shandy asking her husband when he was in the middle of that operation which resulted in Tristram nine months later, whether he had wound up the clock.

"My dear girl!" I cried. "Bother the Station Staff Officer and all his reports. Come! I am hungry for another sweet go! I want this! and I slipped my hand under her belly and between her thighs, and my middle finger into her palpitating cavern.

"No!" she said, forcibly pushing my invading hand away. "No! Not one more until you have gone and reported yourself! Ah! you don't know the regulations, I see! But *I* do! I have not been in India all these years without learning what they are, and Major Searles, the Brigade Major here, is a perfect beast and devil! You may depend upon it he knows you are here, and he would be only delighted to get a chance of sitting on you, and he will be able to do so if you don't report yourself before dark—mind! you got here early this morning!"

CHAPTER SEVEN: MASTER PERCY AND THE OPPOSITION

No ONE WHO WISHED to be the Casanova of our century would start off by calling himself Percy. And even for memoirist of youthful love and lust, the handle must be something of a handicap. Forget Jean-Jacques for a moment—would we still be reading the *Confessions* of Percy Rousseau? The story in question comes from a yellow-wrapped novel, *Forbidden Fruit . . . and More Forbidden Fruit, or Master Percy's Progress.*

All of this is only to say that *Master Percy's Progress* owes much to the rumbustious, bawdy, rowdy, bottom-pinching side of literature and very little to pale or intense passions pursued minutely behind silk blinds. The ancestors of Percy and the country woman Phoebe are somewhere in the cartoons of Rowlandson and Hogarth, drinking mightily, burping and snorting, wigs askew and hands full of a barmaid's breasts.

Contrast the romps of this sort with the careful and subtle psychological delineation of *Sweet Dreams,* where we get half a chapter on the curious and ambivalent relationship of the man of the house to the girl of seventeen whom he has whipped for her offence. In the world of Master Perry no one would give a damn about psychology. Master Percy, the landowner's son, fancies a ride. Phoebe, the country wench, is ready to be mounted. Next time she is not ready for it. All right, says Percy, what about one of your daughters then? Oh, all right, say Phoebe. And off they go.

Now this takes no prizes for realism. People don't behave that way, not even in the English countryside of 1905 when the novel was published. It is a joke and, like a good many jokes, it is bawdy. No one believes that such characters as Percy and Phoebe actually exist, any more than they believe in the truth of *Dallas* or *Dynasty*. But there is somewhat more honest and down-to-earth chicanery in the life of our young hero than in most television soaps.

Where did the novel come from? We don't really know. Its title-page simply says, "London, 1905." But the yellow paper wrapper and the rough-edged pages suggest that it saw London only when imported from France. There is a crazy preface in which the author describes how he acquired the manuscript when he happened to find a girl reading it by a Sussex hedgerow. In no time at all there was an "understanding" between them. The girl lent him the manuscript and—hey, presto!—the story of Master Percy was published to the world.

Paris, not London, was its birthplace and the first part of the book had appeared in 1898. It never got past the English or American censors but it showed the gathering rebellion against the "niceness" and "primness" of Victorian etiquette. Publishers like Carrington, even in their erotic, were apt to light a fuse under the edifice of American and English self-righteousness. *Dolly Morton* revealed things about the sexual bondage of girls in the Deep South that the Deep South resented. *The Underside of English Prudery* unmasked the scandal of reformatory masters whipping girls of fifteen like Elaine Cox and having a lot of fun in the process.

Master Percy is different. He merely selects those things that English society thought tasteful and decorous. Then, putting his thumb to his nose and his tongue to his lips, he blows a thunderous raspberry at the lot of them.

FORBIDDEN FRUIT

LUSCIOUS AND EXCITING STORY

AND

MORE FORBIDDEN FRUIT

OR

MASTER PERCY'S PROGRESS

in and beyond

the Domestic Circle

LONDON

—

1905

Our residence stood in large grounds of its own, surrounded by a delightful country stretching away in a long vista to the South Downs. Papa owned several farms in the neighbourhood, so we were generally respected and looked up to by the working class and their families, as Mamma disbursed a good deal in helping any who might be in trouble.

I remember one labourer's family, the husband a carter who never got home till late in the evening, as his work was rather at a distance; his wife, about thirty or a little more, was a fine, handsome, young woman with a ruddy, tanned face, but oh! such brown eyes as she looked at you from under her dark eyelashes. She was a fine woman of her class, and I had once heard Mamma say Peter, her husband, had to marry Phoebe (that was her name) very young as he had got her into trouble; she had three very pretty little girls—ten, eleven, and twelve years old—regular beauties, with the same dark brown eyes and arch looks as their mother, and they were well grown for their ages. This was my mark. I had often been with Mamma on a visit to their cottage when they had any little illness, and carried a basket of nice things for them. I didn't know their family name, but Phoebe always kissed me and so did the girls when they were well. "Master Percy, Master Percy," they would call out as soon as ever I got in sight, because I generally had some sweets in my pocket for them. Now I had not been to the cottage for quite two years, and wondered if Phoebe would kiss me now. I would her if I got the chance. It was only about a mile to walk from our house down an unfrequented lane leading to nowhere but an old farm-house further on.

Mrs Twiggs, our housekeeper, lent me a small basket, so I went into the pantry and helped myself to a good sized cake, some eggs, and a bottle of port wine, as I said I had heard that Phoebe was rather delicate.

I timed myself to get to the cottage soon after their mid-day meal, so as to have a long afternoon in case I found any sport.

Phoebe was all smiles as she answered my rap at the cottage door. "Oh, Master Percy, how you have grown, and how's your Mamma—I hope she isn't ill?"

"No thanks, Phoebe, I heard you were not quite well, so made up my mind to walk over with some new-laid eggs and a bottle of wine for you and a cake for the girls; where are they?"

"How kind of you, Master Percy, who could have told you that? I'm all right, and the girls have gone to see their grand-mother at Becton and won't get home much before dark, so I'm alone; no-one ever comes to see me. Thank you so much. Won't you come in and sit down for a rest?"

"That I will, Phoebe, and I feel done up carrying that basket. You might draw the cork and give me a glass of port, and a drop will do you good."

The cork was soon drawn, and she drank to my health with her "Best respects to you, Master Percy. How you have grown, I shan't like to kiss you now."

"Why not, Phoebe, what harm can it be? I have often sat on your lap and kissed you when my mother was here, and I mean to again."

"Oh, no, it isn't proper only with little boys. They're harmless you know; now you're so big you must only kiss your young lady sweetheart, or Mamma, or your dear aunt, Miss Gertie."

"But you must give me one, or I shall feel quite a stranger. What harm can it be?"

"Well I don't know any harm, and you're a dear,

kind boy to think of us, as you have, but I mustn't do it again before any one," as putting her glass down she stood up and kissed my cheek, and would have sat down again; but my arm was round her waist in a moment, drawing her close to me, my lips kissed hers, then her cheeks and lips again."

"You only gave me half a kiss, Phoebe, I must have a proper one," pushing her back on her chair, and seating myself on her lap. "This is how I want it, just as you used to do. Now kiss me nicely."

Her rich-colored face crimsoned, and I felt her splendid bosom heave with emotion as I fairly glued my lips to hers, and tried to push my tongue between her lips, and one hand tried to get inside her neck-kerchief.

"You mustn't, you wicked boy. What a flutter you have put me into! now get away do, Master Percy. You ought not to kiss me like that."

But she only struggled faintly; my hand slipped inside her bosom and felt those still lovely firm orbs, as her heart palpitated and her lips gradually relaxed till my tongue fairly met hers tip to tip.

"Ah, you rogue! how bad you make me feel!" returning my caresses, and rubbing one hand up and down my back, as if she only wished she dared put it in front."

"Percy, Percy, Master Percy, for shame, don't be so rude," as I suddenly placed her hand on my big prick which I had let out of my trousers. "What a size for a boy of fourteen, and I believe you know a lot."

"Yes, Phoebe, I know what 'cunt' and 'fuck' mean; shall we have a game? We're all alone, and it is so nice you have made me feel wild." I was now raising her skirts and soon had my hands up a splendid pair of thighs, fit for Venus herself, and quite innocent of drawers, as a delightful aroma of cunt made me feel still more randy. Separating her legs, as she lay back in the chair, I could see what a splendid white skin she had, and the lips of her cunt just peeping out from a profusion of almost black brown hair. Not a word passed between us as I tried to get into her, but I could hear the heavy breathing and the almost audible palpitation of her heart. I was a little awkward, but her hand helped me to go straight: the head of my eager prick got in, and, she pushing herself forward, I progressed upwards within the folds of her vagina and found myself at full length in one of the hottest cunts I had yet felt. "Wait a moment, don't hurry, dear; let me enjoy it—this is a treat, Master Percy. I couldn't help myself, but it is so awfully wicked you know."

She kept me like that for quite five minutes, the inner folds of that amorous cunt of hers pressing and nipping the head of my prick, her arms were tightly clasped round my back, so I could scarcely move, whilst her lips seemed as if they would eat mine, and her tongue was regularly fucking my mouth.

"Let me fuck you, Phoebe, you're making me come. I can't stop it, dear. Ah, oh! There it is shooting up you. Can't you feel it?"

"Yes, yes, I'm spending too, Percy, you love; what a grand prick to hold in my cunt—Peter's isn't near so big—you fill me up so beautifully, besides he only fucks me on Sundays; he is too tired to do it during the week. Will you come and see Phoebe as often as you can? Now fuck me well, you dear boy."

Without losing my stiffness, I went on drawing right out to the head of my instrument and pushing it slowly in again, which soon drove her quite wild.

"Faster quicker, fuck hard, darling!" she almost screamed, and as I did so with all my force, she lay back and gave quite a neighing squeal in the excess of her lubricity. I came again at the same moment. So finished my first fuck with the splendid country woman, who was indeed a rough jewel in her way. She would not permit any more just then, so I took leave of her after we had kissed each other's parts, and she made me promise not to be long before I called again.

* * *

But hot on the heels of Master Percy came the squadrons of a moral majority who had no intention of allowing country life to degenerate into a caper of this sort. After all, Master Percy and his kind were to be the leaders of the nation at some time in the future and, even though some of those leaders turned out to have a pretty shaky record anyway, this was no way for them to spend their early years.

Perhaps worst of all, Percy hinted at the animal indecencies of rural life and also at the spectre of incest, which was rather more common in primitive communities than most of the moralists at the time cared to admit. Small inbred villages or settlements began to take a more than casual interest in such matters. The marriage of cousins and of a man to his dead wife's sister was reluctantly sanctioned by law. But the problem and the scandal of such things was not, of course, confined to the poor and the rural. That most unfortunate of British kings, George III, was said to have had a spot of bother with his children. The Duke of Cumberland, who later ruled Hanover and would have ruled England as well if Victoria and her cousin had never been born, took a fancy to his sister, the Princess Sophia. It was said that he "triumphed" and fathered upon her a son, who grew up to be known as the mysterious "Captain Garth." The best that the royal public relations department could do was to admit that Cumberland had tried to ravish his sister but that she, stout girl, had beaten him off.

But one way and another it looked like time for a little moral backbone to be introduced in high society and low society alike. To that problem there was a single answer. "Bring back the lash," or in this case continue using the lash but do it more frequently. The newspapers began to sing its praises and soon there was no doubt that those who fancied one another, closely related or not, had better do it with a whip in their hands. No moral majority ever objected to that. In 1889, Mrs Walter Smith set up her famous "chastising service for young ladies" in London and the provinces. She was overwhelmed by business and advertisements appeared in such papers as the *Church Times* and the *Daily Telegraph*. Master Percy and his passions seemed to be on a very short leash.

Without the least hint that there was anything odd about such enthusiasm, for both Mrs Walter Smith and reformatory enthusiasts like James Miles thrashed women in their twenties, testimonials to the virtues of flagellation began to appear in slim volumes. In case anyone should suppose that Master Percy was typical of his life and times, here is a sample of the other side of the argument.

"Delightful sport! whose never failing charm,
Makes young blood tingle and keeps old blood
warm."

G. Colman.

———

Experiences
of
Flagellation

A Series of Remarkable Instances of Whipping
Inflicted on Both Sexes

WITH
CURIOUS ANECDOTES OF LADIES
FOND OF ADMINISTERING BIRCH DISCIPLINE.

COMPILED BY
AN AMATEUR FLAGELLANT.

LONDON:
PRINTED FOR PRIVATE CIRCULATION
1885.

REVELATIONS OF BOARDING-SCHOOL PRACTICES

At the age of seventeen I was sent to a fashionable boarding-school, near Exeter, in Devonshire. I was sent there owing to the influence of my aunt, who was always praising this establishment up to my mamma, and strongly recommending it as a finishing academy for young ladies. My aunt was a maiden lady of forty, a tall, handsome, buxom woman.

Neither myself nor my mamma ever thought she was an advocate for the rod, and liked administering, and seeing it administered. It turned out afterwards, as the narrative will show, that she was really in league with the schoolmistress, and would frequently call at the establishment and indulge herself in her favourite pastime, for which she no doubt paid large sums annually, being a strong and fervent advocate for corporal chastisement, at times as unseen observer and with some of the elder young ladies being the operator. In all there were twenty-four young ladies in this fashionable establishment, their ages varying from twelve to nineteen. I was as tall, fine-shaped, and handsome as any young lady in the school, and no doubt when my mamma gave her consent to my leaving home, my aunt thought there was a great treat in store for her.

A few days after arriving, I soon found out what sort of lady principal I had to contend with, and her assistants were not much better. The first sample I saw her administer to one of her pupils was after I had been there four days. A young lady, about fifteen, had committed some trifling error, for which madam told her in plain terms that she should give her a good whipping when class was over, and this she did and in front of the whole school. She was taken by the arms and legs by two of the assistant teachers, and thrown face downwards over a desk sloping each way and firmly held there. Madam then approached with a flat piece of wood about an inch-and-a-half in thickness, and shaped like a hair-brush, but much bigger. After addressing a few words of advice to us, and admonishing the culprit, she took hold of her garments at the bottom, then without any further to-do, she lifted the "spanker," as this piece of wood was called by my school-fellows, and inflicted a tremendous "spank" across the girl. A loud yell followed, and a strong effort to free herself from the grasp of her tormentors, but all of no avail, for they, no doubt owing to their previous experience, could hold a young lady in any position. She received about a dozen stripes before she was released.

We had a system of making so many marks, and if any young lady had not made so many by the end of the week they were sure to receive a whipping. I have known as many as seven young ladies whipped on a Saturday. It was at these whippings that my aunt and her friends were present as unseen spectators, through the medium of small glass panels being inserted in a door to an adjoining closet.

In fact, during my two years at this establishment I was whipped several times. I shall never forget my last experience. I think the lady principal had made up her mind that I should be flogged on the Saturday, for at the early part of the week, however good I did my lessons, fault was found with me, and I got careless towards the latter end. On the Saturday I found my name on the "Black List," as it was called. I was number three on the list, my two school fellows, both young girls about fourteen, had gone in and received their punishment. I was then ordered in. I need not tell you that I entered the room trembling from head to foot. Madam called me by my Christian name "Emily," and informed me she was very sorry to have to inflict punishment on such a big girl as me, but the rules of the school must be enforced, winding up by ordering me to prepare for punishment. I dropped on my knees in front of her, and begged of her to take into consideration my age, size, etc.; in fact I hardly remember what I did say. She was inexorable, and, with a smile on her face, ordered me to obey, or she should have to call assistance, and my punishment would be much more severe. I made some remark, when she seized me by beautiful long hair, and beat me about my ears, head, cheeks, and arms, with the birch, until I was compelled to give in and promise obedience in future.

Soon after I found means to send a letter to my mother, informing her of the circumstances related above. She accordingly took steps for my early removal, and I was soon afterwards married, but my mother and aunt have never been friends or spoken to each other since.

* * *

"Medical Student" writes: "With regard to the Whipping of Girls, I think, that as "this is the age of the ladies," there is no reason why girls should not be whipped as well as boys. But let me remind some of your correspondents that the days in which Milton was whipped at Oxford are long gone by, and if the girls require to be whipped at sixteen they will require it all their lives. I suppose that their husbands are the only persons on whom the duty will devolve after they have left the parental mansion. Now, as husbands are punished for thrashing their wives, why should not schoolmistresses be punished for doing the same by young ladies of sixteen or seventeen committed to their care?''

* * *

"Gratitude." "I own, as you see, one of the most honoured names in England, and call myself 'Gratitude', because I am anxious to show my gratitude for the fact that I owe my present position as a useful happy English lady to the firm discipline I experienced at the very turning-point of my life. I was brought up in a loving home, I had every possible advantage; but amidst it all I became sullen, self-willed, and disobedient and idle. I was the grief of my parents and a byword to my companions. However, soon after I was fifteen I most fortunately was sent to Mrs.——'s school for young ladies, in Brighton, where I showed the same evil disposition which I had evidenced elsewhere, but where, most fortunately and happily for me, it was checked and cured. In school and out of it, during the first month, Mrs.—— and the other teachers reproved me, set me tasks, and 'kept me in.' But I only grew worse; and one night after I had refused to do an 'imposition,' as boys call a punishment lesson, Mrs.—— came and sat in my room after I was in bed and talked to me most impressively. The next day, however, the impression of what she had said wore off, and I was as bad as ever. But a change was at hand, for in the evening, when we had just gone to our bedrooms, Mrs.—— again came to me, and said, 'Miss W., you will to-night occupy the dressing-room adjoining my room. I

will show you the way.' I was half inclined to diso-
bey. However, I followed my governess through
her bedroom and across a small sitting-room,
which opened out of it into a room comfortably
furnished, in which was a small low bed, and telling me to undress and go to bed, Mrs.—— left me,
locking the door after her. I had been in bed about
a quarter of an hour when Mrs.—— came to me,
holding in her hand a long birch-rod. Placing the
candlestick and the rod on the table, she told me
that but one course was now open to her after my
behaviour, and that she was going to flog me, and I
was to get up. But though the twigs of the birch-
rod stood out in ominous shadow in front of the
candlestick, and while I noted the thin, closely
wrapped handle of that rod, and its fanlike-
spreading top, I never attempted to obey. Three
times Mrs.—— told me to get up, but I stirred not.
She then very deliberately turned down the bedclothes, and again told me to get out of bed. I
began to feel that I was going to be conquered, but
I stirred not. Mrs.—— returned to her own room,
and came back with a small, thin riding-whip, and
said, 'must I use this?' There was something about
her which quite awed me—it was more her manner
than her tall powerful figure—and as she swung
that whip about in her hand I at once stepped out
of bed and stood before her. 'Give me your hands,'
she said, but I put them behind me, when slash
across my shoulders came six or seven smart
strokes of her whip, and screaming I put out my
hands, which she fastened together with a cord by
the wrists. Then making me lie down across the
foot of the bed face downwards, she very quietly
and deliberately, putting her left hand round my
waist, gave me a shower of smart slaps with her
open right hand—a proceeding which so surprised

and humiliated my proud self that I could hardly believe in my own identity, and as I screamed and struggled, she merely said, 'This is for not doing *now* as I told you, and it will not only punish you for *that,* but will increase the pain of the birching I am now going to give you.' Mrs.—— then, as I lay, spoke to me for a few minutes with great kindness and earnestness. She then rose, took the birch in her right hand, and swooping over me, pressed her left hand tightly on my shoulder so as to hold me as if I were in a vice; then raising the birch, I could hear it whizz in the air, and oh, how terrible it felt as it came down, and as its repeated strokes came swish, swish, swish, on me! yet I felt, in spite of the terrible stinging pain, that I deserved it all—and it *was* painful. I was a stout fair girl, and very sensitive to pain. I screamed, I protested, I implored, but it was of no avail; Mrs.—— heeded not my cries, but held me down and birched on till she had finished a whipping which seemed to have lasted an age, but which quite changed my character. At last it *was* over. I was permitted to rise, my hands were unbound, and, burning and smarting, I raised my tear-stained face to my true friend's, on whose face no sign was visible, of the slightest anger or passion. Calm and serene, she wished me 'Good-night' and left me conquered. Henceforward I was a different girl; and though a few weeks afterwards I relapsed, yet another night spent in Mrs.——'s dressing-room and another similar application by her of that wonder working birch—I did exactly as she told me this time—sufficed finally to cure me. I became cheerful, obedient, unselfish. My parents and friends the next holidays could hardly believe that I was the same girl. I stayed three years with Mrs.—— at Brighton, leaving her when I was nineteen with much regret. I am now twenty-four, and hope to be married at Easter to *the best man in the world* who never *could* have loved me had not sensible, wholesome, discipline changed my evil nature, as *the* means under Higher Power of doing so. I am thankful to publish my experience, and so to express not only my gratitude, but confirm what others have so well said and told on this subject.''

* * *

"Emma" (near Newcastle) writes: "A while ago I undertook to bring up two nieces of the ages of twelve and fourteen. I soon found them to be most stubborn tempers and impudent. Thus they have often caused me much trouble and annoyance. Though not an advocate of corporal punishment, I was much struck with the description by 'A Schoolmistress' of a most ceremonious method of inflicting punishment that I determined to follow exactly the same method and try it the same morning. I prepared a woollen dress; not being able to procure a birch, I sent and had made a pair of very long pliant leather taws. In the afternoon I found the eldest of my nieces in a gross fault, and on being found fault with she was very pert. I therefore took her to my bedroom and made her don the garment and follow me to the drawing-room, she never thinking for a moment of what was to follow. I then quietly told her of her bad conduct for some time past, and that I was determined to try what a whipping would do. On ordering her to lay across an ottoman she distinctly refused. I told her if she did not at once comply I would ring for a servant to compel her. Still refusing, I rang for assistance. Hearing the servant coming upstairs, and seeing me determined, she lay down rather than be seen by the servant in this predicament, wherefore I went to the door and sent the servant back. I then fastened her across the ottoman. I then proceeded to administer a few strokes of the taws, which soon elicited cries for forgiveness and promises of future good conduct, but being determined to try the efficacy of this method, I continued until I had given her a severe flogging. I then allowed her to rise, and on her knees to thank me for the correction, then sent her off to bed for the day. Up to this time the perfect subjection and submission of this girl is such that I most heartily recommend all parents and guardians to try the same method in all cases of disobedience. I think that in all whippings of grown children a large amount of cool ceremony is most effectual.

CHAPTER EIGHT: VILLA ROSA

FUN IN THE SUN is the nearest modern dream to fulfilment. Somewhere, always just over the horizon, is the summer resort where the ocean rollers rumble on the sands and the flags of the promenade stand out stiffly in the breeze of the bright morning. In the dreamworld, the resort is often in France, probably that south-western coast with its long beaches rather than the crowded and torpid Mediterranean.

And there, as Edward Sellon described it, behind the pink-tarmac'd tennis-courts and the casino, surrounded by high walls and isolated by wide gardens, stands the ideal villa for the wealthy *bon viveur*. A square Spanish-style tower at one corner, no doubt. French windows and green shutters against cream stucco. A quiet paved drive with the sun sparkling on a pair of the most expensive German and Italian cars that money can buy. The name on the gate invites us to the Villa Rosa.

When it comes to such fantasies the novels of erotic dreaming tell us what we want.

> *The hot days were passed in the naked pleasures of elegant rooms, among brooding lamps and silent carpets. Her pale aloof beauty was the complement to ornaments of jade and ivory in cool recesses, alabaster and porcelain on painted shelves. Afternoon drives in a shaded carriage took the lovers along the elegant boulevards of white stucco, the imperial Parisienne grandeur of hotels and the little boutiques with coloured sunblinds. The brilliance of the summer tide glinted on the fresh paintwork of the corniche, where pink tamarisk moved with feather-lightness in the warm breeze and yellow*

broom flamed in the gardens. The smell of tide-washed sand hung in the afternoon air as the emerald sea darkened in the heat to a black horizon band.

Read this on a bleak foggy day in Trenton or Detroit and see if you can keep your hand away from the phone and a call to American Express, booking a priority reservation in dreamland.

And after such a day, there comes the evening and the night, tall camelia trees and pampas grass in the dusk of the private gardens, Italian cypress and white flowers in the shady depths of warm twilight. In the grounds of the Villa Rosa, the glass moons of the lamps on their wrought-iron mounts glimmer among dark evergreens.

Our destination in this case is a very private and very select dinner-party to be held in the secret and vine-shaded courtyard of the villa. There, under the light of the Spanish lamps, the diners are attended by a pair of young waitresses, Sian and Helyn. Redhead and brunette, they are as different in their characters and sexual attitudes as in the colour of their hair. Perhaps one ought to guess that it is Sian the redhead who is dreamy and lascivious, while Helyn the brunette is demure and bashful. Why do redheads get all the blame?

Tear up your ticket for a White House reception, there is more important business on hand. As the last of the sun gathers across the western ocean, the invited guests put on their evening suits and black ties, preparing to answer the summons to dinner with Anton and Merle at the Villa Rosa.

VILLA ROSA

* * * * *

Pleasures of a Summer Coast

EDITIONS LION D'OR

SIAN AND HER MISTRESS

We caught only a glimpse before dinner of the two girls who were to be our waitresses during the meal. I cannot tell you how Sian and Helyn had been acquired by Anton but I assure you they were not volunteers for the duties soon to be demanded of them. They were both shopgirls or something of the kind and there was no great refinement or breeding about them. But I believe Anton's purpose was to show what could be done with such unpromising material: how two girls who had known one another only in the common rituals of their working life could be made to put their relationship on to a new and intriguing foundation.

It would be quite wrong, however, to deny the two girls their individual characters. They represented innocence in Helyn's case and experience in that of Sian. I glimpsed them, as I say, very briefly beforehand. Merle, the young negress with her vein of black-eyed cruelty, accompanied them one by one down the corridor to the room where they were to be prepared.

Both girls were only of moderate height and Sian was the elder of the two by a few years. She was, I believe, twenty-two at this time and the wedding-ring suggested that she was well-used to regular exercise on a man's erection. Indeed, her appearance suggested that she might like it a good deal. She was a redhead, the lightly waved hair combed back and its ends clustering over her collar and forward a little on either side of her fair neck, so that it lay on her lapels. Sian had a fair-skinned sensual face with a rather creamy complexion. The blue eyes were dreamy and distant, as if contemplating some fanciful vision of their own. The nose was a little crude and prominent, the chin a little weak.

Her mouth was quite large, the lips generously lipsticked and lightly parted as if in a thoughtful mood. In profile the points of her cheeks seemed quite prominent and then, when she turned to look at me, I thought the slope of her cheeks appeared rather flat.

I was able to anticipate the appearance of Sian's lower figure by the snug fit of the jeans she was wearing and which I suppose she normally wore at work. Her thighs and hips, as well as the cheeks of Sian's bottom, had that first slight softness or fattening of a girl whose teenage trimness is just beginning to yield to fuller womanhood. There was just the beginning of a rear-cheek swagger in Sian's walk, of the kind one detects in girls who are not very tall and past their maidenhood. In the company of her dark-skinned mistress, I watched her walk down the corridor. Then Merle opened a door and handed Sian over to those who were to supervise her preparation.

I did not think that Helyn was more than nineteen. Whatever her age, she was an extremely pretty brunette with firm-set lines to her young face and wide brown eyes. The rich darkness of her hair was tied back in a little tail with red ribbon. By the time that they had prepared her, this collar length of dark hair was a mass of tiny ringlets, rather fluffed out for effect. When I saw her first, she was wearing tight silk matador pants, black with a leaf-pattern, which showed her figure to be softer than Sian's. But in this case, Helyn's bottom-cheeks and thighs had retained a natural softness of girlhood rather than acquired the slight fattening of womanliness. I think this young charmer was naturally quiet and affectionate, though understandably apprehensive at what was about to happen to her now. I judged that she had yielded a little to a man of whom she was fond, but she had not been ridden as regularly and energetically as the young redhead.

The courtyard of the Villa Rosa was prepared in good time, long before the twilight of the hot summer day and the first flutter of beautiful moths or the metallic rasp of the cicadas. Anton had given instructions that the table with its white linen was to be set at the centre of the old paved enclosure near the disused well, under the wrought-iron of the heavy Spanish lamps. It was far too big for three of us, being quite six feet square. Yet it suited Anton's purpose. We were to be served from the stone arcade that ran round three sides of the leafy cloister, leaving uncovered only the wall up which the vine and the bougainvillaea climbed to the upper windows.

Though we had all the comforts that civilisation could devise, we were as remote from the fashionable society of the resort as if we were in one of the remote little valleys at the foot of the Col d' Ispeguy. The hushed summer tide was barely a whisper. Round the enclosed and leafy courtyard lay the sumptuous apartments of the villa. Beyond that, the lawns and paths stretched for a quarter of a mile on every side. Then there were the screens of poplar trees and beyond that the high walls which the most nimble maiden would never climb. The only gate was locked securely and the key remained in Anton's possession. But had the bell in the wall outside rung on that evening, it would have rung in vain.

Having dressed for dinner, I joined Anton and Merle in the library where one of the footmen was waiting with cool glasses of Frascati. The conversation was entirely about events at Bayonne, the new piece at the theatre by Duval and the latest exhibition at the Musée Bonnat. It was as if the arrangements for our bizarre dinner-party had been quite forgotten.

Presently, the footman returned and Anton led the way out to the courtyard. We took our places at the table, sheltered from the warm night-wind that was already beginning to gather somewhere off the shallows of the Bidassoa. In a moment more, our two waitresses appeared, one carrying a decanter and the other a tray of cool melon slices.

It was their characters rather than their appearance that still intrigued me, though their costumes—if one can call them that—were designed to make them feel with every movement that they were slaves in attendance upon their masters and mistress. They were dressed alike but Sian came in first with the tray. A simple band arched over her head to prevent her red hair from falling forward about her face as she bent to serve us. From breasts to waist she was encased in a bodice of tight black silk with a black leather collar round her neck to make her hold her chin up. Below the waist, she was bare-legged, though Sian wore the high-heeled shoes she always affected in order to give a little extra height to her young figure. But those who prepared her had also obliged her to wear what looked like a leather chastity-belt—a strange garment for such an occasion as this!

Round the young redhead's waist was a tight-fitting belt that had been locked at the small of her back by a tiny key. A little triangular piece ran down from the belt at the front, just concealing her sex. It narrowed to a polished strap drawn tightly back between her legs and up between the slightly fattened and sluttish cheeks of Sian's bare bottom. It was locked, as I say, in the small of her back. But the true ornament was a plume of hair, a pony-tail that exactly matched the redhead's own colour. I guessed how it had been fixed. A thumb-sized leather butt, inserted in Sian's anus, was the base of the tail. The stem ran up under the strap whose tension held the butt in place. The plume itself arched out—under and over her waist-belt at the rear, for all the world as if the red-haired tail sprouted from the base of the girl's spine.

But what intrigued me was the expression on Sian's face, for it had scarcely altered. I cannot think there had been screaming and holding-down and compulsion when the tail was fastened in place. Her blue eyes still had the same dreamy voluptuous languor, her wide lipsticked mouth was still lightly open. She walked calmly across with the tray and, as she passed me, I saw that the falling plume of the redhead's tail brushed lightly to and fro across the squirm and tremor of Sian's pale bottom-cheeks.

Merle turned to us.

"Does she tempt you? I hope so. It is Sian who must accomplish Helyn's seduction on the table after dinner. Before the strap was drawn tight, three of those little Japanese geisha pleasure-balls of smooth metal were inserted between her legs. As she moves, they move within her. I promise you they give Sian a delicious and exciting feeling. Look at the young bitch! Can you see how much Sian loves it? She has been well broken-in, well ridden by her man. A girl in one of those back-street bedrooms learns not to refuse her husband's demands."

Sian walked to the serving table and set the tray down, as if quite indifferent to the comments made about her. Merle looked at me and said quietly.

"There is another smooth metal globe in the set. Or, rather, an oval. The size of a small egg. Sian's

· 176 ·

bottom carries it, so that her sensitive nerves will be stimulated there by its movement. She is to be your bedfellow tonight. You will prefer her to be conscious of all her possibilities, will you not?''

Sian turned and began to serve us. If she heard what Merle said, it certainly brought no blush to her young face. Indeed, when she turned from me to serve Merle, she seemed to stoop a little more than was necessary and the slightly fattened pallor of Sian's bottom-cheeks were offered to me, the girl herself turning so that the redhead pony-tail slid aside and revealed them. The strap was drawn sensually tight and deep between Sian's bare buttocks but still visible as it separated them by its strained tautness.

Helyn was similarly dressed, though Merle had denied her the three smooth metal balls and the lascivious oval. Sian's power alone must seduce her. Pretty Helyn with her wide dark eyes and the firm lines of her young face, the little ringlets of dark hair clustering over her bare neck, was a charming study in apprehension. In her case, a brunette plume of pony-hair brushed across the softer milky-pale cheeks of Helyn's bottom as she walked. She looked so intently and beseechingly at each of us as she poured our wine and tried not to bend over in a pose of blatant provocation as she waited on us.

There could be no doubt that we were about to witness Helyn's initiation in the art of lesbian affection. Our lewd young Sian walked here and there, the pale red pony-tail bum-brushing across the young redhead's pearly rear cheeks as she seemed to swagger a little. Helyn walked with cautious steps and her lovely brown eyes were lowered, as far as the leather collar round her fair throat would permit her to dip her chin. It was as if she feared to provoke us by meeting our gaze or allowing her hips and backside too free or seductive a movement.

There was a moment when Sian turned, her hands empty and the characteristic dreamy vacancy in her blue eyes. She came to pick up the empty plates from which we had just eaten the *terrine de la maison*. She stood beside Anton and leant right over the table in a most ungracious stoop to collect Merle's plate. As she did this, I saw that Sian seemed to turn her creamy fair-skinned face with its lipsticked bow of a mouth and its rather crudely prominent nose. She was half looking sideways at Anton, as if to see how he would react. To pause and watch Sian bending over to her ordinary shopwork in high-heels and tight jeans is to smile at the slight lascivious fatness assumed by her bottom-cheeks in such a posture. She bent now and the pale bare cheeks of Sian's bottom swelled suggestively—all the more seductively for the plume of her red-haired pony-tail whose silky fall brushed the outward curve of her young buttocks.

Merle took the leather collar round the girl's neck and held Sian like this, pulling her over. Anton studied the view she offered, laying aside the pony-tail so that it now fell over the flank of her hip rather than her seat. Sian seemed to be rising on her toes in a slight exertion and tensing her bare thighs together unmistakably. There was surely no doubt that the young redhead was giving herself a good time in anticipation of what Anton might do to her.

The answer to that came soon enough. His mouth tightened a little and he administered a sounding cheek-smack on Sian's bare bottom, which made her sleekly broadened buttocks jump and quiver. But she never ceased to tense her thighs self-lovingly together. Another smack rang out on the same cheek of Sian's twenty-two-year-old bottom, and then another. For the first time Sian's red tresses swept her neck and she tried to twist round to look at Anton. He turned in his chair a little to spank the young slut more soundly, while dark-eyed Helyn looked on with a troubled and apprehensive stare.

Sian was not enjoying herself quite as much now, the tensing and twisting of her seductive young bottom was evidence of that. But as Helyn watched, the redhead lay over the table, hips still jigging a little as she squeezed herself, eyes not yet responding to Merle's gaze. The callous negress was able to inflict the most vindictive spite on the young redhead, knowing that Sian's shrillness, however frantic, would be heard only as a faint owl-cry at the distant walled boundary.

While Merle conveyed the sense of this with her dark eyes, Sian responded in a reproachful and self-pitying manner but I was fascinated to see that the squeezing and tensing, agitating the three smooth globes in her loins, still continued. Sian might sing, "No!" and "Please!" up every note of the scale until the force of her soprano wildness almost made one cover one's ears. She would still not persuade Merle to pity her.

Merle held her over the table like this, gripping Sian's collar for a while longer. There was naturally some reproachful glancing from the young redhead and a subdued mewing of self-pity at the threat in Merle's eyes. But of the three of us it was Helyn with her cloud of brunette ringlets who was watching in most astonishment. Sian was slowly beginning her squeezing and tip-toe movements again, even while she lamented the callousness of brown-skinned Merle and her master Anton.

"You see, Helyn?" said Merle, looking up at the young brunette, "Sian is quite different to you. She is a lover of luxury and voluptuousness. But she is rather too slow and preoccupied in her pleasures for such an occasion as this. It requires something sharp to give her passion a keener edge. Sian needs to be stung or pricked a little to get the most out of her climaxes. It hurts her. But that is the spur she needs."

And so it seemed to be, for Sian was certainly tensing and squeezing all the harder upon the smooth little globes in her loins, as if to offset the prints of the smacks that glowed upon her bottom-cheeks. I was to see far more evidence of this in the future. Pretty Helyn shed tears and mourned after scolding and whipping. But Sian sought refuge, even while being tanned, in the distraction of sensual enjoyment.

When the meal was over we took our coffee and armagnac at leisure in the comfortable armchairs at the wide table. Sian and Helyn stood by obediently, waiting for us to finish and give them our commands. Two footmen closed the doors and stood with their backs to them, guarding us from interruption and preventing any escape. It was now the hour when the warm southern night comes on, the bats hardly discernible any longer against the sheer blackness of the vault. Anton and I lit our cigars while another footman cleared the cups from the table.

"Get yourself ready, Sian," said Merle quietly.

Sian put one bare knee on the edge of the table and drew herself up with a pretty squirming of her thighs. She stretched out so that Merle could unlock the leather belt at the back of the young redhead's waist. Then Sian lifted her hips a little for the dark-skinned young mistress to draw the belt clear. She opened her legs for Merle to free it from between them. Sian was naked now except for her hair-band, the black silk corselet that ended at her waist, and the suggestive plum of the pony-tail.

Merle gave another command. As the redhead obeyed, it was intriguing though rather lewd to see the butt of the tail being squeezed cautiously from Sian's bottom. A further word of instruction was spoken and Sian delivered the egg-shaped metal globe from her behind into Merle's hand. Even while Sian did this, there was no sign of a blush. She had been well trained to obey such commands, her natural timidity or modesty long since suppressed. The squeezing of the metal play-balls in her loins or the expulsion of the silver egg from her bottom would be performed with the same dreamy look in her blue eyes, the same insolent self-assurance in her fair-skinned face, with which she received the admiring glances of those who passed her at her work.

"Come to me, Helyn!" said Anton, as Merle attended to the redhead. Helyn obeyed, walked apprehensively towards him. "Turn your back, Helyn. Bend over and rest your hands on your knees."

Helyn obeyed without protest but, though the little cloud of dark ringlets fell forward round her pretty face as she stopped, it was just possible to see the blushes playing in her cheeks. Anton unlocked the belt in the small of her waist and drew it from her.

"Now put yourself face-down over my lap, Helyn," he said.

Still wearing her brunette pony-tail, she obeyed him, lying like a little girl about to be spanked. But Helyn was not to be spanked and she was a far more suggestive and voluptuous burden over his knee than a girl-child would have been.

"Release your pony-tail, Helyn," he said.

It was the easiest thing in the world to do, but in her confusion the pretty brunette could not bring herself to do it. The act required something that she had never done in front of anyone since infancy and which she had never done at all in the presence of a man. Anton did not raise his voice to her. But Helyn with the delicate modelling of her pretty face must be trained all the same, for her own sake. He tapped ash from his cheroot and considered the soft pallor of Helyn's nineteen-year-old bottom-cheeks. He drew the havana bright and stroked the nearer cheek of Helyn's backside. I watched with great curiosity as Helyn's wildness rang round the courtyard walls. She cared nothing more for who might see her. Indeed, the three of us watched her as she expelled that leather thumb-shaped holding the tail in place.

Merle told her to compose herself at once and climb on to the table round which we sat. Helyn and Sian were stretched out side by side, lying so that they faced one another closely. Sian's blue eyes met Helyn's with a faint and lascivious reassurance. But the wide dark eyes of the other girl were troubled and almost fearful from the brief moment of anguish.

"Make love together," said Merle casually, "I'm sure you know by instinct what to do."

There was no possibility of refusal unless displeasure and penalties were to follow. Both Sian and Helyn knew that. In a charmingly awkward way, they drew close and kissed each other's lips. Helyn hugged the young redhead but only with the awkward affection that girl-children show each other. Sian, however, brushed back the dark little ringlets, kissing Helyn's sensitive bare neck and ears so that the nineteen-year-old brunette shuddered with excitement and anticipation.

Helyn drew back and kissed Sian repeatedly on the lips, as if she did not know what else to do. Sian ran one hand down the younger girl's back, slid her fingers between the cheeks of Helyn's bottom and came to the sensitive feminine flesh by a rear approach. But at this touch, as if stung by an electric shock, Helyn bucked her lips back to escape the caress of the randy young redhead.

Sian drew her hand away and stroked the cloud of brunette ringlets instead. Helyn would permit kisses and ˚cuddles but could not bring herself to share more than that. Merle frowned.

"Get down from the table, the pair of you."

They obeyed, Helyn standing before the mistress with confusion and apprehension, Sian's lips parted to suggest pleasure interrupted. Merle summoned the two footmen. She spoke in Spanish, which neither of the girls understood. One of the footmen took Sian by the arm and led her to a room adjoining the courtyard. Before the door closed I was able to see that the other man was holding a short tailed strap of thin leather. Through the closed door we heard a dozen measured impacts of the strap on the bare smoothness of Sian's rear cheeks. They brought her out in some disarray. The smart had brought sharp tears to the redhead's eyes and her mouth was wider open as if a cry might escape at any moment. And yet, as I later heard, Sian had bent over as seductively as possible and had tried to make her tanning as enjoyable for the two men as she could.

"She is so sensual," Merle assured me, "that Sian's bottom seems to flirt with the spanking-strap."

But Helyn uttered a wail of dismay as they now

led her to the same room. Sian stood like a little girl in disgrace, the prints of the strap scarlet across her bottom-cheeks and one or two across the backs of her legs. This time, before the door closed, I saw that they had Helyn bending over, head down to her knees, thighs sloping back, the full soft pallor of her bottom-cheeks presented as their target. They gave her eighteen and we heard Helyn shrill and frantic before it was over. The footmen brought her back in a very mournful state, the wailing portrait of a punished little girl. The pallor of Helyn's backside was flushed with the deepest blush of all.

Merle turned to me.

"You think it unjust that both should suffer a little for the fault of one? In that, my friend, you are mistaken. Pretty Helyn has had the strap in order to heat her up and overcome her reluctance. She was too cold and indifferent but she has a warm and passionate nature. As for Sian, a taste of the strap will make her try harder to overcome her friend's bashfulness. I promise you it will inspire them both. They know that if they have to be taken back there again, the second time will be far worse than this."

I had no doubt of that, nor did the two girls. They clambered back on to the table and this time Sian took command of the unwilling brunette without delay. They did not lie as before but head-to-tail. Each girl lay on her side and presented herself to the face of the other in what I would call an upward squat. Sian guided Helyn to draw her knees up a little more. Helyn's thighs and hips, as well as her bottom, were offered to Sian's kisses and caresses in a more fully spread and revealing posture. At the same time, the lascivious young redhead posed so that her femininity peeped between the rear of her thighs while she almost sat naked on Helyn's face. They made a charming study for a camera portrait.

We leant forward round the table for an hour or more and watched at close range the seduction of innocence by experience. It was evident that the two had never before had amorous feelings for one another, not even of the most secret kind. In the case of the young brunette, there had never been such yearnings for any girl. That being so, it was Sian who took the initiative and Helyn who became the pupil, copying what was done to her.

A further delay would have meant another visit to the room where the footmen waited. Sian's fingers gently and comfortingly took Helyn's sensitive femininity, stroking and rousing it. She worked slowly but coaxingly, no doubt judging that what she had sometimes done in private to herself would cause arousal when she did it in the same way to another girl. In this she was proved right, as Helyn's hips began to stir. Sian also kissed the soft bare cheeks of Helyn's bottom, as if soothing the lingering smart of the strap. Helyn was almost gasping as she drew breath and she could not keep her thighs from squirming a little.

Meanwhile, the swelling cheeks of Sian's bottom and her spreading thighs were presented patiently and expectantly to Helyn's gaze. The brunette's pretty face with its wide dark eyes was a study in hesitation. Her own enjoyment troubled her. As one watched, it was clear without any question that Helyn was receiving pleasure. At last her fingers tentatively stroked the peep of Sian's feminine flesh between the rear of the girl's thighs. Sian lifted her upper leg a little, crooking it back from the knee, to make herself more fully accessible.

Helyn closed her eyes as if to create some vision

of her own while Sian caressed her. Her own
fingers began to fondle Sian's intimacy, although
she did it rather inexpertly.

"Keep your eyes open, Helyn," said Merle, chid-
ing her gently. "You mustn't hide your feelings
from us while Sian makes love to you."

The beautiful brown eyes opened again, startled
at the command and a little dismayed. But she
looked closely at what her fingers were doing, as if
fascinated by Sian's secret anatomy. Despite herself, Helyn was intrigued by the other girl's body
and the effect that her caresses were having upon
it. Helyn's eyes grew gentle and loving as she continued to gaze at the moistening and roused feminine flesh.

"Use your other hand as well, Helyn," said
Merle coaxingly. "Sian's arse is beautifully presented to you. You needn't be shy about doing
anything to her. Sian is sensitive there as well."

There was no protest from the pretty brunette.
Helyn looked lovingly and tenderly at the lightly
parted cheeks of Sian's backside. While her other
hand remained busy with more important matters,
she also stroked the young redhead's bare rear
cheeks. Then, as if imagining what she would like
Sian to do to her, Helyn's fingers slid gently
between the cheeks of Sian's rounded arse, feeling
and stroking.

Soon there would be no more difficulty in per-
suading Helyn to play the part of a boy with
another girl. She began to kiss the backs of Sian's
bare legs, starting behind the knees and working
up. Sian, excited at this, touched her lips to the
brunette's roused sexual flesh, kissing it lightly and
then beginning to flicker her tongue upon it. Helyn
shuddered and moaned but never ceased to kiss
the redhead's thighs. Without more ado, they

settled down to kiss and nuzzle and tongue-tease one another in the most intimate and sensitive place.

Both would have reached fulfilment in a few minutes more, but Merle and Anton drew the girls' heads back and held their hands away. There were two bereft little sobs as the pleasure was interrupted. But it was interrupted only in order that it might be prolonged. When Sian and Helyn were permitted to resume, they did so in the most hungry and passionate manner. It was true love-making now, where each was as eager to feast upon the other as to be feasted upon herself.

It was delightful to see Helyn, after so much reluctance, quite unable to hold back. Her fingertips played lightly and tantalisingly on the young redhead's secret places. At the same time, Helyn kissed the cheeks of Sian's bottom which Sian now thrust out more fully. Helyn hesitated and then, flinging caution aside, kissed between them.

"Kiss her there, Helyn," murmured Merle encouragingly, "No need to be afraid or shy. Don't hold back, Helyn. Enjoy being rude with her there. Use your tongue between her cheeks, Helyn. Make her cry out with excitement. Don't you want to hear that, Helyn?"

Sian herself was manualising Helyn with great skill and had brought her close to a crisis. An excruciating pang of pleasure seemed to paralyse the young brunette. Then, in its spasm, Helyn's tongue was stuck out, firm and urgent, its tip disappearing where Sian's bottom is better imagined than described. Helyn was shuddering with the first release of her tension. Merle and Anton held her firmly while she was having it. When it was over, there was a danger that Helyn would burst into sobs of relief and remorse. She might lie there in dismay, cold and ashamed at what she had done. They held her so that there should be none of that. The caressing would continue so that the last spasm of her release would merge with the first tickle of the next arousal.

"Lie still, Helyn," whispered Merle, "You'll come half a dozen times on the table tonight. Was this the first one you've ever known? You'll be with the African and Jamaican girls soon. They'll make you let yourself go like this several times a day and once or twice during the night. You need to have your climax often, Helyn, before you know yourself properly."

As she said this, Merle began to milk Sian with quick expert fingers, bringing the redhead to a gasping and shuddering conclusion.

"Lie still, just as you are," the young negress said to the two girls, "Now begin all over again."

And so they did while we watched them. This time there was no holding back. They hurried to regain the heights of excitement from which they had just gently descended. There was no doubt of the exertion which the labour involved during the warm night. A gloss of sweat shone on the soft pallor of Helyn's bottom and hips, the wetness slippery between her legs and rear cheeks. Merle took a white linen napkin and wiped her over, though without interrupting the nuzzling and caressing, the tongue-tickling and kiss of the two girls.

This time, Sian reached her reward first. Her back arched and she flexed her legs, her mouth opened in a long soft cry and her blue eyes rolled back as if she might swoon. But she never ceased to caress her brunette girl-friend. When Helyn had finished as well, they lay together, touching lightly and apparently exhausted by their labours. I think they could have slept then and there, upon the table.

It was Merle whose cunning prevented that. Gently with her own hands she began to rouse the moist and sensitive flesh of each girl again, one hand attending to Helyn and the other to Sian. Despite their langour, it was not long before they stirred, squirming and sighing. The second bout of love-making had been hurried and eager, this one was slow and luxurious. They were like contented and sleepy female animals, playing with one another's bodies rather than bacchantes going to it with desperate passion. The girls studied each other's loins and thighs and bottoms, fingers examining and testing rather than caressing. The slipperiness of their sweat made them look like two beautiful girl-wrestlers making up to one another and sleepy after combat.

Without inquiring too deeply, it seemed evident that both Sian and Helyn were destined for a private collection. They knew this and probably understood that it was futile to protest or argue against their destiny. I later heard Helyn begging Merle to arrange that she should be allowed the same destination as Sian. Merle refused this, the arrangements being already made. But she consoled Helyn by assuring her that the dark-skinned beauties in such places were experts in love between women. In a life where amorous idleness was the only occupation, a soft fair-skinned brunette would be irresistible. Several hours a day were passed in the kind of kissing and caressing we had just witnessed. Again, Merle assured her that Helyn would have her climax several times before each sunrise on the busy fingers of the native girls. Sian, on the other hand, was spoken for by an Arabian master. That arrangement was not to be altered.

The separation of the two girls was not the

doom of love but merely the end of an infatuation. Indeed, if Sian and Helyn were now deeply in love, this exclusive passion would not have been welcome to the man whose household they joined. Merle understood this and was wise enough to prevent it. The separation of Sian and Helyn must be permanent when it came, but it would not come for a few days or even a few weeks. During that time, they were permitted to sink deeper and deeper into their mutual attachment. They might kiss, caress, and play with one another all night and most of the day. It was to be encouraged, so that Helyn's reluctance in such matters would be quite overcome.

It was long past midnight on the occasion of Anton's dinner when the two loving girls on the table sank back from their third mutual release. Anton lit a fresh cigar and stood up, leading us over to the side-table where we might refresh our glasses. We stood there talking for a little while, ignoring the redhead and the brunette who lay humidly and sleepily together. It was almost ten minutes later, as we were still in conversation, that I turned to say something to Merle. As I did so, I looked towards that spacious table under the wrought-iron Spanish lamps. Sian and Helyn stirred sleepily again. But Sian's fingers were gently examining Helyn's intimate flesh which was moistening readily. And Sian in turn was dewing Helyn's fingers and lips with her copious feminine excitement. Without being commanded, and indeed doing it furtively because they were not commanded, Sian and Helyn were beginning all over again.

The first still light of summer dawn caught the dark silhouette of the eastern roof of the Villa Rosa before our two girls ceased playing the boy with each other on the table. I led Sian up to the cool light of the bedroom where, upon silken covers, she was to yield me the pleasures that Helyn had lovingly prepared. After what I had witnessed, it would have been absurd for the young redhead to pretend to modesty at front or rear when required to present herself in either way. Nor did Sian pretend to it. So much time went by before I was finally satisfied with her, that we fell deeply asleep and woke only when the sun had passed its highest point.

CHAPTER NINE: ELAINE COX, A TOMBOY WELL CHASTISED

IN THE GALLERY of female types who populate underground fiction, some seem more typical than others. The frivolous and pampered young beauties of *Flossie* or *School Life in Paris* were hot favourites. They had silvery laughs and teasing giggles, wasp-waists and figures frail as the parasols they carried. In reality they also had the physical constitution of Rasputin and a piercing or accusing glance that would have had Sigmund Freud babbling away on his own couch in no time at all. Most of their kind would make a modern feminist look like a simpering wallflower.

But just as there was the dreamworld estate of Edward Sellon, so there was the more melodramatic Gothick fantasy of the subterranean vault or the reformatory chastising room, where dark deeds were hidden behind high walls and barred windows. Here too there were favourite types, to judge from the fiction. An extended tale of *Pearls of the Orient* illustrates this. For the disciplinarian of wayward adolescent girls there was the cheeky imp or the pretty teaser, the long-legged nymph or even the petite snub-nosed young wife. We know that in reality the ages of delinquent beauty at the chastiser's call, sanctioned by official morality, ranged from as young as thirteen to as old as twenty-eight.

But from the titles of books in such series as "Social Studies of the Century," let alone from their contents, we also know that there was one type thought to be in special need of corrective treatment. She was the "boisterous" and often "insolent" adolescent girl, "sturdy" or "robust," over whom the reformatory masters and justices toiled painstakingly. At the most sexually repressive time, here was one indulgence which the whip-wielding moralist could find simultaneously exciting and righteous. In some cases, he was paid a salary by the authorities for enjoying himself in ways that would have cost him a small fortune in a brothel.

What made such books officially unwelcome was that tales like this from *Pearls of the Orient* were merely the fictional tip of a massive factual iceberg, disclosed in French-published works like *The Underside of English Prudery* and *Studies in Flagellation,* prominently circulated through magazines like *La Fin du Siècle.*

Of course, it has to be said that later accounts of Pauline Cox and a younger daughter Elaine towing a harem owner's garden-carriage round his estate are an extravagant additional fantasy. Over the bar side by side, the slattern and the tomboy present bare to the drive "the comparative anatomy of two female bottoms in the same family, at varying stages of development." And the afternoon drive is erotic circus at its most zany. "*Smack!* went the whip and round went the wheels." Pauline must sound her post-horn for a keeper to open a gate and the last slope is known, without any attempt at subtlety, as Horsewhip Hill.

They came to the steep incline which ran straight between the chestnut and beech trees for quite two hundred yards to the top of the ridge. The groom rose from his seat. It was not Pauline but the tomboy daughter with whom he began. Elaine had struggled so wildly over the bar that the tail of her blouse had slipped down once more aslant her buttocks. He tucked it up under the harness-strap. Pauline and Elaine were struggling to obey. Their feet pushed and their thighs strained, their pale hips were tense and surging with effort. The slope of the path and the labour required as they bent between the shafts caused Pauline's bigger seat and hips to arch out and squirm in the most provoking manner. Meanwhile, it almost seemed as if Elaine was deliberately flaunting her adolescent backside at him, for the strain and the labour made her arch and thrust her tomboy bottom-cheeks out vulgarly at every strenuous step.

By contrast, the memoir from *Pearls of the Orient* tells a story of the origins of such a half-forgotten cause *célèbre* from the one point of view that had yet to be heard—that of the worthy official who had caused all the trouble. However true the events, the reality of his desires is unambiguous.

PEARLS OF THE ORIENT

The Third Volume

ELAINE COX: A "TOMBOY" WELL-CHASTISED

****

By "A Believer in the Efficacy of the Bamboo"

A rod
To check the erring and reprove.

Wordsworth, Ode to Duty

LONDON
Published by the Society for the Improvement of Manners

ELAINE COX: A TOMBOY
WELL-CHASTISED

There are girls whom no man or woman could regard as being beautiful or charming, nor ever likely to become so. And yet for reasons that only the most learned investigator of the human passions could divine, they become objects of fierce desires and long-matured yearnings. Sometimes the very fact that they are vulgar or impudent, dismissing with contempt the lascivious gaze of their admirers, seems only to heat up the determination of their followers to possess them. From time to time this gives rise to a public scandal of some kind and those who hear of it shake their heads. How could a respectable gentleman "make a fool of himself" over such a young slut? How could he "throw away everything" in order to enjoy her by fraud or force?

There was, I recall, such a bother over a common young woman of twenty or so, Janet Bond, for whom a man nearly ruined himself. When one saw her, she was a plump slut though with appealingly timid brown eyes and a hint of freckles to her soft features. Her dark brown hair was piled on her head with the aid of a tortoiseshell comb and its length trimmed and worn in a Roman helmet cut round her face. Imagine her pushing her infant up the road and the respectable gentleman following. A rear view of Janet Bond in short jerkin and tight brown working-trousers, so that the hem of her knickers arched in a visible ridge on each buttock. The seductive fatness of Janet Bon's backside quivering and squirming. Whatever he did to her was little enough. A word or a smile. A photograph or two as a keepsake of the ludicrous sight she offered. Perhaps a smack or so.

Next thing, the young baggage tries to make a

fuss and ruin him. I will not disgress but I assure
you that the opinion of men of substance was
unanimous, though it was indiscreet to voice it
pubicly. They would rather have given the plump
bare cheeks of Janet Bond's bottom a taste of
whip-leather, stood her on a cart with the hempen
halter round her neck and trundled the cart away.
They would do that, before they would have seen
the ruin of a man who was so much the more use
to the nation than a bitch who would whelp again
soon enough and be a charge to the public purse.

How can a gentleman have so little sense of his
rank or his security as to compromise himself over
such a slut as that?

Now you may be sure that the "gentleman" himself would be the last one who could answer such
a question. And yet I should not be surprised if
every man at some time in his life has not felt one
of these freaks of powerful feeling towards an
unlikely object of desire. The girl I am about to
speak of now is not unknown to the history of
such scandals. Others have written of her that,
"there can be no harm in revealing now that a
number of respectable middle-aged gentlemen
coveted Elaine Cox since she was no more than
thirteen years old." I write to acknowledge that I
was not merely one of those aimed at in such a
charge—I was the sole defendant!

How strange it is to see oneself written about in
such a way, stranger far than the reports of the little scandal as they appeared in the columns of the
press. I have never before put my own side of the
"case" with utter frankness, nor would I do so
now unless I was safe from reproach or inquiry.
But I came so well out of my "little trouble" that
my remuneration was increased and fresh powers
given me to continue as I wished. I do assure you

that I am now quite beyond the reach of those self-regarding busybodies who had tried to make life disagreeable for me.

Very well then. I shall tell my story, since others have told theirs. I promise you that I shall do so without evasion or hypocrisy, concealing nothing of my feelings. If plain speaking about my sexual and disciplinary feelings towards a schoolgirl tomboy is not to your taste, I beg you to turn to some other choice volume.

It would be foolish and quite unnecessary to conceal the interest that I had taken in Elaine Cox for some time before finding myself in a position of authority over her. To begin at the point when I first set eyes on her, or perhaps first noticed her, I suppose she must have been about thirteen. But there was no conscious hint of desire at that time. My knowledge of her was purely casual then, merely becoming aware that she walked to and from school every day and that I saw her go by. From this realisation there grew a habit of waiting and watching, which I think the girl herself soon became aware of.

I do not quarrel with the description of her given in the Studies of Flagellation and other historical accounts. At fourteen or fifteen she was a sturdy adolescent schoolgirl, a shouting and striding tomboy, defiantly tossing the lank fair hair that lay loose on her shoulders. Combed from its central parting, it framed the broad fair-skinned oval of her face whose thin lips and narrowed eyes composed what the historian has called "a portrait of snub-nosed insolence."

If I and the other "middle-aged gentlemen" relished the sight of her figure, it was because Elaine dressed so as to display it. She taunted her elders and betters with something that she reserved only for ruffian boys of her own age. She wore a school uniform, the white blouse and striped tie. Her skirt was the regulation kind, grey and pleated. But it was quite scandalously brief, covering her hips and only the upper six inches of her sturdy bare thighs.

At the same time, there was nothing of the coyly seductive nymph about this fifth-form tomboy. With her slum-child impudence, the contemptuous tossing of her lank fair hair as she strode by, she expressed her indifference to the admiration of her middle-aged followers. Such a young slut inspires two reactions in men and women. Most men and even more women would like to strap her over a table, take off her skirt and knickers, and whip the tomboy cheeks of Elaine Cox's bottom long and hard. Some men, while she was thus positioned, would first need to take their pleasure with her, in such a way as to teach her a lesson about the male sex. Most men, given the opportunity, would be ravishers and disciplinarians with such a girl.

In other words she presented, did she not, an intriguing problem in human psychology?

I confess that my own feelings were of the most complex. I gave her no indication of this and at first, as we passed in the road, she would favour me with a smile. In Elaine's case her smile, at thirteen years old, was something of a hard and knowing leer. When she first guessed my thoughts about her, I do not know. Soon, however, I was treated to the same contemptuous indifference as so many others. I made no secret of my wishes any longer, though only she and I could guess them. It was intriguing to follow the same way with her after school, watching the slight heaviness of her pale thighs left bare by the scandalous little skirt. On the hill, a full length of her bare legs was visible from behind as she walked. Occasionally, a breath of wind fluttered the skirt, lifting it, so that one had a view of her white elasticated briefs and the sturdy young cheeks of Elaine Cox's bottom which they tightly moulded. She changed her schoolgirl knickers every day, I think. The wash-line always displayed a row of them, though some no doubt belonged to her big sister. A good many gentlemen, three or four times her age, paused and gazed thoughtfully at Elaine Cox's plain white briefs on that wash-line.

To study her at more leisure, I was often equipped with a camera and took a hundred photographs at one time or another as she walked by or as I followed her. Several of these are before me as I write. Looking at them, the bare thighs and the little skirt, the insolence of her expression, I cannot regret anything that has happened to the youngster since.

From time to time, when she was slipping out to meet some boy of her acquaintance or going to work of some sort, she was differently dressed. This sturdy fifth-form girl would choose a white short-sleeved singlet and working-trousers of smooth grey-blue lavender cloth. Elaine Cox's trousers fitted tight and smooth on the slight heaviness of her adolescent thighs and hips. She had drawn them in to a narrow waist by a broad leather belt, so that it strained them tighter still over her hips and seat.

As one walked behind her, it was amusing to see how the strained cloth gave a somewhat fatter or heavier look to the cheeks of Elaine Cox's bottom. I greatly enjoyed this vulgar and suggestive appearance, thinking that it perfectly matched her conduct and character. It showed her for what she was—the child of a slattern who was growing up to be one herself!

She would always draw the belt so tight that from the rear the youngster's backside seemed almost to form a circle. If she chose to wear her little grey skirt short to show her bare thighs, then the tightness of her lavender trousers was equally deliberate. What a brazen little tart she was!

Even at fourteen years old, she would dress like this when she went out to meet boys of her own age. She walked openly through the streets, dressed in these same tight pants. I look this moment at a couple of photographs taken as she strode up the hill with her big sister Pauline. They show Elaine Cox's fourteen-year-old bottom-cheeks and hips, vulgarly fattened as she walked out to meet her boy-friend in the tight lavender trousers. Elaine and Pauline would wear one another's clothes from time to time. The brief pleated grey skirt of Elaine's school uniform was, I believe, Pauline's cast-off. These trousers of smooth blue-grey cloth had also been worn by both sisters.

I tell you all this in order to show how one's enthusiasm may be stimulated by the most unlikely object of desire. It would be tedious to recount the misdemeanours which caused Elaine and her sister to be brought before the justices and consigned to the custody of that institution where I found myself in authority over her. Sufficient to say that it happened and that I found myself unexpectedly and excitedly the possessor of the two sisters, the eighteen-year-old who did not much interest me being a plump slut, and the fifteen-year-old who interested me a good deal.

Yet I assure you I was a pattern of duty and rectitude. Not for one moment did I give way to the urges that prompted me. It was several weeks before the first encounter. Others have spoken as if they were the victims of the girl's impudence while sitting at the study window. Perhaps they were. I daresay she tried it a number of times to see how "green" her reform-school guardians might be. I can only say that it happened to me first.

Whatever else might be the truth, it was certainly my habit to deal with the business of the day by sitting at a table in the window of my study. The room was on the ground floor and looked out immediately on the pleasant flower-beds and lawns of the courtyard. The first of these beds was no more than four feet in front of me as I sat at the window-table and studied my papers. I noticed that the fifth-form girls had been allotted various gardening tasks, but for the moment I thought nothing of that. Indeed, if my eyes strayed at all they alighted on Antoinette Hope or Lena Tyndall, who had the best claims to a man's attention.

It was usual on these occasions that the girls should discard their skirts in favour of working-trousers. I noticed that Elaine Cox had been detailed to the flower-bed immediately outside my window. I afterwards thought that this had been done deliberately by one of the mistresses to see if the little scrubber would try to play me up. No doubt an insolent youngster of her sort would want to discover whether a man was "green" and treat him accordingly.

Elaine stood there in her usual attitude of contempt for her betters. The lank fair hair was worn plain and straight from its central parting, in her customary manner, so that it lay loose on her shoulders and framed the broad oval of her impudent face. Her eyes were narrowed and her thin lips pressed tight.

One of the reformatory matrons ordered her sharply to bend over and begin weeding the flower-bed immediately outside my window. With a toss of her lank fair hair, the youngster stooped grudgingly to her task. I watched from no more than four feet behind her. As she bent over, the cheeks of Elaine Cox's fifteen-year-old bottom were fuller and broadened more provocatively still under the thin smooth cloth of her trouser-seat.

To have Elaine Cox bending over like this immediately in front of me made it impossible to attend to my paper-work. I knew that I should pass the whole morning earnestly studying the full-cheeked young backside of this schoolgirl tomboy! When they ordered her to bend over and weed the bed, the posture made the cheeks of Elaines Cox's bottom temptingly bigger and fatter. I enjoyed see-ing this, for it made her look like the bullying and sluttish girl that she was. The rear-cheek move-ments of her smoothly tightened trouser-seat as she stooped and shifted, straining the blue-grey cloth this way and that, entranced me completely. By admitting that, I confess what most men would feel but might not care to acknowledge.

Free from the need to conceal my interest, I leant forward and studied Elaine's behind as she bent. Elaine Cox still had the bottom of a fifth-form schoolgirl but of the sturdier sort. When she bent over a little more, her behind had a decidedly womanly fullness. But seeing her as I did at that moment, I feel sure most young beauties would have thought a rear view like Elaine Cox's too vul-garly robust for elegance! I watched Elaine's young arse as she bent more fully and then as she turned it a little this way and that in her labours. Elaine Cox's bottom-crack was nicely indicated by the tight seat of the smooth lavender cloth. I liked to see how the tomboy swell of her bum-cheeks curved in together and how the cheeks sloped round to the flanks of her hips. I enjoyed the slight tensings and shiftings of the youngster's broadened buttocks as she reached this way and that in bending to pull the weeds. I did not yet know what fault I should find with her, but I was determined that I must use the reformatory cane across Elaine Cox's behind that afternoon.

As I studied her, I knew I should want to use the bamboo across Elaine Cox's bare bottom. There are those who would have caned her bottom through her thin trousers as she bent or else across the stretched white briefs of Elaine's school knickers. But I did not consider that at all satisfactory as I studied her. She was going to get it anyway. There could be no objection in that case to Elaine Cox's backside being bare. It would enforce the moral of the punishment-lesson for her to feel herself bare-bottomed. Moreover, I did not wish Elaine Cox's underpants or trousers to spoil the effect. I truly wanted Elaine to feel the ferocity of the naked smart of bamboo across her bare adolescent buttocks.

You must remember that since she was thirteen or fourteen I had witnessed the contemptuous toss of her lank fair hair, the snub-nosed insolence in the broad oval of her slum-child face. I had endured her shouting impudent manner. In dealing with a sturdy ruffianly girl of fifteen a punishment is not a punishment if she can bear it. I intended to inflict upon her a discipline whose anguish would be far beyond the ability of Elaine Cox's young arse to contain. I had badly wanted to teach her a lesson in manners with the whip even earlier, when she was a year or two younger. Had I possessed the authority, I would have done it. I therefore had no compunction about it now.

You may be sure that Elaine sensed my interest in a moment more, for I moved my head so that she should see I was surveying her young arse with a certain intent vindictiveness. Again and again, she tossed the lank fair hair clear and glanced back at me. The insolence and contempt in her tightened lips and narrowed eyes was plain. But the master of such girls as Elaine and her big sister Pauline finds added pleasure in this. It is good to show a girl of Elaine Cox's sort that one is having a good look at her tomboy arse-cheeks as she bends—without hypocrisy—showing that one wishes to intrude and pry without permitting her any privacy. I leant forward to make a keener study of her broadened and fattened rear cheeks as the tight smoothness of her trouser-seat presented them while she bent over to her weeding.

She shook her hair clear and glanced back again at me. In order to show more plainly what my interest was, I let the youngster see me lean forward a little more and make a blantantly lewd inspection of Elaine Cox's rear cheek-swell and her robust young thighs. I wanted her to watch me as I did it. And once again I resolved that I was going to thrash Elaine's bare buttocks with the cane that afternoon on some pretext or other. I cannot tell you how my heart pounded with excitement at that thought. There are some readers who may protest at such injustice. But I make no apology. A youngster like Elaine has an adolescent vulgarity at fourteen or fifteen which makes it enjoyable to whip her bare bottom for her defiance. By twenty years old the appeal of an insolent schoolgirl would turn to the drabness of a fattened slut with a squalling crowd of brats at her apron strings. Harem masters do not permit such things and take a course that severe gentlemen suggested with Janet Bond. After a final riot of extreme pleasures and severity the leather collar would be adjusted with sinister and final effect about Elaine Cox's throat before her tomboy charms had faded. Here we are more civilised than the barbarous East and order things otherwise. However, it was surely wise that Elaine should be well disciplined while she could still offer satisfaction to her chastisers.

Elaine responded to my examination of her by ignoring her work and staring back at me disdainfully as she bent! One of the matrons reprimanded her sharply. Resentfully, the youngster began to pull the fledgling weeds. I endeavoured to read the papers on my table. But I could think only that there is a pony-lash kept in the stable, a short tail of woven snakeskin. I imagined myself using it on the bare backside of this fifth-form schoolgirl. The rules authorise such an implement only after a girl has reached her sixteenth birthday, which was not yet the case with Elaine. But one does not always feel bound by rules in such a blatant case as this. I looked up and saw confronting me the same vulgarly fattened cheeks of Elaine Cox's arse a few feet before my face. The thought of the pony-lash recurred to me. I would not have scrupled to use it on her bare buttocks at once.

As I leant forward again and studied the view which the little scrubber was offering me, she showed deliberate defiance. She bent to her task—but her hands were idle. I was a milksop, she thought, and so she was treating me with contempt for it! Neither Elaine nor her big sister was shy of being lewd and vulgar. Elaine knew I was eagerly admiring her adolescent behind in its tight trouser-seat. But she did not straighten up with ladylike dismay. Indeed, she was now exaggerating a little the swell of her sturdy schoolgirl bottom-cheeks in the smooth blue-grey cloth as she bent over in idleness. Elaine is the sort of girl who would defy and torment her teachers. There was no mistaking that she now showed her broadened buttocks with contempt and derision. How she misjudged me! I found her rear view an irresistible challenge! She cannot have realised how this view of her fifteen-year-old backside hardened my resolve. My heart pounded as I opened the window. and called the matron in charge. The woman came across. I informed her that I should want Elaine Cox brought to the punishment-room after lunch and that I should require several proper prison canes from the boys' reformatory.

The adolescent impudence in the broad oval of Elaine Cox's snub-nosed face faltered. She bent over to her work again. I was an unknown quantity to the girl. To be sure I would cane her. But I might be green enough to recoil at the first scream, or I might give her light strokes which she would scorn and boast about to her cronies. Or I might thrash her sadistically. She did not yet know. For all her bravado, I could see that her teeth pulled at her lower lip from time to time in a nervous and involuntary manner that she has. Yet from time to time, she would still toss back her lank hair as she worked and give me a defiant glance. I could afford to respond with a knowing smile, assuring the girl of how much I was going to enjoy myself with her in another hour or two. There was still impudence in her. But I had never caned her before. And that made the youngster uneasy.

I kept Elaine working at her weeding in such a manner that she was obliged to remain bending in her big-bottomed posture and the lavender trouser-seat was smooth and tight over her strapping young schoolgirl buttocks. Any man might enjoy watching this rear view of her closely and intently, as she worked. But I had good reason now. I was examining a view that must be offered bare to the punishment cane presently. The rounding and shifting of Elaine Cox's backside as she stooped and tensed, her bum-cheeks well broadened and stretched apart, held my attention so completely that I scarcely looked away from her schoolgirl trouser-seat until the garden labours were over.

I waited impatiently for two o'clock to come. By way of preparation I discarded my jacket and rolled up my sleeves. I also changed into a pair of tighter trousers whose fit was so close at the front that a mere glance would show that their wearer was a well-endowed man. I thought that my manhood would be bigger and harder when dealing with Elaine and I wanted the youngster to see it while she was caned. I had always thought it an error for teachers and others to appear crestfallen and reluctant while tanning a rebellious adolescent girl of her sort. I believe the moral of the punishment is better enforced by showing her that I am excited at having an excuse to thrash her and that I greatly enjoy doing it to her. She will know better than to hope for leniency next time.

The scene of retribution on these occasions is always the same. It is a tall brick outbuilding set apart from the main reformatory so that punishments may be given without the danger of eavesdropping or keyhole peeps. It contains a large stone-flagged room with small windows securely barred and set almost at the top of the high whitewashed walls. To increase the brightness, we always light the rows of gas-jets in their iron brackets along each wall. This give a harsh but brilliant illumination to the scene. The sole disadvantage is that the rear wall adjoins the neighbouring institution for delinquent boys of Elaine's age. Though they themselves are whipped for the transgression if caught, some of these young scamps will shin up and peep down from the rear windows to enjoy the sight of the girls under discipline.

We have a "block" in there but the word may be misleading. It consists of a raised surface about the height and dimensions of a sofa, though the restraining straps riveted to it strongly are not such as most sofas could boast. At one end of this rises a stout wooden frame padded with leather. It is an open frame over which the girl kneels with her arms drawn down the far side.

Ten feet to the side of this, a tall stool is bolted to the flagstone. It is used when the chastiser merely requires the girl to bend over it in the common way. This is well suited to willowy nymphs of sixteen with veils of silken hair, like Tracey Hope or Angela Irvine. To the other side, is a heavy kitchen-table of scrubbed pine, six feet long. It is often used when the discipline is severe and the subject is a mature young woman of twenty-five or even thirty or more, not infrequently a wayward wife. She lies fastened face-down with the leather bolster under her loins to raise and broaden the swell of her bare buttocks. One might, for example, use the pony lash on the rather full and heavy bottom-cheeks of Trish Mitchell or Many Worth or Joy Webster. The intended discipline is so prolonged that their own legs would not support them by the conclusion. I soon saw the truth of it, after dinner the following evening. Joy Webster with her coquettish womanly looks at twenty-five, her stylish boy-crop of blond hair, her narrow waist and swelling bottom-cheeks was the seductive whip-marked burden which the table bore by midnight.

It was just before two o'clock when three of the

most burly females brought Elaine Cox to the room. You may be sure she affected contemptuous indifference, striding bare-thighed in her short pleated skirt, tossing her lank fair hair and shouting to several cronies that she would see them after the show. The matrons seemed resolved to check that at once.

Those who constructed the place had the foresight to add a room at one side with the usual pedestal and handbasin. At the matrons' suggestion, two of them led Elaine in there and closed the door so that she might hear what went on in the main room but could not see it. The third matron explained that she had a small account to settle with the elder Cox sister, Pauline. She was duly brought, a plump and rather slatternly girl of eighteen or nineteen with a roundish face and fair hair drawn back and worn in a collar-length tail.

The matron ordered Pauline Cox to shed her skirt, which she did most unwillingly, and then to bend over the tall stool. Her wrists were secured and the tight briefs of Pauline's knickers were drawn down to her knees. I watched closely, not missing the chance to become acquainted with the comparative anatomy of two bare female bottoms in the same family. The matron took the short lash and disciplined the fat cheeks of Pauline Cox's bare backside with great agility. The whip smacked and curled and cut for a minute or two, quite enough for Pauline Cox's screams to rise shrill and clear. Through them I heard a cry or rather a bellow of fury from the younger sister beyond the door. The matrons finished and unfastened the culprit.

"Pull your knickers up, Pauline Cox, and put your skirt on," the matron said, removing any doubt in Elaine's mind as to the identity of the whipped delinquent. Pauline obeyed and was led slowly away. But the result of this was to fire Elaine's fury at all of us.

The youngster was now brought in. Her lips were tighter and her narrowed eyes shone. But smiles played upon the lips of all the adults as we met her gaze. Still smiling at her, I said.

"Take your skirt off, Elaine Cox. Take it right off."

She shook her lank fair hair back contemptuously, undid the scandalously brief skirt of her uniform at the waist, let it drop to the floor and then stepped out of it.

"Kneel over the birching-block, Elaine," the first matron said quietly. As if it were preferable to being touched by them, Elaine turned and knelt on the flat surface, then knelt forward over the frame with her arms down the far side, her hips and seat raised. The stout waist-strap was strongly riveted to the frame. The woman drew it round Elaine's waist, next to the bare skin, and buckled it tightly in the small of the girl's back. Elaine, drawn forward over the heavy scroll by the straps, tossed back her spilling fair hair and turned the thin mouth and narrowed eyes of her slum-child's face upon me. The mouth was still tight with fury. The dark eyes with their fleck of green were narrowed with anger.

Now I could study this fifteen-year-old tomboy in her underpants. The elastic tightness of her white school knickers shaped the full swell of Elaine Cox's backside, broadened and fattened by her posture. Though she was not yet bare, I could not help thinking how the middle-aged admirers who followed her home from school would have enjoyed seeing her like this. She had struggled hard in the grip of the matrons. This had caused the elastic hem of her briefs to ride up at one side, laying bare a pale fattened crescent on the lower curve of that bottom-cheek! It was delightful to see her in this state of disordered undress. Though she was one of the bigger girls in her class, it gave Elaine a suggestion of childish slovenliness, which was true to her character.

The women had fastened her down by the waist-strap and leather anklets, but her hands were still free.

"Reach back and pull your knickers down, Elaine Cox!" the matron said, "Pull them right down so that your master may cane the backs of your thighs as well if he wants to."

She obeyed. I suppose that, as before, the girl did it so that she would not have to feel our own hands doing it for her. But under her breath I heard her cursing us.

"You bastards! You fucking bastards!"

She tossed her lank fair hair back, half looking round as she reached to the waistband of her white stretched briefs and drew them down to her knees. Elaine Cox's behind was pale and full-cheeked as she presented it to us now. Kneeling right forward over the frame, the posture made her seem quite a big-bottomed girl for her age.

"The tail of your blouse, Elaine Cox!" the matron said, "Tuck it right up under the waist-strap so that your bottom is properly bare."

This time the girl reached back with a little more difficulty to catch the rear hem of her white blouse and tuck it up above the strap. Then the two women stooped down. Each of them took one of Elaine's arms, drew it down at full stretch an fastened it by a leather cuff to the base of the frame.

The three women stood forward and I let them have a good look at the full pallor of Elaine Cox's bare bottom-cheeks. The youngster was holding herself rather tense, which was understandable. But the women had never seen her bare. A woman will discipline such a girl even more severely than the male sex would do. These good ladies were therefore as interested as any man in the fullness of Elaine's rear cheek-swell and the target offered by her broadened buttocks.

"Her bottom needs a good thrashing, sir," said one of them, "Most teachers would want to tan Elaine Cox. She's a young ruffian, sir. She needs the cane across her young bottom hard and long. I'd take her to one of those prisons, sir, where they'd whip her backside with a proper lash. There's four canes over on the table, sir. There's a pony-lash in the cupboard. If you should use it, sir, you'll hear no complaint from us. And Mrs Brace is coming to unfasten Elaine at seven o'clock, sir. If you should want the little scrubber tanned with the spanking-strap then, you need only leave it on the table here when you finish with her presently. It's the normal sign we give, sir. If Mrs Brace finds it there, sir, she says she'll know what to do. Nod and a wink, sir, if you take my meaning."

With that, these honest women left me to my task. I went across and bolted the door, so that there should be no interruptions. For those with such tastes, the prospect of having a bare-bottomed tomboy like Elaine Cox over the block for the afternoon is profoundly stimulating.

Elaine now wore only her white school blouse with the tail tucked up and her striped tie. She shook her lank hair clear and twisted her impudent face round, as I studied the swelling pallor of her bare rear cheeks. As any teacher might have done, I sat down on the surface upon which she knelt, just behind her and inspected this profoundly

interesting rear view of my adolescent tomboy. I
strapped her sturdy bare legs together firmly, just
above her knees. The entire summer afternoon was
at my disposal. There was time to fondle the slight
heaviness of her pale adolescent thighs. She gasped
and cursed but I was not to be denied.

I was almost bursting in the tightness of my suit-
ing and longed to unbutton in front of her, manhood fully armed. I did not doubt that one or two
boys of her own age had shown her their young
instruments and that she had been intrigued. But
that of a middle-aged gentlemen was not at all to
Elaine's liking. I stood before her and smiled at her
impudence as I drew the cloth tighter and showed
her the hardness under it. I thought she would be
less likely to argue or plead, if she saw the state of
the tool that must determine the length of her punishment.

I sat down behind her again to make a survey of
the bare target she offered.

"Get forward over the block, Elaine Cox!
Bottom-upwards! Right over it! Tighter than that,
you little scrubber! Show your backside properly,
Elaine!"

I smiled to myself as I sat a few inches behind
her on the edge of the block. I was confronted by
the fattish adolescent pallor of Elaine's broadened
buttocks. I gave her a sounding smack on the
nearer cheek of her bare backside and then another
lusty smack on the same one. The impact of my
hand stung her enough to make her squirm and
curse me in the foullest language imaginable. Even
this was gratifying, in my present mood, and I
avenged the insults by a further rear-cheek smack
or two that made the bare walls sing.

"In a moment you'll get the bamboo cane across
your bare bottom, Elaine Cox. And you'll ask for

your punishment. You'll call out the number of each stroke before you get it, asking me to give it to you. If you refuse, you'll get it anyway, Elaine. But it won't count towards the total I'm going to make you have. It's time you had a proper punishment-lesson, Elaine Cox! I've set aside the whole of the afternoon for you.''

At these words she gasped and struggled in vain against the straps, cursing and fretting.

''Lie still, Elaine,'' I said, meeting her eyes with a smile again, as she now craned round in uncertainty and apprehension.

The rules of discipline entitle the chastiser to familiarise himself with the object of punishment. I handled the full pallor of Elaine Cox's bottom-cheeks, finding them smooth and cool in their nudity. I drew them hard apart, prying into the rude rear valley between them. I ran my hands over her smooth bare thighs and pressed their softness apart to examine the intimacy which they concealed, feeling her shiver with excitement or apprehension—or perhaps a little of both! Having coaxed and fondled these warm folds, I allowed her firmly-strapped legs to close over them again. My lips touched the pale mounds of her broad young buttocks and browsed upon them. A dozen times I paused and gave her a vigorous smack on one of her bottom-cheeks to relieve my feelings.

My attention wandered to the heavy pallor of her young thighs, then to her broadened adolescent backside once more. I parted its cheeks and enjoyed another long close inspection of the tight little blow-hole. Elaine uttered a sound of rejection in her throat and flinched as I applied a pouting kiss. Ignoring such protests, I rewarded her adolescent vulgarity with my own, settling down and applying intrusive nuzzling kisses. Her bottom-cheeks brushed my face as she tensed and squirmed. I was intrigued and delighted to find that even an insolent slum-girl like Elaine can burn with outrage and disgust! How absurd that seemed! Consider the impudent and sluttish way in which she had shown her young bottom while she was bending over that morning. She and Pauline have not even the nymph-like hesitation or self-consciousness of the Hope sisters, Tracey and Antoinette. I now became strictly formal with her.

"Get tighter over the block, Elaine Cox!"

Almost an hour had passed since she was put over the apparatus. Let me confess that under urging stiffness a couple of buttons had popped open, as if the imprisoned hardness had a will of its own. Not that this deflected me from severity. Quite the contrary. With a bare-bottomed tomboy like Elaine Cox over the block, I was going to be absolutely implacable with her.

I stood behind her as she knelt. Then I leant forward to ease her hips more tightly over the leather-padded frame, drawing the waist-strap more firmly. I wanted Elaine Cox bottom-upwards, her rear cheeks swelling more fully. In doing this, I naturally pressed hard on her, the swell of my pants' front against the smooth pallor of her adolescent buttocks. The warm tool grew stiffer at this and, I fear, slipped out and touched the cooler smoothness of Elaine's bottom, which naturally caused such an erection a spasm of excitement.

Though she could not see what was happening, this defiant youngster could feel it. Elaine Cox tossed her lank fair hair clear as she twisted her face round and cursed me for a dirty filthy thing. Far from regretting what had happened, I allowed it to stroke its big head on her young backside. My lips touched her ear and I softly confessed to Elaine

Cox how I had followed her and admired her when she was a year or two younger, waiting for her return from school, and my thoughts and wishes then.

There could be but one conclusion. Passion grew exquisitely sensitive. It lay in the warm humid valley between the double cheeked swell. The first pulse came and I kept it between the pale fattened cheeks of Elaine Cox's schoolgirl backside. A second and third there before she pulled away and Cupid's warm gruel fell in jet and splash upon the cheeks of Elaine Cox's behind. One might deplore this, but such accidents will happen on these disciplinary occasions.

She shook her hair back and twisted round again. Thinking me a milksop, I suppose she imagined I should look aghast at my folly and forgive her at once, begging her only not to reveal this terrible lapse. But when she directed the fury of her narrowed dark eyes with their fleck of green upon me, I was smiling open-mouthed with delight at what I had done. I stood in front of her and showed her what she had to thank for her present state, obliging her to have a good close look at it. I asked her if she liked the feel of the tribute that now adorned her bare backside. There was no response beyond the indignation and cursing of an adolescent slum-girl.

I composed myself, obliging her to wait with the shining dew of passion giving a most suggestive look to the fullness of Elaine's pale bottom-cheeks. Fortunately, her discarded briefs of white cotton make an excellent mop when pressed to a wad and decency was soon restored again. It was by no means too soon. I heard the first tell-tale scrape of a boot against the brickwalk on the outside of the rear wall. High in that wall, dividing my own domain from the establishment where delinquent lads were confined, was the row of small barred windows. Imagine a dozen young scamps of Elaine's age who knew what was going on in that room. At the risk of being thrashed themselves, they shinned up to perch on the ledge, looking down on the view she offered.

Not every culprit shows such indignation at being spied on by the lads during these sessions. The older delinquents, young women of twenty-five or thirty whom we position bottom-upwards on the table, betray a certain excitement at being watched by such boys. I observed it in Trish and in Joy but I do not think they would admit it for the world.

I pretended not to hear the furtive movements outside the windows. There were seven or eight apertures. The next time Elaine tossed back her lank fair hair and craned round at me, the insolence and contempt in her narrowed eyes failed her. Her glance round showed her the grinning faces high in the wall behind her. It was a salutary lesson for her. The lads were allowed no other access to her and had no need to indulge in the pretence of courtship. They caught Elaine's eye, grinning at her as if to assure her how greatly they would enjoy watching her given a lesson in discipline. Each of them showed her his young manhood as he began to manualise with excitement at her present state.

I chose the longest and most supple bamboo, a cane which I am sure many of Elaine's teachers at school would have longed to use upon her.

"Thirty-six strokes of the bamboo across those big cheeks of your bare arse, Elaine Cox. You know the rules, Elaine. Call out the number of each stroke before you receive it or it will not count towards your total."

A gasp of anticipation came from the lads crouched at the barred windows. I flexed the supple bamboo, then touched it lightly this way and that across the robust pallor of Elaine's behind while I took my aim. She flinched from the feel of the cane, her bare buttocks tensing and shifting. But the strap round her thighs and another round her waist held her kneeling over. Elaine Cox's bottom-crack was pressed to a thin line as she tightened. Then her rear cheeks slackened only to tense in alarm again at the cane's new touch. Elaine's young bum-cheeks squirmed as if she might be squeezing something between them. How her teachers must have longed to have her like this over the schoolroom desk!

"Call for the first stroke, Elaine Cox," I said quietly. She would not. Her adolescent defiance showed the contempt she felt for a middle-aged master and a fury at the whipping she had heard us giving her big sister Pauline. Pauline Cox's screams were a sound that Elaine would never forget nor forgive.

I brought the supple cane down hard and sharp as I could across the defiant fifth-form girl's bare buttocks. I assure you the bleak whitewashed walls rang with a pistol-crack smack of the bamboo across the broadened cheeks of Elaine Cox's bottom. The youngster gave a gasp deep in her throat at the ferocity of the smart and tightened her buttocks inward as if to contain the anguish.

I knew that the pain of the impact would swell for several seconds and I always tried to catch her with the next stroke at the point when the agony of its predecessor had reached a climax. With such robust thighs and buttocks, Elaine Cox was a ruffianly adolescent girl. It was therefore necessary to take every opportunity to enforce the severity of the discipline. I gave a warning little touch of the cane low down on her bottom-cheeks and saw Elaine force her knees together as if to brace herself. I whipped hard with the bamboo just above the flesh-crease dividing her buttocks and thighs. She gave a wild gasp, her pale hips rose a little with the pressure of her knees and Elaine Cox's bottom-crack was urgently drawn into a thin tight line as she tried to compress the surging torment.

And still she had not called out for the first stroke. I caned her low across her fattened young bottom-cheeks again, and then again with a lash of bamboo as sharp as a ringmaster's whip. This time her breath was caught in a short hard cry. Her strapped hands were clenched into fists and her toes curled with the intensity of the smart across her young backside. She tossed her lank fair hair back and craned round, her teeth gnawing frantically at her lower lip as she watched me take the next aim across her behind.

By now there were a half-a-dozen crimson bamboo-prints raised across Elaine Cox's bum-cheeks. Despite that, her fury at what we had done to Pauline was such that she continued to refuse to ask for the first counted stroke of her discipline. As she craned round and the first sign of consternation appeared in the broad oval of her snub nosed face, I met her narrowed eyes with a knowing smile.

"Ask for your punishment, Elaine Cox!" I said, teasing her a little, "Call for the first stroke. You must ask me to thrash you."

That fired the impudence and defiance in her young face. But I had been intrigued by Elaine Cox for too long to show leniency to her now. I lashed hard and repeatedly causing her pale bottom-flesh to jump and quiver at the impacts. She was fighting not to surrender by crying out. Her mouth was distended in a wide silent grimace. At each stroke she uttered a deep urgent gasp, as if she were panting in fright and under some desperate labour or exertion.

To enforce obedience, I decided to aim repeatedly at one weal of bamboo on the lower curve of her young arse. I brought the cane down across it with a whip-like impact that made my ears sing at its sharpness. Elaine gave a short hard cry and writhed her buttocks gently. I heard her gasping, "Oh, shit! Ahhh! Oh, my arse! My arse! Fuck you, you bastard!"

I smiled again at this.

"Six extra strokes to curb your insolence, Elaine Cox! Add them to your punishment when you call out for it. Forty-two to count, Elaine! Call for the first. Your judicial caning hasn't even begun yet."

I let her feel me measuring the next stroke across the same stripe.

"No!" cried Elaine, tossing her hair and looking round at me in startled dismay, "I can't bear it again across there!"

But I set my teeth and thrashed her across that stripe with all the spring of the supple cane. The smart of it across an already painful stripe was atrocious and, quite unable to check herself, Elaine Cox farted with all the adolescent vulgarity of a schoolgirl tomboy. She tossed back her hair and this time craned round with a wild and entreating look. Elaine had given me the best pretext for adding to her punishment and her mouth was rounded in an "Ooooooooo!" of fright.

The reformatory lads were grinning at her from their perch, each licking his lips and showing her the stiffness in his hand. They were thoroughly enjoying the spectacle and greatly hoped that it would be prolonged.

"Eight extra strokes for rudeness, Elaine Cox," I said firmly, not bothering to hide my smile from her. "You'll count them in addition at the end!"

I knew Elaine was trying to convey to me that in her present state the next ringing smack of the cane was going to make her young bottom repeat its rudeness. I let her see that I understood. I held her eyes with a smile as I touched the bamboo lightly again across that same smarting welt. I quietly assured her that when she began to count, I would still make her take every stroke of her discipline. It was good to see her snub-nosed insolence give way to mournful self-pity. In fury at her big sister's punishment, Elaine had defied me till she could bear no more. She was frantic now. Her prison caning had not even begun. Unable to bear another agonising smack of bamboo, she dared not call for it. Yet by refusing, she would add dreadfully to her ordeal. It was a delightful predicament in which to have a fifteen-year-old tomboy like Elaine Cox, if one enjoyed giving her a proper punishment-lesson. I greatly wanted to teach the bare fattened cheeks of Elaine Cox's schoolgirl arse a long lesson in discipline.

"I'll have absolute obedience from you, Elaine," I said, still smiling.

I let her see my mouth tighten. I touched the bamboo lightly across the throbbing tenderness of that ominously raised stripe. As she craned around at me in consternation, Elaine Cox's tomboy bottom retorted impudently a second time. The lads at the windows laughed delightedly. I accused her of deliberate vulgarity. I think I was right. Elaine was desperate to interrupt her punishment, even for a moment's respite. But a fifteen-year-old schoolgirl pays a severe penalty for such misconduct if she commits it while her bare bottom is being thrashed. Michele Page was taught manners for her young backside's insolence. So was pretty Jane Mitchener's arse at fourteen. It would be impudent to deal so severely with young Jane in public. Behind closed doors and thick walls, however, the bare cheeks of Jane Mitchener's bottom tasted bamboo and snakeskin. No tale-telling of this was permitted.

"I shan't add to your strokes for that insolence, Elaine Cox," I said at last, "but you'll have the last ten across your bottom with the prison lash."

I drew back and caned her hard again across the same place. There was much work still to do upon such a target, despite the plum-coloured tapestry across it. One does not judge by tears and frenzy, which may be pretended, but by the view presented for discipline. The slight adolescent heaviness of her hips and seat, the broadening and fattening effect of kneeling over the block, made Elaine Cox appear a rather big-bottomed youngster. This inclines one to severity rather than leniency. I began to cane her very hard and rapidly. The room rang with the *whip!* . . . *smack!* . . . *whip!* . . . of the bamboo across her bare bum-cheeks. I caught her with a beauty aslant her fifth-form backside and Elaine Cox screamed. After that, repentance followed at last. She sobbed out that she could not bear any more and I informed her that I should make her bear it anyway. When she turned her face, the narrowed eyes brimmed over and the mouth was like a tragic mime. Her protests ended in another smack of the bamboo and a wild teenage shrillness. She drew breath frantically and let it out in a ringing shriek.

"One!" she screeched, "One! Let me count! Please! One!"

I felt excitement and anticipation at having

forced her to obey. Elaine was now asking to be caned. She was desperate not to miss the count, though she did so several times when the agony of bamboo across her bare backside paralysed her shrieks. I heard her yell, "Two! . . . OW! . . . Oh, shit! . . . Three! . . . OW! No! . . . Not there! . . . AAAAAHHH! . . . OH, my bottom! . . . Four! . . . O-O-OWWWW! . . . F-i-i-i-ve!" Sometimes, when I paused, I would hear her tearful and urgent panting, "Oh, my arse! . . . You fucking bastard!" A vicious lash of bamboo across her tender bottom-striping curbed her rebellion and made her yell, "Eighteen! . . . AHHHHH! Not there again! . . . Ple-e-e-ase! No! OOOOOWWW! . . . NINET-E-E-E-N!"

By the time I exchanged the prison cane for a lash, the tomboy cheeks of Elaine Cox's bottom were a teacher's delight. They smarted the colour of fire, marked across by deeper-toned and finely embossed bamboo prints. As a matter of prudence, I say little of ten curling kisses that the snakeskin imprinted upon the young cheeks of Elaine Cox's backside. The last three or four were carefully-aimed crack-shots and Elaine reached the peak of her voice-range.

When such a girl has been punished, it is a rule that she is left fastened over the block until dinner-time that evening, which was then about three hours away. The intention is that she is made to reflect upon her insolence and her misconduct. To assist her in this, the chastiser ensures that the youngster continues to feel the smart of her punishment keenly during those hours. We keep a jar in that room. It contains the fat of salt bacon, with which a further heavy salting has been melted. I do not deny that the crimson-blushing cheeks of Elaine Cox's bottom were already sore enough to make her squirm. But I dug out the fat and spread its salty harshness over her. Elaine's big-cheeked schoolgirl bottom was soon blushing a brighter red and sleek with grease. The heavily salted bacon fat stung like fire on her young backside after such a whipping. She jammed her knees hard together, tensed her thighs and buttocks, struggling to contain the throbbing tenderness.

"You'll kneel like that, Elaine, until Mrs Brace comes at seven o'clock."

She shook her hair clear and turned the broad oval of her face, her eyes still narrowed and mouth tight despite her punishment-lesson. I left the building and locked the door. But there is a little spy hole with a locking cover, to which the master alone has a key. It is his privilege to spy without ever being spied upon! I opened it and observed her secretly. She continued to squirm her hips and tense her rear cheeks as far as she could, holding her breath and releasing it in frantic gasps as she endured the smarting fat. She was not alone for long.

On a warm afternoon, one cannot avoid the bluebottle blow-flies getting in through the little windows. As Elaine knelt forward, strapped over the block, the sheen of salt fat on the youngster's buttocks was naturally a great attraction to these persistent and rudely intrusive pests. Strapped down as she was, how Elaine must have wished she had a tail to swish them away! And how glad I was that she had none! Two or three large flies landed on the shining tomato-red swell of her tanned buttocks. Elaine gasped and twisted, dislodging them. They rose a moment and then landed again. She dislodged them by squirming and they returned at once, about ten or a dozen of their black big-winged companions joining them.

Certain male members of the human species might have envied them their afternoon of such sport! They crawled over the cheeks of Elaine Cox's fifteen-year-old bottom, licking and tickling her for the salt. She squirmed at the torment of it. Some of them scented their way between her rear cheeks, drawn by the suggestive intimate bouquet of Elaine Cox's bottom-crack. The youngster emitted a curse of anger, disgust and dismay. She strove to writhe over the block but the flies were by now well used to such restricted movements. They refused to be dislodged at all. A dozen or more of them settled down to explore Elaine's tomboy backside, allowing her no privacy whatever.

The randiest admirer of her adolescent charms could not have behaved more outrageously than the large black flies. They were peremptory with her and would permit no evasion or concealment. Several of them settled on each crimson-tanned an fatly-salted cheek of Elaine Cox's arse. They fussed and buzzed intently over the suggestively swelling and sleekly-greased bottom-cheeks of this ruffianly schoolgirl, licking their lips and squeezing their back legs in excitement. Others tickled the rear of her thighs, making their way high up to see what they could find in between. Several nosed between the cheeks of Elaine's young bottom, pursuing the moist and musky scents naturally gathering between her fifth-form buttocks on a warm summer day. Three or four interlopers gathered round the tight little vortex. They would tickle and nuzzle from now until dinner, thinking themselves the luckiest fellows alive.

After more panting and struggling, Elaine gave a cry of defeat and ceased to squirm, submitting to their persistence at last. The insects fussed and hummed industriously, becoming busier and more excited with her young bottom.

While this was happening, I saw that the boys had opened one of the little windows. They were dappy lads, agile and accurate in every kind of sport. From somewhere, probably a cupboard in their master's room, they had purloined one of those teachers' spanking-straps, about eighteen inches long and three inches wide, made of thin leather and split into tails at the end. I was puzzled by this for there was no way that they could reach Elaine with it! Then one of them slipped his hand through the open window. Gently he lobbed the strap, so that it fell lightly on to the large scrubbed table a few feet to one side of the block over which Elaine knelt.

And then I understood their prank. The one who lobbed the strap had been Elaine's boy-friend until they were apprehended and remained to the separate institutions. There was no chance that they would be permitted to meet and he could no longer have her kneeling behind some convenient wall and taking in her mouth the tension that plagued him. Elaine, like the other girls, could provide excitement to these peeping lads only by being tanned. Even her own boy-friend wanted to see her get the strap from Mrs Brace and knew that if it was found on the table at seven o'clock her fate would be sealed. Having dealt with her quite severely myself, I though the addition of a spanking with the strap would be imprudent. But these lusty young scamps had no such scruples. Even Elaine's boy-friend no longer concealed his enjoyment.

You may be sure that when our schoolgirl tomboy saw the strap now lying on the table, she went mad with panic.

"No!" she shouted frantically, "No! No! No-o-o-o-o!''

She tossed her fair hair and craned round at them in dismay. They grinned down at her. Elaine tried in vain to squirm and twist against the leather pinions holding her wrists and waist, thighs and ankles. But in her present state of bare-bottomed fright, she truly could not keep still. The lads at the high windows behind her teased her a little. They assured her that her boy-friend was devising a way of helping her pass the time until seven o'clock.

There were more chuckles at this. I waited to see what they would do. Fortunately, I was able to watch through my peep-hole in the door, so that I was hidden from the youngster herself and the lads at the windows. Presently I heard a bump and scrape against the rear wall. They opened one of the little windows again and intruded a slim pole about the thickness of a thumb. They were about ten feet behind the girl as she knelt and six feet above her. The device was like a proper fishing-rod and seemed long enough to reach her.

And then I understood what the clever young devils were about. Let me explain.

Several years before this date, there had been a master appointed over the delinquent lads, a man who pursued in his leisure the science of botany. He had been in the East and brought back with him various unusual species. There were rhododendrons of a kind seldom seen outside northern India or Tibet, but which now flourish in the shrubbery of the institution. Among his other successes was a tall dark-leaved nettle, known colloquially as the Scorpion Leaf. It flourished in large banks about the buildings and was reckoned to be as good a barrier as barbed wire and broken glass. A lad who tried to walk through it would gasp and jump back if it touched his hand, however lightly. The Scorpion

Leaf was to the common stinging nettle as the bite of the viper is to the touch of the innocent earthworm.

What these ingenious young scamps had done was to wrap their hands and pick a bouquet of Scorpion Leaf with its angular serrated fronds and the little hairy spikes of its sting-tips. This bouquet, the size of a nosegay, they had tied to the tip of the slender rod. The one who was sliding the rod forward had an intent expression, tongue pressed to his lips in concentration. He looked greatly concerned that the fiendish device might not reach Elaine.

But then he saw that it would do so quite easily. His face relaxed in a grin of delight and his companions began to smile. Elaine was craning round at them as she knelt strapped over the block. She looked uneasy at what was happening but did not yet guess the truth. Perhaps they were merely devising a whisk to keep the troublesome flies from her smarting backside.

There was no mistaking the excitement in the lad's eyes, however. He and the others ignored the girl's backward look at them, their gaze directed intently at her full-cheeked fifth-form backside. The spiked leaves of the "nosegay" touched her bare buttocks lightly and Elaine Cox screamed as if she had just sat on a red-hot stove. The shock of this shrillness was hardly enough to make the lad draw the nettle-stings from her blushing and smarting bum-cheeks for more than a few seconds. Guiding the rod carefully, he began to brush the dark leaves up and down the nearer cheek of Elaine Cox's fifteen-year-old bottom. In her wildness she twisted her face round, mouth stretched wide in a piercing cry and eyes frantic at what was happening to her.

Presently he drew the leaves away and one saw

a deeper beet root red on that cheek, with the little sting pricks clearly raised. Half in anger and half in desperation, Elaine yelled at them that she was going to get the strap at seven o'clock. She shouted that her bottom was already smarting too fiercely to endure that spanking and pleaded with them not to put her in an even worse predicament. They grinned at this, several younger ones showing her their manly stiffness, telling Elaine to shut her mouth and keep her bottom still.

"They'll give you a hard time with the strap anyway, Elaine," said the leader of the boys, teasing her, "Don't you want to find out what it's like being tanned when your bottom is smarting too badly to be touched? Wouldn't you rather have some real excitement in the room while you're getting it? You'll have the spanking-strap anyway, Elaine. You might just as well let them enjoy themselves with you properly. They get a big thrill when they see that you're sore to begin with. Get your bottom ready for the nettles again, Elaine!"

Then they settled to their task. One of them took the pole and brushed the leaves up and down the rear of one of Elaine's bare tomboy thighs. He did it, slowly and held it there for a while. All her frenzied tugging at her straps, and all the squirming of her hips made no difference. But the goad of the fiercely stinging nettles made it impossible for her to keep still.

"We're going to ginger you up properly, Elaine," said her first admirer.

A crimson sting-rash covered the rear of one of her thighs before the boy began to stroke the other. He let her calm herself for a moment after that.

"Is your bottom really smarting yet, Elaine?" he asked presently, "Time for you to be really hotted up now. You might just as well keep your arse still for it, Elaine. You'll get it anyway. Settle down and take it calmly.''

"No!" Her face was twisted round to them as if stuck in that position, mouth wide and yelling. "No!"

"You're a fat-arsed little scrubber, Elaine Cox!" the lad said smiling, "One cheek of your bottom hasn't been touched yet. We'll start there. Is that making your hair curl, Elaine? . . . The other cheek of your bottom now, Elaine . . . Just a tickle down the backs of your legs . . . Behind your knees . . . And now your bottom again, Elaine. . . .''

The wildness of her open mouth rang back from the whitewashed walls. A third lad brushed the bare flanks of her hips and thighs. The true artist was the one who followed. He began at the backs of her knees, brushing up in slow lingering strokes, trying to tickle between the tightly closed thighs as much as possible. He reached the sensitive tops of her legs and just caught pussy at the rear. Then it was the big schoolgirl cheeks of Elaine Cox's bottom for the third or fourth time. She howled and bellowed and shrieked with all the power of her lungs. But this did not distract him. At last he steadied his aim and tucked the nosegay in between the cheeks of Elaine's young backside.

I watched all this, greatly intrigued, for it shows what even the lads of her own age feel about such a girl as this. This one had tucked the nosegay between her rear cheeks and was giving Elaine's tomboy crack a severe time of it. It was interesting to witness a situation with lads of her age and class, in which they could see that she was unable to bear the atrocious smart, and yet they made her bear it all the same. They soon had Elaine yelling and pleading, cursing and farting, all of which seemed only to add to their zeal.

To my surprise there was a sudden movement and the lads began to scramble down from their perch, as if about to run away. I heard footsteps and prudently withdrew to concealment. It was Mrs Brace, making a preliminary visit an hour or two before her seven o'clock rendezvous. I caught only a glimpse of her in the room and heard something of the words exchanged between her and the girl. Her mouth opened in visible delight at the sight of the spanking-strap lying on the table. She stood behind Elaine, the good woman's lips rounding in amusement and astonishment at the sorely blushing rear cheeks and thighs of this impudent pupil. The eagerness and delight of Mrs Brace's features was all too plain to the youngster herself. Elaine bellowed and cried out at her, pulling helplessly at her straps. She demanded to be released and shrieked that the boys next door had stung her and put the strap there.

The truth of this seemed undeniable from the sting blisters on Elaine Cox's arse and thighs. But Mrs Brace smiled teasingly at her.

"Don't add deceit to your other misconduct, Elaine Cox. I'll be back at seven to give you the strap, never fear. You shan't escape your due punishment. I can guess how you stung your bottom on a nettle, you dirty little slut. Lying on your back, skirt up and knickers down, for some young ruffian to have his way with you. You'll get it all the worse for that, Elaine. I've got a few scores to settle with you, my girl. I'll be here prompt at seven, so that we have a full half-hour before dinner. Ever been tanned properly with a spanking-strap, Elaine? Your teachers were afraid to send you home after school in a real state! You'll be in one by the time you leave this room!"

Mrs Brace walked away with Elaine shrieking after her. The door closed. I heard the boots of the lads on the wall as they scrambled back. The rod, adorned by a fresh posy of Scorpion Leaf, intruded at the open window again.

"She won't be back for an hour or two, Elaine," said her younger admirer, "We're going to give you some real thrills with the nettles before then."

"Better get into the mood, Elaine," said another, "We're really going to tickle up your bottom and legs this time. I bet the old woman's looking forward to what she's going to do to you at seven o'clock! I'd love to change places with her, Elaine. Would you enjoy it more from a man, Elaine?"

It was now late in the afternoon and I had business to complete. I could intervene and send the lads scampering, even report them for a birching, or I could leave Elaine at their disposal. I studied her through the peep-hole. This sturdy fifth-form girl was wailing in anticipation, all the impudence gone from her brimming eyes and howling mouth. She might be exaggerating her ordeal. By viewing her adolescent bottom as she presented it big-cheeked over the block I would make my decision. I studied Elaine Cox's schoolgirl backside and conceded that its cheeks were blazing and smarting fiercely. I had bamboo'd her soundly. The snake-skin had kissed her bottom scorchingly a dozen times. A frenzy in her face as the nettles again brushed her flaming buttocks suggested a hangman tightening a noose about her throat.

But in her present posture, Elaine Cox's fifteen-year-old bottom also had a look of big-cheeked impudence. Her insolence had been such that even when she was thirteen or fourteen I would have thrashed her young buttocks soundly. I had not been able to deal with her then and so I felt that she needed it all the more now. I smiled as I remarked how she had bent over that morning in front of me, scornfully and idly. The conduct of the young scamps with the nettles was not to be condoned. Yet it was understandable. Once again, I studied Elaine Cox's bottom, the sturdy adolescent cheeks swelling so blushing and tender, curving in together in her tomboy crack. Unless I intervened, the youngster would hear the walls ring with her own frenzy until dinner time. Her bottom would be smarting most violently by the time that Mrs Brace came back. And then there would be half an hour during which the tailed strap would make its intimate acquaintance with Elaine Cox's young backside. Half an hour whose every second she would remember vividly for the rest of her young life.

I stood undecided. I took another long peep at her. Not knowing that I was there, Elaine twisted her sturdy teenage hips urgently at that moment, so that she turned her bare bottom fully towards me. As she tried in vain to pull from the block Elaine's schoolgirl bum-cheeks swelled a little fuller and fatter, parting to offer a suggestive glimpse between them. There was a certain impudence even in the way she presented her behind to me now. It seemed absurd to argue that she would not be able to bear a spanking with the leather strap. So long as she was securely held over the block, and so long as the mistress remained implacable with her, Elaine must learn to bear it. I smiled, my tongue running loose at my thoughts. I spent a minute or two more studying the broad snub-nosed oval of her full swell of this fifth-form girl's bottom-cheeks and my eyes eagerly mapped the rear cleavage of what I call Elaine Cox's tomboy crack running between them. Though it was not quite correct to leave her to the attentions of the delinquent lads with their Scorpion Leaf, I still hesitated. In a twinkling, the lad with the nosegay created havoc in that same rear cleavage. I listened to Elaine's ringing descant a moment and then I walked quietly away.

I noted in the register that Elaine Cox had received exemplary discipline. Whether it was an example to the other girls, I do not know. It did not change her own conduct, nor did I ever suppose that it would. I had watched her since she was thirteen and knew that insolence and contempt for her betters was part of her nature. I was not concerned. "What cannot be cured must be endured." To be frank, it is no bad thing. Fourteen to eighteen is the only time when a girl of Elaine's kind is desirable, as a nymph like Tracey Hope may be from sixteen to thirty. It is then she must be savoured. I do not know a better way than the moral discipline of the strap or cane, nor a better subject than Elaine Cox.

She is not my only charge, of course. There is quite a tale to be told about an appealing youngster like Jane Mitchener with her lank brown hair on her shoulders, her little fringe, the firm openness of her fair-skinned face and the taut pallor of her figure's fledgling femininity. Pretty Jane knows that I treat her in quite a special way. The little teaser appeals so easily. Jane Mitchener's name appears regularly in the list of those who must pay the penalty for some fault or other. Her rendezvous in that whitewashed room is with me alone and generally at an hour when all others are in bed for the night. Jane is soulful and promises to be a good girl for the future. But she never escapes the present. The session is always a long one and Jane Mitchener has twice occupied that table reserved as a rule for amazons of twenty-five or thirty. Although the youngest of the girls, the provocation offered by the taut bare cheeks of Jane Mitchener's bottom is perhaps the greatest. The imperious kiss of snakeskin bears witness to it. But do not think I neglect the moral training of Elaine. I am praised everywhere for my inflexible resolve with her. But I must now say publicly that her adolescent insolence and defiance stiffens my middle-aged resolve quite remarkably.

AFTERWORD

A GOOD DEAL OF EROTIC FICTION was pure ornament and imagination, a literature of suggestion. Edward Sellon's houses and gardens are places that we admire and contemplate. It scarcely matters if nothing goes on there. We are invited to dwell on the scenery and imagine what might take place. The events themselves, detailed precisely, may come as an anti-climax.

The girls offered for admiration, even in a collection like *Pearls of the Orient,* range from the nymph and the *gamine* to the tomboy and the trollop. A companion piece to the downfall of Elaine Cox shows the appeal of the "working-girl," a daughter of the lower orders who by some quirk of the libido excites her elders and betters. Noreen's appeal and her downfall are sometimes hinted by images alone. As the narrator says later, we become more intimately acquainted with this nineteen-year-old wench than her boy-friend or bridegroom would. Noreen, lying on her belly over the pillows and bare from the waist down, would make a "living sculpture" in Sellon's garden. The story insists that Noreen, like Elaine, cannot be permitted to have her way in the world. Her rebellion requires that she be dealt with behind closed doors. Her fate is a Gothick variation on Sellon's private pleasure-dome.

There are ogres in such a world, no two ways about it. They exist as surely in underground fiction as they do in detective novels or real-life politics. Those with political ambition may even claim to be doing us all a moral favour while having the time of their lives at our expense. Hardman, who supervises Noreen in his private reformatory, is one of that breed. The narrator admits it. Do we condemn Mr Hardman? Or do we smile and secretly envy him? The story knowingly suggests an answer. Noreen at nineteen years old needs "to be taught a lesson." Who better than Mr Hardman to teach a girl of this type?

PEARLS OF THE ORIENT

The First Volume

NOREEN: A STRAPPING YOUNG TROLLOP

＊＊＊＊

Private Conduct-Training for a
Rebellious Shopgirl of Nineteen
By her Master, Mr Hardman

PARIS: SULIS MINERVA PRESS
For the Corrective Education of Working Girls

Of the two types of erotic fiction, there can be no doubt at the opening of the tale of *Noreen* that even if the girl does not know it herself, we are entering the world of the sexual Gothick.

It is strange to reflect now that, of the three girls who were busy with the window of the shop, it was Claire who caught my attention first. She was eighteen years old and, though you would hardly call her a beauty, Claire had a hint of the perverse and promiscuous about her. She was a redhead with a rather pale red or ginger coloured cut of straight hair. It looked as if she had put a pudding basin on her head and trimmed straight round it, her hair so boyishly short and plain with its brief fringe on her forehead. Claire was thin and pale with rather pert and enigmatic features, a certain vicious slant in her green eyes. The tight pants and top that she wore while setting out the merchandise, showed the slimness of her young body, the narrow back and trim rear-cheeks as she bent, the slender thighs.

I cannot pretend that I was attracted by her charms. On the contrary, it was the air of the perverse about her that caught my long and admiring glances as I passed by. Unlike the two other girls who worked with her, Claire would often dress with some sophistication after work, choosing a smart caramel-coloured skirt and jacket with matching parasol and high heels.

Vivienne, I scarcely noticed by comparison. Indeed, Viv was a soft young beauty of rather timid aspect with a page-length brunette hairstyle. Perhaps she had not yet been mounted by a lover and was in no hurry to be. The third girl, Noreen, was about sixteen or so when I first set eyes on her. I hardly noticed her beyond observing that she was dark-haired and quite strongly built with a rather hard and vulgar look.

It was some time later when redheaded Claire with her basin-cut and perverse glances was employed elsewhere at another task. For the first time I gave my attention to Noreen in the absence of her rival.

Noreen was kneeling behind the glass with her back to me, sitting on her heels, working the cloth on the floor with a vigour and determination that were reflected in the firm set of her jaw and the wide points of her cheekbones. She was dressed as usual in the snug-fitting cotton singlet and the faded light blue of her tight jeans. A stout leather waist-belt drew the thin denim smoother and tighter over her hips and thighs, making her lower figure an object of great interest. It was certainly enough to make one pause and study the view that the sturdy young trollop offered. Knowing that she was being watched, Noreen responded with a pretence at indifference or a contemptuous flick of her finger.

She inclined her back forward a little with the energy of her polishing and one saw that the faded blue denim of her jeans was drawn skin-tight over Noreen's sturdy bottom-cheeks and hips, which naturally swelled fuller and broader as she sat on her heels. To this day I do not think Noreen realised the rear view she offered to casual passers-by and the tempting thoughts she provoked as they admired her! Such was her disdain for them that I do not suppose she cared. Sometimes, when one of them stood over her watching, she stopped her work and turned the firm features of her fair-skinned face with an insolent stare of her brown eyes, as if to dismiss the man.

When she needed to reach further, as I watched her polishing the surface, it was necessary for Noreen to lift her hips and go forward on all fours, the collar-length of her lank dark hair falling loose about her face. As she raised her haunches from her heels and went forward on hands and knees, it was possible to hear a sharp intake of breath from some of the men who saw her. In this posture, each of Noreen's rear cheeks filled the tightened jeans like a smooth and taut balloon swell. But she was strongly-made rather than plump and her thighs had the firm-muscled line of a well-exercised working-girl. Her broad leather waist-belt pulled the washed-out denim of the Falmer jeans still tighter on her rear curves!

How suggestive was the rear view she presented to the street! The faded blue jeans were skin-smooth, shaping the firmly-stretched mounds of Noreen's buttocks. As she knelt down on all fours, the stout central seam of the denim seat was drawn deep and taut between the slight fat-ness or heaviness of Noreen's swelling bottom-cheeks. The tight fit of the jeans strained the seam forward under her legs almost parting the lips of her sex where its soft flesh was clearly moulded by the tight denim between the rear of her thighs! She was eighteen or nineteen years old by this time. Her backside in such a posture appeared robust and full-cheeked but firm and

*well-shaped at the same time. The elastic hem of
Noreen's knickers was clearly outlined through
the thin taut denim of her jeans-seat. She was
wearing the briefs of elasticated cotton common
to girls of her age and type. From the rear opening of her legs, the ridge of the hem arched up
high and tight over each of her sturdy buttocks,
showing that the cheeks of Noreen's backside
were half bare under her jeans.*

*She worked vigorously in this posture for five or
ten minutes, polishing the waxed surface with
the cloth, rounding her hips this way and that,
sometimes backing on all fours towards her
admirers who smiled quietly at the sight she
presented. Sometimes, as one gazed at her, she
became aware of it. Noreen would stop, immo-
bile on all fours, flicking back her level fringe
and watching the watcher under her shoulder or
even turning her firm young face round with a
look of defiance or contempt. Sometimes she
would sit back on her heels and wait until the
man whose attentions she rejected had walked
on.*

*It was impossible not to wish that she might
pass from her boy-friend's possession into the
keeping of a gentleman who would know how to
train and employ her properly. It would be
indiscreet of me to say how it happened or how
I heard of it. But my friend Mr Hardman,
employer of the three girls, was the presiding
genius of a philanthropic institution to which
hoydens of Noreen's sort might be committed by
justices of his acquaintance and "improved."
There came a day when their admirers no
longer saw Noreen, or Claire, or Vivienne on
view.*

Nothing has taken place in this prelude except admiring gazes and an exchange of glances but there is not the least doubt that we are firmly in the territory of erotica's own *roman noir*. Edward Sellon had favoured enclosed gardens and remote luxury villas, designed so that even the servants were prevented from seeing what was going on. The Villa Rosa seems to have been planned by an architect of like mind. But in the case of Mr Hardman, the emphasis is on the sinister walls and thick doors, the barred windows and the soundproof rooms of a darker fantasy. When Noreen is whipped before the justices, it takes place at dead of night in a vaulted room. But when Mr Hardman goes to collect her for this, there is once again far more posing than acting.

By opening the door, there was enough light from the passageway to illuminate the room where Noreen lay sleeping. The guardians who supervised her had positioned the young window-dresser on her belly without a sheet or blanket over her. She was a strongly-built girl and it was of the greatest importance that she should not be permitted to offer violence to those who had charge of her. For that reason, her wrists in their soft leather cuffs were attached to the frame at either side of the bed. The light from the doorway showed Mr Hardman that his young shopgirl was asleep. Noreen's head lay in profile on the pillow, the lank collar-length of her dark hair falling on her neck and jaw-line. He could see that her eyes were closed in profound slumber and her lips were parted a little.

*As usual, Noreen was naked except for her short
pale blue singlet, whose hem ended across the
back of her waist. And, as always, the turnkey
who had attached her face-down for the night
had wedged two pillows under her loins and
pulled the singlet hem high at the rear. Noreen's
backside and hips, her thighs and flanks, were
properly bare. The pillows under her loins and
belly emphasized the spread of her strong young
thighs and gave a fuller and broader swell to
the firm cheeks of Noreen's bottom. Not only did
this make her admirably available for whatever
purpose her master might choose, it also made
Noreen appear to be offering herself in the most
blatantly provocative manner, which was the
last thing she had intended to do.*

Like the hero of Elaine Cox's ordeal, Mr Hardman seems content to stand and stare like a born
voyeur. As it happens he sits and stares, perched
on the bed while the girl sleeps. His mouth is set
hard and vindictively as he makes his survey of the
"areas that interested him" at what is called "kissing distance."

*His breath was a little uneven and his lips only
a few inches from the bare rear slope of her
strong young thighs. He mused upon the fair-
skinned and blue-veined hollow behind Noreen's
knees. His lips and tongue almost touched the
cool pale smoothness of the backs of her sturdy
young thighs. He spied eagerly between her legs.
A well-built working-girl of nineteen like Noreen
gives off the tang of her sex's instinctive arousal
while she sleeps. In the warm air, Mr Hardman
inhaled this suggestive perfume.*

· 245 ·

The hem of her singlet at the rear had been drawn up to her waist so that he was able to dwell on the firm broadened mounds of her buttocks. As he studied the robust young cheeks of Noreen's behind at such kissing-distance, Mr Hardman's expression was amorous and yet severe. Tight-lipped he considered the strapping double cheek-swell of the young window-dresser's bottom, the curving out and the sloping in together, the fatter flesh low down on her nineteen-year-old backside. As she lay relaxed in sleep, her bum-cheeks were parted a little, showing the dark forbidden rear cleavage and permitting him to ponder at leisure the tight buttonhole of Noreen's anus. His nostrils flared a little, for the warmth had made her humid in her cracks and crevices, enabling him to savour the humid femininity between Noreen's rear cheeks.

Like all the best ogres from such dark romances, Mr Hardman is not the least bashful about his desires. As a matter of fact he wants to flourish them in the faces of his girls. Having woken Noreen by his stroking, the girl flicking back the collar-length of her lank dark hair and looking round at him, "He brushed the rear of her legs and the backward peep of her femininity between them with light kisses. Noreen grew tense, her head bowed away from him as if to hide her face, her breath exhaled through clenched teeth. Mr Hardman kissed the cool smoothness of Noreen's bottom-cheeks. He parted insistently and kissed Noreen between. Her knees jammed hard into the divan as he applied a tauntingly suggestive kiss to Noreen's tight rear dimple. There was nothing he would shrink from with her."

No one could accuse Mr Hardman of shrinking from anything. There is no access to Noreen's body from which he turns away. With a whip he becomes extremely imaginative and, not to be denied, he lights a Corona cigar and punishes her rebellion by administering a "touching-up" to her bare bottom. But even so, a good deal of the action is only static and suggestive. We leave Mr Hardman perched on the side of the girl's bed, considering the rear view offered by Noreen. But like the eye of the camera travelling upwards, the narrator notices the shelf running along the wall beside the bed. The objects on it may never be used on Noreen. It may be pure coincidence that they are there at all. On the other hand, she may be about to get the lot. "There was a finely erected tool of India rubber, a lime glass squirt in a bottle of liquid soap, a perfume spray and a jar of vaseline. These stood next to the china pot and paper roll. A bamboo cane and a length of whipcord lay with a short black lash and straps that would impose absolute stillness on Noreen and hold her in whatever posture Mr Hardman commanded."

Leaving Noreen in the capable hands of Mr Hardman, in a world of vaults and whips and soundproof rooms where she and the other girls are to learn respect, obedience and the rest of it, one turns to that other world. It is out of doors and daylight. People are not on the whole held by straps or anything else. It is the world in which Edward Sellon lived and there is nothing much Gothick about it.

* * *

After so much languid hothouse fantasy, like the enervating steam and perfume of a Turkish bath, comes the cold shower of reality. Edward Sellon not only wove rich erotic fantasy, he also wrote an account of his own career. He called it, *The Ups and Downs of Life,* a title that must have seemed more sexy to his own time than it does to ours.

There was far more of the extraordinary and the bizarre in Sellon's life than in most erotic fiction. He was one of those who swung from apparent wealth to penury, from indigence to comfort, and then back to poverty again. He scraped a living for the most part and turned his hand to anything. He never told his own story in his novels but he did put into them a good deal of his own experience. Apart from the diarist of *My Secret Life,* Sellon was one of the most forthright chroniclers of the sexual reality of his time. He wrote bluntly and graphically about it.

If there is any truth in his adventures at all, Victorian women were not quite the prudes and the shrinking violets that their stereotype image suggests. A countrywoman like Phoebe might yield easily to the "young master," just as at a much later date, a reform-school girl like Elaine Cox would pull her briefs down for punishment and show herself quite contemptuously. No screams of horror or swooning among such girls. Maria and Eliza would, in reality, be intrigued at the thought of having a school of boys with their pants down.

This was mere confirmation that human nature and its enthusiasms remain immutable from one age to another. But the last word should go to Edward Sellon himself. Here is his own sketch of his life as edited by Henry Spencer Ashbee just after Sellon's death. Ashbee adds to it a brief notice of the author's death and an account of Sellon's last fling before that failed officer and gentleman booked into Webb's Hotel with a pistol and a bottle of whisky, to do "the decent thing."

* * *

"The son of a gentleman of moderate fortune, (the author informs us) whom I lost when quite a child, I was designed from the first for the army. Having, at the age of sixteen, been presented with a cadetship, so soon as my outfit was completed, I started by the Mail for Portsmouth, on a cold night in February, 1834."

In India he remained 10 years, and at the age of "six and twenty found himself a captain, a rare thing in the company's service." The greater part of the volume is devoted to his Indian career—a duel, and amours of various kinds among the European ladies and native females, the latter he thus portrays: "I now commenced a regular course of fucking with native women. The usual charge for the general run of them is two rupees. For five, you may have the handsomest Mohammedan girls, and any of the high-caste women who follow the trade of a courtesan. The 'fivers' are a very different set of people from their frail sisterhood in European countries; they do not drink, they are scrupulously cleanly in their persons, they are sumptuously dressed, they wear the most costly jewels in profusion, they are well educated and sing sweetly, accompanying their voices on the viol de gamba, a sort of guitar, they generally decorate their hair with clusters of clematis, or the sweet scented bilwa flowers entwined with pearls or diamonds. They understand in perfection all the arts and wiles of love, are capable of gratifying any tastes, and in face and figure they are unsurpassed by any women in the world.

"They have one custom that seems singular to a

European, they not only shave the Mons Veneris, but take a clean sweep underneath it, so that until you glance at their hard, full and enchanting breasts, handsome beyond compare, you fancy you have got hold of some unfledged girl. The Rajpootanee girls pluck out the hairs as they appear with a pair of tweezers, as the ancient Greek women did, and this I think a very preferable process to the shaving.

"It is impossible to describe the enjoyment I experienced in the arms of these syrens. I have had English, French, German and Polish women of all grades of society since, but never, never did they bear a comparison with those salacious, succulent hours of the far East."

On his arrival on furlough in England, he learned that his mother had arranged to marry him. This was not to his taste, but finding the bride destined for him to be "a young lady of considerable personal attractions," and "a reputed heiress with an estate of twenty-five thousand pounds, an only child," he consented, and his intended's parents objecting to her going to india, he resigned his commission. They were married and spent the winter of 1844 in Paris. Returning to England he was disgusted to find that his wife was not so rich as he had been led to suppose, that her allowance would be but four hundred a year; and his mother in law plainly told him that they must retrench, and he must go and live in "a pretty cottage in Devonshire which she had furnished for them." Recriminations ensued; he left his wife, and took up his abode with his mother in Bruton Street. For two years he remained thus separated from his wife, consoling himself in the arms of a "dear girl" he had "in keeping at a little suburban villa"; but the relations coming to an understanding, his wife returned to him to his mother's house.

"For the first month all went well, but unhappily, among my mother's servants was a little parlour maid, a sweet pretty creature, the daughter of a tradesman. She had received a pretty good education, and was not at all like a servant, either in manners or appearance. I had seduced this girl, though she was but fourteen, before my wife came up to town, and the difficulty was, how to carry on the amour after her arrival, without being discovered."

The discovery soon took place. On her return from church on a Sunday morning, his wife found Emma's cap in her bed, her husband having feigned a head ache, and not risen before she left the house. A scene naturally followed, and our hero assuming great coolness, and refusing to give a satisfactory explanation, the outraged lady lost her temper, and flew at her husband like a panther, planting such a tremendous blow on his right ear, as nearly to knock him out of his chair.

"I very calmly flung the remainder of my cigar under the grate, and seizing both her wrists with a grasp of iron, forced her into an arm-chair. 'Now you little devil,' I said, 'you sit down there, and I give you my honour, I will hold you thus, till you abjectly and most humbly beg me for mercy, and ask my pardon for the gross insult you have inflicted on me.'

"'Insult! think of the insult you have put upon me, you vile wretch, to demean yourself with a little low bred slut like that!' and struggling violently, she bit the backs of my hands until they were covered with blood, and kicked my sins till she barked them.

"'I say, my dear,' said I, 'did you ever see Shakespeare's play of Taming the Shrew?'

"No answer.

" 'Well, my angel, I'm going to tame you.' She renewed her bites and kicks, and called me all the miscreants and vile scoundrels under the sun. I continued to hold her in a vice of iron. Thus we continued till six o'clock.

" 'If it is your will and pleasure to expose yourself to the servants,' said I, 'pray do, I have no sort of objection, but I will just observe that John will come in presently to clear away the luncheon and lay the cloth for dinner.' A torrent of abuse was the only answer.

" 'You brute,' she said, 'you have bruised my wrists black and blue.'

" 'Look at my hands, my precious angel, and my shins are in still worse condition.'

By and by there was a rap at the door. 'Come in,' said I. John appeared—'Take no notice of us, John, but attend to your business.'

"John cleared away the luncheon and laid the cloth for dinner. Exit John.

" 'Oh, Edward, you do hurt my wrists so.'

" 'My ear and face are still burning with the blow you gave me, my hands are torn to pieces with your tiger teeth, and will not be fit to be seen for a month, and as to my shins, my drawers are saturated with blood,' said I.

" 'Let me go! let me go directly, wretch!' and again she bit, kicked and struggled.

" 'Listen to me,' said I, 'there are 365 days in the year, but by God! if there were 3,605, I hold you till you apologize in the manner and way I told you, and even then, I shall punish you likewise for the infamous way you have behaved.' She sulked for another half hour, but did not bite or kick any more. I never relaxed my grasp, or the sternness of my countenance. My hands were streaming with blood, some of the veins were opened, her lap was full of blood, it was a frightful scene.

"At length she said, 'Edward, I humbly ask your pardon for the shameful way I have treated you, I apologize for the blow I gave you, I forgive you for any injury you have done me, I promise to be docile and humble in future, and I beg—I beg,' she sobbed, 'your forgiveness.'

"I released her hands, pulled the bell violently, told John to run immediately for Dr. Monson (the family physician), and fell fainting on the floor. I had lost nearly a pint of blood from the wounds inflicted by the panther. When I recovered my senses, I was lying on the sofa, my hands enveloped in strapping plaister and bandages, as were also my shins. Ellen (sic) and my wife knelt at my feet crying, while Monso kept pouring port wine down my throat. 'Could you eat a little,' said he kindly.

"'Gad, yes,' said I, 'I'm awfully hungry, bring dinner, John.'

"They all stared, it was ten o'clock; however dinner was served, though sadly overdone, having been put back three hours. John had only laid covers for two, presuming my wife and I would dine tete-a-tete. I told him to bring two more. Monson and my wife raised their eyebrows—'Doctor, stay and dine with us, call it supper if you like; Emma, I desire you to seat yourself.' She made towards the door. 'Augusta,' said I, addressing my wife, 'persuade Emma to dine with us, I will it.'

"'You had better stay,' said my wife, with a sweet smile. Emma hesitated a moment, and then came and sat beside me."

Our hero drank during this strange dinner a bumper to the man who knows how to tame a shrew, and obliged his wife to pledge him in the toast; the Doctor lectured her, and advised her to restrain her temper in future.

"I had one of my bandaged hands up Emma's clothes while he was saying this, and was feeling her lovely young cunny. It was nuts to crack for me. Dr. Monson gone, I rang the bell, 'John, you and the servants can go to bed,' said I. John cast an enquiring glance at Madam and Emma, bowed and retired.

"I asked Emma for my cigar-case, as for Augusta, I did not notice her. I lit a cigar, and drawing Emma on my knee, sat before the fire and smoked. 'You can go to bed, Augusta,' said I, as if she was the servant and Emma the wife, 'I shall not want you any more.' The humbled woman took her candle, and wishing us both good night, went to bed.

"'Oh, Edward,' said poor little Emma, 'what a dreadful woman she is, she nearly killed you, you nearly bled to death! Dr. Monson said two of the great veins at the back of each hand had been opened by her teeth, and that if she had not given in when she did, you would have bled to death.'

"'But here I am all alive, my sweet.'

"'But you won't have me to-night, mind.'

"'Won't I though!'

"'Now, Edward! pray don't, you are too weak!'

"'Then this will give me strength,' said I, and I drank at a draught a tumbler of Carbonell's old Port. I made her drink another glass, and then we lay down on the couch together. I fucked her twice, and then in each other's arms we fell asleep.

"It was six o'clock the next morning when I woke up. I aroused Emma and told her I thought she had better go to her own room, before the servants were about; my hands were very painful, so arranging with her when and where she should next meet me, I went up stairs to bed. My wife was fast asleep, I held the candle close to the bed and looked at her, she was lying on her back, her hands thrown over her head. She looked so beautiful, and her large, firm breasts rose and fell so voluptuously, that I began to be penetrated with some sentiments of remorse for my infidelities. I crept into bed and lay down beside her. I soon fell asleep. I might have slumbered some two hours, I was aroused by being kissed very lovingly. I was sensible that a pair of milky arms clasped me, and that a heaving breast was pressed to mine. I soon became aware of something more than this, which was going on under the bedclothes. I opened my eyes and fixed them upon the ravisher! It was Augusta. She blushed at being caught, but did not release me. I remained passive in her arms. My hands I had lost the use of; inflammation had set in in the night, I felt very feverish, in an hour more I was delirious; I became alarmingly ill.''

* * *

His illness lasted a month, during which time he was tended by his mother and wife. Emma is sent away; and on his recovery he went with his spouse to Hastings. There, as bad luck would have it, his discarded mistress met and accosted him. There was another scene and they again parted. Our hero continues:

"Then came a series of disasters. Our family solicitors, a firm that had managed the affairs of the family for three generations, turned knaves, my poor mother was plundered of all her property. She was obliged to dismiss all her servants, and send her furniture and carriage to the hammer. For two years I drove the Cambridge Mail, but not under my own name. I made about three hundred a year, and have reason to think I was much liked on the road. The adventures of that part of my life, alone, would form a volume, but as this purposes to be an erotic auto-biography, I abstain. The advance of the railway system closed this avenue of my career at last. Then I started some fencing rooms in London. Sometime after I had been thus engaged, my wife, I could never learn how, found me out. She called upon me, she was beautiful as ever, there was a scene of course, it ended by my agreeing to live with her again. The gods alone know how many infidelities I had committed since we parted six years before. She never knew them. I accompanied her to the depths of Hampshire, to a certainly charming cottage she had there in a remote hamlet, not a hundred miles from Winchester. Now it was an anomaly in her character, that she with all her fanaticism, all her pride, should condescend to a meanness. I thought it paltry, and I told her so frankly on our journey, but she represented to me that she had always spoken of me, as her husband, Captain S—, and nothing would do, but I must be Captain S—."

Our hero settled down again to a quiet country life. He proceeds:

"Now let the casuists explain it, I cannot, but the three years I passed in this delightful spot—

'The world forgetting
By the world forgot.'

were the very happies of my checkered existence.

"Augusta would strip naked, place herself in any attitude, let me gamahuche her, would gamahuche in her turn, indulged all my whimsies, followed me about like a faithful dog—obtained good shooting for me in the season, and a good mount if I would hunt. I was faithful for three years.

"A rake, I! a man about town, fond of gaiety, of theatres, of variety, of conviviality, say—ye casuists how was it? But so it was; and, sooth to say, I was very happy.

"And thus passed three golden years, the happiest in my life. From this dream I was awakened by my wife becoming enceinte; from that moment 'a change came o'er the spirit of the dream.' Her whole thoughts were now given up to the 'little stranger' expectant, all day long nothing was to be seen but baby clothes lying about the room, she could talk of nothing but baby—drew off from marital amusements, cooled wonderfully in her manner, and finally drove me, as it were, to seek elsewhere for the pleasures I no longer found at home.

"When the child was born, matters became worse, everything was neglected for the young usurper.

"My comforts all disappeared, and at length I became so disgusted, that I left her, and going up town had a long interview with my relative Lord E—."

The poor ill-used captain remained in London, indulging in every kind of debauchery.

"And whose fault was it, (he resumes) that I committed these adulteries? Surely my wife's. Had I not been faithful to her for three years! had I not let slip many chances during that time? Venus! thou art a goddess, thou knowest all things! Say how many divine creatures I neglected during that time? for though buried in the depths of the New Forest,—

'Full many a flower (there) is born to blush unseen,
And waste its sweetness on the desert air—'

So saith the Poet, and true it is.

"And the baby she idolized and loved so well, he grew into boyhood, and she spoiled him, and he grew to man's estate, and became a curse and a disappointment. Go to! now ye fond mother's (sic), who drive your husband's (sic) to infidelity, and what the correct world calls vice, that you may devote yourselves to your children. What profit have ye? Go to! I say.

"But in six months this woman began to feel certain motions of nature, which told her there were other joys besides the pleasure of spoiling her breasts to give suck to her brat, and she wanted to see her sposo again. She was virtuous, was this woman, so ought to have been 'a crown to her husband.' God knows it has been 'a crown of thorns,' but let that pass.

"She came up to Town, and called on the Earl. She was all pathos and meekness, of course. She told her 'sad tale.' My relative was moved, a 'woman in tears' is more eloquent with some people, than 'the woman in white!' I received from my relative a very peremptory letter. I had some expectations from this man; it would not do to offend him; I consented to live with her again."

Sellon returned then once more with his wife to Hampshire, but as may be imagined, this renewal of domestic bondage could not last long. Having gained entrance into a girl's school, he was detected by his wife just as he was conducting his young companions "into a wood for a game at hide and seek."

"After this escapade, I could no longer remain in Hampshire, so I packed my portmanteau, and was once more a gentleman at large in London."

The volume closes with the following note

signed by the editor, but in reality written by the author himself:

"The narrative here abruptly terminates, and as far as it has been possible to ascertain, it would appear that the writer died shortly after, at all events he was never again seen alive or dead by any of his numerous acquaintance."

The sad truth is this—Edward Sellon shot himself in April 1866, at Webb's Hotel, No. 219 and 220 Piccadilly, then kept by Joseph Challis, but since pulled down; its site being now occupied by the Criterion of Messrs. Spiers and Pond. There was an inquest, but through the influence of his friends the affair was kept out of the newspapers, and hushed up. Before committing suicide he wrote to a friend informing him of his intention, but the letter only reached its destination the following morning, when all was over. In that letter were enclosed the following lines, addressed to a woman who was fond of him, and who, when he got into difficulties wished to keep him.

"NO MORE!"

"No more shall mine arms entwine
"Those beauteous charms of thine,
"Or the ambrosial nectar sip
"Of that delicious coral lip—
                              "No more.

"No more shall those heavenly charms
"Fill the vacuum of these arms;
"No more embraces, wanton kisses,
"Nor life, nor love, Venus blisses—
                              "No more.

"The glance of love, the heaving breast
"To my bosom so fondly prest,

"The rapturous sigh, the amorous pant,
"I shall look for, long for, want
                              "No more.

"For I am in the cold earth laid,
"In the tomb of blood I've made.
"Mine eyes are glassy, cold and dim,
"Adieu my love, and think of him
                              "No more."

"Vivat Lingam.
"Non Resurgam."

Here then is the melancholy career, terminating in suicide at the early age of 48 years, of a man by no means devoid of talent, and undoubtedly capable of better things.

Sellon was a thorough atheist, and fully believed in the maxim with which he concludes the poem above quoted.

"Ups and Downs," the MS. of which had been sold to W. Dugdale shortly before the author's death, is no fiction, but, allowing for a little colouring, portrays truthfully enough Sellon's career.

The following letter I am induced to give, inasmuch as it to some extent, fills up the gap between the abrupt ending of the autobiography, and the equally sudden termination of the writer's own life. It was addressed to the same friend to whom Sellon had communicated his intention of destroying himself, and was of course intended exclusively for his amusement and not for publication. In it, as in his book, Sellon shews himself the same thoughtless, pleasure-seeking scamp, unchanged to the very last.

"London, 4th March, 1866.

· 260 ·

My Dear Sir,

"You will be very much surprised no doubt to find that I am again in England. But there are so many romances in real life that you will perhaps not be so much astonished at what I am going to relate after all.

"You must know then that in our trip to the continent, (Egypt it appears was a hoax of which I was to be the victim) we were to be accompanied by a lady! I did not name this to you at the time, because I was the confidant of my friend.

"On Monday evening I sat for a mortal hour in his brougham near the Wandsworth Road Railway Station waiting for the 'fair but frail,' who had done me the honor to send me a beautiful little pink note charmingly scented with violets, in which the dear creature begged me to be punctual—and most punctual I was I assure you, but alas! she kept me waiting a whole hour, during which I smoked no end of cigars.

"At length she appeared, imagine my surprise! I! who had expected some swell mot or other, soon found myself seated beside the most beautiful young lady I ever beheld, so young that I could not help exclaiming, 'Why my dear you are a mere baby! how old may I be permitted to ask?' She gave me a box on the ear, exclaiming, "Baby indeed! do you know sir, I am fifteen!' 'And you love Mr. Scarsdale very much I suppose? said I as a feeler. 'Oh! comme ça!' she rejoined. 'Is he going to marry you at Vienna, or Egypt?' I asked. 'Who's talking of Egypt?' said she. 'Why I am I hope my dear, our dear friend invited me to accompany him up to the third Cataract, and this part of the affair, you I mean my dear, never transpired till half-an-hour before I got that pretty little note of yours.' 'Stuff!' she said, 'he was laughing at you, we go no farther than Vienna!' 'Good!' said I, 'all's fair in love and war,' and I gave her a kiss! She made no resistance, so I thrust my hand up her clothes without more ado. 'Who are you my dear?' I enquired. 'The daughter of a merchant in the city who lives at Clapham,' said she. 'Does you mother know your out? I ejaculated. 'I am coming out next summer,' said she. 'That is to say you were coming out next summer,' said I. 'Well I shall be married then you know,' said the innocent. 'Stuff!' said I in my turn. 'Who stuff?' she asked angrily, 'do you know he has seduced me?' 'No my angel, I did not know it, but I thought as much—but don't be deceived, a man of Mr. Scarsdale's birth won't marry a little cit like you.' She burst into tears. I was silent. 'Have you known him long?' she asked. 'Some years,' said I. 'And you really think he won't marry me?' 'Sure of it, my dear child.' 'Very well, I'll be revenged, look here, I like you!' 'Do you though! by Jove!' 'Yes, and,— I give you my word I was into her in a moment! What bliss it was! None who have not entered the seventh heaven can fathom it! But alas! we drew near the station, and I only got one poke complete. She pressed my hand as I helped her out of the Brougham at the Chatham and Dover Station, as much as to say 'you shall have me again.' Scarsdale was there to receive her. Not to be tedious, off we started by the Mail, and duly reached Dover, went on board the boat, reached Calais, off again by train. Damned a chance did I get till we were within ten or twelve versts of Vienna. Then my dear friend fell asleep, God bless him! The two devils of passengers who had travelled with us all the way from Calais had alighted at the last station—here was a chance!! We lost not an instant. She sat in my lap, her stern towards me! God! what a fuck it was, 'See Rome

and die!' said I in a rapture. This over we were
having what I call a straddle fuck, when lo! Scarsdale woke up! I made a desperate effort to throw
her on the opposite seat, but it was no go, he had
seen us. A row of course ensued, and we pitched
into one another with hearty good will. He called
me a rascal for tampering with his fiancée, I called
him a scoundrel for seducing so young a girl! and
we arrived at Vienna! 'Damn it,' said I as I got out
of the train with my lip cut and nose bleeding,
'here's a cursed piece of business.' As for Scarsdale
who had received from me a pretty black eye, he
drove off with the sulky fair to a hotel in the *Leo-
poldstadt,* while I found a more humble one in the
Graben near St. Stephen's Cathedral, determined,
as I had £15 in my pocket to stay a few days and
see all I could. But as you will find in Murray a
better account of what I did see than I can give
you, I will not trouble you with it. I got a nice little
note the next day from the fair Julia appointing a
meeting the next day at the *volksgarten.* How she
eluded the vigilance of her gallant I don't know,
but there she was sure enough in a cab—and devil-
ish nice cabs they are in this city of Vienna, I can
tell you. So we had a farewell poke and arranged
for a rendezvous in England, and the next day I
started and here I am, having spent all my money!

"So there's the finish of my tour up the Nile to
the third Cataract, to Nubia, Abu Sinnel, etcetera. It
is very wrong I know, I deplore it! but you also
know that what's bred in the bone, &c., so adieu,
and believe me

"Yours very truly
"E. SELLON."

Selected Blue Moon Backlist Titles

J. Gonzo Smith
SIGN OF THE
SCORPION
Clara Reeve's amateur
sleuthing to find her sister
catapults her into a thrill-
seeking world, and a
labyrinth of sexuality.
#161 $7.95

Patrick Henden
BEATRICE
An aura of eroticism
surrounds Beatrice, as well
as her equally attractive
sister, Caroline, who is into
the strange fulfillments of
their desires. #81 $7.95

Daniel Vian
SABINE
A beautiful but naive demi-
mondaine travels from
France to South America
with her rich patron, who
tells her upon their return
that he has no money for
her. #29 $7.95

**David (Sunset)
Carson**
LAMENT
Carson's western is, in the
words of Hubert Selby Jr.,
"bawdy, bizarre, satirical,
Rabelaisian, iconoclastic,
and zany. It is also
gruesome, and funny as
hell." #153 $7.95

Akahige Namban
WOMEN OF GION
When a respectable
councilor is murdered in
old Miyako while enjoying
his new concubine, there
are a plenitude of suspects,
including the councilor's

wife, her ambitious lover, the beautiful blonde Rosamund and even the governor of Miyako.
#36 $7.95

Don Winslow
IRONWOOD
The harsh reality of disinheritance and poverty vanish from the world of our young narrator, James, when he discovers he's in line for a choice position as "master" at an exclusive and very strict school for young women.
#22 $7.95

Edith Cadivec
EROS
The Meaning of My Life

The author of this book, a Viennese schoolteacher during the 1920s, was a well-known advocate of corporal punishment. Her position as a schoolmistress provided her with a continuing source of "culprits" to satisfy her erotic needs.
#158 $7.95

Olga Tergora
MARISKA I
The beautiful ballerina of the Russian Imperial Theater, Mariska is trained in the baronial mansions of the Ukraine, where she first resists, then yields, and then later becomes a willing whipping girl for her master.
#65 $7.95